THE EX EFFECT

A WASHINGTON WOLVES NOVEL

KARLA SORENSEN

DEDICATION

For the women out there, just like Ava (and me), who often clutch their big feelings tight to the chest. Find the people who allow you to let those out, the ones who meet your emotions with love and acceptance.

And to those people in my life- you know who you are.
Thank you.

CHAPTER 1
AVA

WASHINGTON WOLVES

This might seem difficult to believe, but once you've seen one naked football player, you've seen them all.

No, really.

The first time I walked into a locker room—a fresh-faced, pink-cheeked college intern—I was completely and utterly unprepared for the amount of ass I'd be confronted with. And it wasn't even just the ass or the unabashed way they walked around one thousand percent *naked*, but the fact that I was standing in the midst of men who made millions of dollars by honing their bodies into flawless machines of muscle and strength.

Please allow your imagination to wander in the way that that sentence intended.

Only once did I allow myself a full-on gape at the abs. And pecs. And biceps. And ... everything else. None of them saw my drool or the way my jaw practically came unhinged, thank the holy ghost of Vince Lombardi up in football heaven, because if they'd noticed my reaction that very first time, I never would've made it this far.

Fast forward six years, and as the public relations manager for the Washington Wolves, I could walk through a locker room of three dozen naked men and not blink.

"You owe me a Twitter takeover, Robinson," I told our newest wide receiver. When he grinned, lazily toweling off his broad chest, I didn't so much as blink. "You were supposed to start fifteen minutes ago. Where the hell were you? People are asking you questions, and I don't want to lose our audience; otherwise, we'll pop out of the trending searches."

I got a couple of confused blinks before he finally decided to yank his boxer briefs up his legs.

"Coach had me run some extra routes." He shrugged, showing me his heavily tattooed back before tugging a T-shirt over his skin. "I can't exactly tell him I'm ready to leave. I'm the new guy."

It was the off-season, but that didn't mean jack shit as far as the hours we all worked.

"How long until you're ready to go?"

"I dunno. Coach wants me to come talk to him after I'm dressed."

Narrowing my eyes at him, one of my most effective weapons against men who were bigger, stronger, and a hell of a lot more intimidating than my five-six self, I took satisfaction in seeing him shift uncomfortably.

"Fine," I said after a long silence. "Give me your Twitter log in, and I'll do it."

"What?" he yelped. "You can't do that, can you?"

One of the veteran players, Dayvon, strolled past us, winked at me, and smacked Robinson on the back of the head. "She sure can." He chuckled under his breath as Robinson—I couldn't even remember his first name yet—rubbed the spot on his scalp that was probably now bruised from Dayvon's ham-sized fists.

My voice turned soothing, and I made sure to pat his arm gently. "I promise, I won't check DMs or respond to anything except the takeover hashtag, okay? You can change your password as soon as I'm done."

His dark eyes were still skeptical, and I exhaled patiently.

"No DMs?" he said after a beat.

"No DMs," I assured him. And I meant it. Internal shudder. There was not much I hated about my job, but the accidental viewing of propositions being sent back and forth between single (or not single) players and groupies was definitely at the top of my list.

Robinson finished buckling his belt and leaned in close. "Robinson4MVP2017. My password."

I smothered a smile. "Got it. It won't take longer than twenty minutes, I promise. And if you have time to jump on at the end with some more personal stuff, then you can do that."

"You got it, boss," he answered.

"Swing by my office if you get done with your meeting early," I called after him as he sauntered through the door.

My hand slid into the pocket of my dress and found my phone. Everything I wore had pockets because my phone was always, always within reaching distance.

Like always.

If the press caught wind of a story and I needed to issue a statement, the worst thing that could happen was for me to be caught sleeping, literally or figuratively, on the job. Thumbs flying over the screen, I logged in as Robinson.

Ah-ha, *Levi*. That was his name.

Quickly, I answered a few of the questions, randomly throwing in some phrases I saw on his Twitter feed so it wasn't glaringly obvious that a twenty-eight-year-old woman was answering each tweet.

@levirobinson4real: Best part of playing 4 the Wolves so far? #AskAWolfWednesday

To @cassidycowgirl: Leveling up to my teammates, learning from the best. It's legit around here.

· · ·

My surroundings barely registered as I scrolled and typed, paused to check the ding of an incoming email, then tapped out a text response about when I'd have the analytics from the new website.

Someone cleared their throat.

My eyes snapped up, and I saw three defensive players strolling out of the shower. Two had towels frozen around their waists, and one was stark-ass naked. My eyes never even considered dropping. That was how hardcore I was now.

"Sorry guys, gotta get the work done where you can, right?"

I gave them a brisk smile and wiggled my fingers in a wave as I walked out, phone still clutched in my other hand. There was an open conference room across from the locker room, so I yanked out a chair with the toe of my bright pink heel and sat indelicately.

Once I was down, I stretched my feet and groaned. The shoes were hot AF, boosting my average height by a solid four inches, but sweet merciful heaven, I wanted to die by the end of the day from how they made my feet feel.

After allowing myself sixty seconds to breathe and stretch, I flew through the tweets as best I could, only taking the time to reply more than once on a couple of threads. Fourteen new DMs came in while I did my stint as Levi Robinson, but gross, I wasn't touching those with a ten-foot pole.

When I felt comfortable logging out and letting Levi handle the rest, my phone started vibrating in my hand.

"Oh goody," I muttered under my breath when I saw my mom's name flash ominously across the screen.

I knew why she was calling. Oh, as sure as Tom Brady would be a first round hall of fame pick upon his retirement, I knew why the woman who birthed me was calling. Casting my eyes up to the ceiling, I sighed heavily. Dramatically. That gust of air came from somewhere down in the depths of my very soul.

"Hello, Mother," I said.

She sniffed. "I expected it to go to voicemail."

I rubbed my lips together before answering. "Nope. You caught me at a good time. What can I do for you?"

No, *How are you? How's Dad?* There was none of that in our phone calls. Abigail Baker always called for a reason. That purpose would be revealed quickly, with little emotion, though it would be loaded with subtext no matter how I answered.

"You haven't sent in your RSVP."

If there was a prize for being right, like a car or a big paper check that could never be cashed, I just won. Sitting on my desk was the ridiculous invitation for my older sister, Ashley's, ridiculous vow renewal for her ninth anniversary.

That's right. *Nine* years. Not ten. Because Ashley couldn't do things the way everyone else did them.

The heavy paper with rose-gold engraved letters probably cost more than my rent each month, but the golden child would always, always get what she wanted.

"I figured my attendance was a given, Mother. Sister of the bride and all." Well, hey! Listen to me, being all calm and shit. Make no mistake. My parents and my sister gave zero shits about me as long as I never, ever in a thousand years eclipsed Ashley. In my job or my looks or my relationships (*snort*) or anything. They didn't care if I attended the vow renewal, but it would look bad if I wasn't there. Aunts and uncles would notice.

"It's bad manners not to RSVP."

I saluted with two fingers, wishing desperately she could see it. "I bought a beautiful dress already. You have nothing to worry about."

"It better not be white," she snapped. "Mail it in by next week, Ava."

Click.

My two-finger salute became a one-finger salute aimed straight at the now disconnected phone. For a split second, I grinned as I imagined arriving at the ceremony wearing a pristine white dress. Ashley's smooth alabaster skin would probably melt off.

Alas, my dress was a deep navy with pockets and complemented my dark brown hair and olive skin tone. *I'll look hot, don't you worry about that*, I thought just as my phone rang again.

Oh, hallelujah. No family members this time, though. Just my boss.

"Hey, Reggie, what's up?" I glanced out the doorway when a few players walked down the hall. "I'm still here if you need to see me."

I heard some papers shuffling and imagined him at his always messy desk. "No, no, that's fine. I just shot you an email. We'll need to set up some press about an acquisition we just made on defense."

I leaned over the table and grabbed a Wolves notepad and pen that someone had left behind. "Hit me."

"Matthew Hawkins."

The pen clattered to the table, and I felt the air rip violently from my lungs. "Wh-what?"

"Yeah, I know." Over the racing of my mind, I could hear his voice pitch upward, just like it did when he knew we were about to get great press for something. "I couldn't believe Cameron got him to come out of retirement for a two-year contract. But with Rickson injured, we couldn't leave that hole in the roster. Matthew signed this morning. Real hush-hush."

"Matthew Hawkins," I repeated unsteadily.

"I know." The smile in his voice made me pinch my eyes shut. "You can handle this, right? The press will be humping our legs faster than we can get the press release out."

With a shaky hand, I brushed my hair out of my face. "Yeah, of course." I nodded even though he couldn't see me. "Of course, I can handle it."

"Good. I'll send him down to your office tomorrow morning after we meet with the front office."

Spiky bubbles of hysterical laughter crawled up my throat. If I'd had chocolate in my pocket, I would've shoved it into my mouth for the fake calm it could bring me. "Mmmhmm. Sounds good."

"The email has his full bio. Let me know if you need anything else before you reach out to the press."

I almost laughed out loud.

I knew Matthew's bio.

I could rattle off his stats as far back as college. More than just his height (six five), the position he played (defensive end), or the number of sacks he'd had (seventy-nine, just in the NFL), I knew he was obsessed with peanut butter, he hated beer, he was allergic to dogs but never admitted it because he wanted one so badly, and he'd seen the movie *Rudy* at least fifty times.

"Thanks, Reggie," I said instead.

I knew so much about Matthew Hawkins that the press never would.

How he never treated me like the five-year tagalong to my perfectly shiny, angelically beautiful, and horribly selfish sister. How he didn't even treat me differently when, after four years of dating and six months of being engaged, she cheated on him with another man.

Oh, I knew Matthew Hawkins all right.

My sister's ex-fiancé, and the man I'd had a ridiculous crush on in high school, simply because he'd been nice to me.

And now he was going to be one of the men in the locker room across the hall.

CHAPTER 2
MATTHEW

L iving in Seattle was weird.

Not that I could properly judge whether I liked living in a city after less than forty-eight hours, but it felt like my brain hadn't followed my body yet.

Sitting on the plush carpet in my massive, unfurnished master suite, I bounced a tennis ball from the floor to the wall and back, staring out at the lights of the Seattle skyline just beyond the sprawling balcony outside the glass sliders.

Everything inside the walls was pristine and empty, save for the moving boxes that I hadn't started unpacking yet. It was quiet except for the *thud, bounce, thud, bounce* of the ball, an uneven cadence that was as soothing now as when I'd started doing it in my tiny dorm room in college. The mindless bounce, thud, catch, throw motion helped me think.

"What am I doing here?" I said out loud. No one answered. I could've called one of my two brothers, but they were already worried about why I was doing this. My parents too.

One of the boxes labeled *fragile* by the movers held priceless memorabilia from my eleven years in the NFL. All with the same team. We'd set records as a team, and I'd set records on my own. The awards I'd won were all carefully wrapped inside that box along with signed jerseys from my idols and teammates. Just not *the* award.

The trophy everyone wanted.

Which was the reason I was here. In a city only familiar from the short trips during away games over the years.

Thud, bounce, thud, bounce.

Even sitting on the floor of my bedroom, I had a perfect view of the Space Needle. The spherical top and long, curving base looked like someone dropped it there from a foreign planet as an homage to some strange deity. All around it, blocks of lights set in tall buildings looked squat and simple in comparison.

But once the sun came up, I'd see the jagged edge of the mountains behind it, a sure indicator I was not in Kansas anymore.

Or Louisiana, but that didn't have the same ring to it.

I wasn't used to staring at mountains when I woke up or glittering skylines—unless I was traveling. And even then, I had a horrible tendency to overlook it because I was so focused on whatever game I was getting ready to play.

In the quiet, I knew I should explore and get to know this place I'd call home for the next two years. But instead, I snapped my wrist one last time and then caught the ball when it came back at me. Planting my hand on the California king mattress sitting on the floor, I stood with a small groan.

"Careful, old man," I muttered. If I made too many sounds like that, stemming from a slight twinge that I still felt after my back surgery to fix a herniated disc, Coach Klein and the rest of the Washington Wolves would have no problem buying me out of my contract and moving on to someone younger and faster, who hadn't had back surgery or dislocated elbows or broken arms.

Pushing those thoughts out of my head with both hands, I took a deep breath and ripped open the first box. After my third trip into the closet, folding and stacking the shirts on the long row of white shelves, I heard my phone ring from where I'd left it on the kitchen counter.

Jogging toward the sound, I snagged the call just before my voicemail picked up.

"Hey, Mom," I said as I punched the button to put her on speaker.

"Hey, sweetie. Are you all settled in?"

I looked around my apartment and lied straight through my teeth. "Yup."

She was quiet for a second, and I braced myself. Hurricane Eileen was about to make landfall.

"Are you sure you're doing the right thing?"

No. I closed my eyes before I answered.

"I wasn't ready to be done, Mom." That was the truth. When I thought about what I wanted to do in my life without football, I couldn't see anything. The future was some foggy, undefinable thing without the practice schedule or games to study for, prepare for, and push my body to the brink for. "And I couldn't keep playing there."

"Those assholes."

I snorted. "My contract was up. I can't blame them for wanting to focus on someone younger and healthier than I am."

"They're still assholes." She cleared her throat. "Did your father pressure you into this?"

Yup. This was what I was waiting for. "No, Mom."

"Because he never knows when to quit with you boys. He pushes too hard, and he doesn't take your feelings into account. Remember that time in Pee Wee football? I could've killed him."

I blew out a hard breath. Yeah, I remembered. Some kid jacked me in the nose, and my dad screamed in my face when I started crying. He told me to get my pansy-ass back on the field because winners didn't quit because of a little blood. Maybe my mom could've killed him, but she always wanted to kill my dad. The truth was that my dad taught me grit. He taught me to stop making excuses if I wanted to be the best. And if I wasn't aiming to be the best, then I was wasting my time.

"Mom," I interrupted when she kept ranting about him. Half of my phone calls with her included this same rant. Half of my phone calls with my dad involved something similar. The joys of an ugly divorce twenty years earlier.

"Sorry," she said. "I just ... I worry. You're all alone up there."

"I was alone in New Orleans too," I reminded her.

"Not when you were married to Lexi."

"Mom," I corrected gently, "you of all people know that you can be married and still feel alone."

She didn't argue, but I could tell she wanted to.

"But you had friends there. A life."

It didn't matter that I was in my mid-thirties. To her, I was still her firstborn, and she still worried that I didn't have friends. My smile was slow, but I held in my laughter because I knew she was serious as a heart attack.

"I'll be fine, Mom."

"I know." She sighed.

Another call beeped in, and I glanced at the screen. "Mom, I have another call. Love you."

"Love you too."

"Hello?" I said once I clicked over to the unfamiliar Seattle number.

"Matthew Hawkins?" a female voice asked. Before I could turn it off, wariness made my eyebrows bend in. Crazier things had happened than fans hunting down a player's phone number. I took a deep breath, about to ask who was calling, but she spoke immediately. "This is Alexandra Sutton."

I straightened. The owner of the Washington Wolves. "Of course. How are you, Miss Sutton?"

"Call me Allie, please," she said with a smile in her voice. "Do you have a minute?"

Lifting my eyebrows, I glanced around the empty apartment. All I *had* were minutes. "You're giving me a break from unpacking, so I have all the time in the world."

On the other end, she laughed. I didn't know much about her other than she had inherited the team unexpectedly after her father's death less than a year earlier. That, and she was currently engaged to the team's veteran quarterback, Luke Pierson.

"I'm sorry I missed you earlier at the office. I had to pick up my daughter from school. Cameron told me you got your contract signed."

"No need to apologize," I assured her. "Witnessing my signature is nothing all that important."

"Well, Coach Klein and Cameron assure me that's not the case. They're very excited, as am I, that you've decided to continue your incredibly impressive career here in Washington."

"Thank you," I said respectfully.

"Luke tells me that he has the distinction of never having been sacked by you."

It was my turn to laugh. "He's right about that. Maybe I'll get my chance in practice."

"Oh, you have my permission," she said with clear humor in her voice. "As long as you don't injure him, I think it'll do him a bit of good."

"Yes, ma'am," I said, a bit of southern slipping through after eleven years of living and playing in New Orleans.

"Please, if you call me that, I'll age fifteen years before I can blink."

I swiped a hand over my mouth and tried not to laugh. Allie Sutton was known as much for her looks as she was now for being a great team owner. Aging her fifteen years wouldn't hurt her in the slightest.

"Actually," she continued, "some of the guys like to call me boss lady, which has a nice ring to it. But again, Allie is just fine."

"I look forward to meeting you, Allie."

She hummed. "I'm not sure if I'll be at the office tomorrow. I've got to juggle some other meetings, but Luke and I plan to host a get-together in a week or so for some of the new players and coaching staff. Give you guys a chance to relax a bit outside of practice especially since you're joining us so late in the off-season."

That had me lifting my eyebrows in surprise. Most teams and

team owners knew that late additions to the roster—whether players, coaches, or coordinators—were just part of the game. Injuries happened at any time, on the field or off, and throwing a party for those of us joining later wasn't the norm.

But I didn't really know anyone in the Wolves organization. No one I'd played with during college was here, and no one had transferred from my old team before me. For the past eleven years, I'd been one of the leaders—the guy who the new players sought out for advice, for a welcome, and for acceptance.

Now I was the newbie. The guy with the ticking clock over his head practically screaming with each tick forward, *this is your last shot, don't screw it up.* As if someone dropped me on an unsteady surface that tipped and turned with even the smallest movement, and I had nothing to grab on to, nothing to steady me.

The control freak in me—the one who liked the predictability of where I'd been thus far, knowing everyone and being in charge—hated this part of it. Hated the change.

So a welcome like this was unexpected but good. I sighed. "That sounds great, actually."

"Good," she said briskly. "Now, it's my turn to read my daughter her bedtime story, so maybe I'll get the chance to meet you tomorrow."

"I look forward to it." And I did. Allie was a dynamic shift from my last owner, who was exactly the kind of man her father had been. Rich in life, successful in business, and well into his seventies, both men had spent their time continually expanding their empires.

"And if I don't get there before, I know that one of the first people they want you to meet with is our senior PR person to get some press set up. Her name is Ava Baker, and I think she's expecting you."

My head snapped up. "Ava *Baker?*" My voice rose in shock.

Allie was quiet. "Yeah. Do you know her?"

I laughed under my breath. "I might. I used to know an Ava Baker, but she was in high school the last time I saw her."

In my head, I got a vision of gangly legs and big green eyes, a curious and sweet kid. Instantly, that was followed with a sour aftertaste in my mouth, metallic and bitter, when I thought about the *other* Baker sister. The one I'd been engaged to.

Maybe it wasn't even her. "The Ava I knew would have to be"—I exhaled loudly—"in her late twenties by now, I guess."

"Hmm," Allie hummed quietly. "Without disclosing HR information," she said in a teasing voice, "I'd say that our Ava fits in that general age bracket. But I guess you'll find out tomorrow, won't you?"

I'd always liked Ava. If it was her, then Seattle just got a bit more pleasant.

I smiled in anticipation. "I guess I will."

CHAPTER 3
AVA

WASHINGTON WOLVES

Every woman's wardrobe held a certain number of go-to outfits. A little black dress that could pull double duty for a cocktail hour or a funeral. An interview outfit. A sexy dress for when you want your date to swallow his tongue.

But as I'd learned that morning, my wardrobe did not hold an outfit that I could quickly reach for in the event of "your sister's jilted ex-fiancé, the man you once crushed the hell on, was now your colleague and would be seeing you for the first time as a grown ass woman."

Yeah. You see what I'm saying?

After much deliberation, muttering to my exasperated reflection in the mirror, stripping off outfit after outfit and dumping each of them unceremoniously onto the floor outside my closet, I settled on a winner.

The blousy champagne-colored dress tied around the waist, and with my tangerine jacket, I felt bright and summery, and my eyes popped like gemstones. It was very *adult, professional badass* Ava. After pairing it with my suede, open-toed bootie heels that made my average legs look longer, I was able to strut down the hallways at the office feeling like I wasn't going to vomit at the thought of seeing Matthew Hawkins for the first time in ten years.

And let's get this straight. I never, ever encountered situations at work that made me feel even close to vomiting. I was the one known for keeping my cool. I was the one who was prepared for every contingency.

The Pittsburgh Steeler defense had nothing on me. Ava Baker was the real steel curtain. I kept all that stuff locked down tight.

Until today, apparently.

The last time I saw him, I'd just turned eighteen. The fight from my sister's bedroom—only occupied when she was home on the weekends from Stanford—was so loud that our neighbors had probably figured out fairly quickly that Ashley had cheated on him, then blamed him for it, then tossed the ring back in his face before telling him she could finally move on with someone who *actually* cared about her.

I'd *actually* wanted to kick her bony little ass.

"Get the hell out of my house. You're pathetic," she had hissed at him.

The sight of Matthew, so big and strong and handsome, coming from her room with a flushed face and angry, reddened eyes was something I'd never forgotten.

I thought he'd walk past without seeing me—that was what most occupants of the Baker house did—but he stopped, then crouched in front of me. My eyes watered, so I blinked them away, lest he thought I was being a ridiculous kid. Even though I was just eighteen and a senior in high school, to someone like Matthew, I *was* just a kid.

"She's a fucking idiot," I whispered when I finally looked at his face.

A slow, reluctant smile lifted his lips, and his eyes warmed. He set one of his huge hands on the top of my head and ruffled my hair.

"Don't let 'em keep you down, okay?" he said. Matthew glanced back down the hallway to where Ashley had slammed the door shut behind him. I knew what he meant. After being with Ashley for four years, he'd seen enough of our family to know there was a clear hierarchy of importance.

Ashley was at the top, of course. I fell somewhere at the bottom, an unwelcome afterthought in every facet, down to how I was conceived. My parents weren't mean to me, per se, but it was just very painfully obvious that I wasn't Ashley. They'd had their one perfect child. Then I came along, and even though I'd desperately tried when I was younger, I was nothing like her.

Matthew saw all of it.

"Take care of yourself, Slim," he said as he stood, using the nickname he'd given me the first time he met me as a scrawny fourteen-year-old.

Looking up at him through the haze of my tears, I remember wanting to stand and fling my arms around his huge shoulders to give him a hug and tell him my sister was awful and didn't deserve him. Yet I was so selfishly heartbroken that he wouldn't be part of my family now because he made things better just by being around. He made my life better by being funny and caring and patient and trying to get to know me.

"You too," I whispered instead, tightening my arms where they were still folded around my legs. And he was gone.

"Ava," a voice snapped, and I blinked rapidly. Hello, back to the present, and holy shit, I might have just gone into a memory-induced catatonic state because I didn't even remember unlocking my office. Allie was standing in the doorway, snapping her fingers. "Good grief, where were you just now?"

I pulled in a deep breath, tightening the reins on my emotional state with a firm grip. "Taking a little jog down memory lane, I suppose."

She hummed, narrowing her eyes at me. "Can I guess what this is about?"

When I snorted, she laughed. I leaned back in my chair and spread my arms out. "Sure. You go right ahead and try to guess."

Allie pursed her lips and looked thoughtfully up at the ceiling. "You're thinking about how long it's been since you've seen

Matthew Hawkins and are attempting to mentally prepare your-self to see him again ..." She stopped and eyed my outfit. "Which is also why you wore sex shoes to work."

My jaw was currently hanging around the level of those sex shoes. "H-how?"

She grinned. "When I called him last night to welcome him to the team, I said your name, and ooooh, he remembers you."

"What?" I hissed, standing and grabbing her forearms. "Oh my hell, what did he say? Allie, you need to tell me everything."

Yes, I'm not proud. I basically just accosted my boss's boss, and the woman who could fire me by blinking, but I also genuinely liked Allie, and we had formed an easy friendship over the past year of her owning the Wolves.

There were soooo many men around us at work. So. Many. Men. It was nice to have another woman in the same age range, especially one who wasn't mean or catty or horrible.

I'd grown up with mean, catty, and horrible, which meant I had a radar for it that could not be touched by just about anyone in the world. My mean, catty, and horrible radar was *spectacular*.

Allie laughed at my theatrics, a look of amazement covering her gorgeous face. "Well, I'll be damned. I believe this is the first time I've ever seen Ava Baker even slightly ruffled."

"Shut up," I muttered, then closed my office door so no one would overhear us. On the way back to my desk, I shoved my hand into the large glass bowl that held my precious Dove chocolates. Normally, I tried to limit myself to one in the morning and one in the afternoon.

Somehow, three pieces found their way into my hand.

The first one was unwrapped and in my mouth before I sat back down.

"I'm serious." She took the seat across from my desk and gave me a thorough study. "You're like, *nervous* right now. This is weird."

Glaring at her as I swallowed the last of my milk chocolate, I tried desperately to disagree. But I couldn't. My stomach was in tangled, loopy, swoopy knots, and my heart was clanging behind my ribs. Somewhere in this building, Matthew Hawkins was just strolling around calm as you please.

What a jerk.

"I'm not," I started, then licked my lips and held her eyes. My fingers drummed on the surface of my desk, and her eyes gentled. "Okay, fine, I'm a little nervous to see him, but it's not what you think."

Allie nodded. "How do you know him?"

A flood of words whipped through my head, pushing to get out of my mouth like it was a race they were all trying to win. About my sister and what a bitch she used to be—still was, in fact. Words about how I'd looked up to him during such formative years, words about how freaking weird it was to imagine that if things had gone any differently, Matthew Hawkins would be my brother-in-law right now.

"He and my sister dated all through college." I swallowed. "They met at Stanford freshman year. Got engaged their senior year. Because we lived so close to campus, he … he was over at our house a lot."

Her eyebrows lifted slightly, but she stayed quiet.

"It didn't end well," I said after a pause. "The last time I saw him was the day they broke up. I'd just turned eighteen."

Allie hummed sympathetically. "And he got divorced a few years ago, right?"

Oh, more words, clamoring to get out. Not that I knew all the details, but I'd trained myself to stay casually interested in Matthew over the years. So when he'd married a freaking swim-suit model during his second year in the NFL, I may have scrolled the pictures obsessively when they popped up online. And when she divorced him five years later, after the back surgery everyone thought had ended his career, I may have scrolled those articles compulsively too.

Only it hadn't ended his career because it was *Matthew*.

"Yup," I said. But Allie must have read between the lines because she smiled sympathetically.

"Well, as soon as I said your name, he was surprised. But I think it was a good surprise."

I slicked my tongue over the front of my teeth and studied her. "How do you know that?"

Allie rolled her eyes. "You can just tell. It sounded like ... like he was smiling, you know?"

My heart clenched painfully. Yeah, I knew. This tiny part of me had worried Matthew wouldn't remember me; that I was too insignificant a part of his life since I was so young when he and Ashley broke up.

When Allie spoke again, her tone was careful, her face smooth. "Will this be okay?"

"Will what?" I asked.

"For you to work with him?" Ahh. She was in boss mode now.

Even as I felt a slight pinprick of defensiveness that she even felt the need to ask, I nodded decisively. "Absolutely. The press will piss themselves over this story. No one thought Matthew Hawkins would ever play for another team, and with how well we finished last season and all the work we've done to strengthen our defense, we've given him the best shot at winning a Super Bowl that he's ever had."

Her smile was instant and real. "You're damn right. Luke is thrilled we signed him. He hasn't stopped yammering about it."

"I'll bet." Allie and Luke were so cute that I'd hate them if I didn't love them together so much.

There was a knock on my office door, and my eyes snapped to Allie's. Her grin widened.

"Holy shit," I whispered and stood, smoothing my hands down my dress.

"You look great," she assured me with a wink.

You're a Steel Curtain. A Steel Curtain, I chanted in my head even though the words felt flimsy and inconsequential.

Allie beat me to the door, where through the small window, I could see the slope of one massive shoulder in a light blue shirt and the rounded curve of a bicep straining against the material. So much muscle. There was so much muscle in that one tiny window.

I knew he'd gotten bigger, but when Allie opened my office door, my knees almost buckled at the man I saw standing there.

Matthew Hawkins was a beast. Why, how, how in the eff was he so big? He'd knock his damn head just trying to get through the door.

He zeroed in on me instantly, a smile broadening his face, crinkling the skin around his bright hazel eyes and forming deep dimples on either side of his perfectly fine lips.

My stomach, tangled and loopy as it was earlier, went weightless in an instant, just from the force of that smile. I smiled back.

"Matthew," Allie said, and the connection snapped. She held out her hand, and his smile changed into something more professional. Less personal, but no less potent. "It's such a pleasure to meet you. I'm Allie."

He shook her hand. "Believe me, the pleasure is all mine. It's an honor to be here."

While his attention was focused on her, I took a deep, calming breath and channeled the girl who could walk through a locker room of naked athletes and face a room of rabid journalists without breaking a sweat.

Allie glanced back at me and gave me a reassuring smile. "I'd love to stay and chat, but something's waiting for me in my office that can't be put off."

My ass. What a little liar. Oh, how I loved her.

With a flip of her perfectly tousled blond hair and bright pink dress, Allie was gone.

Matthew had moved to the side to let her leave the office, and when he stepped through the door, the space seemed instantly smaller.

His smile returned. So did mine.

He looked so good.

So. Good.

The dark blond, almost brown hair on his head used to be longer, but now the sides were cropped short. The scruff on his face along the sharp angle of his jaw was just shy of a full beard.

The version of this demigod standing before me that I'd seen ten years ago was almost-a-man Matthew. He'd been big but not this defined. His face was leaner and harder now with lines that showed life and some laughter.

This was Man Matthew.

"I can't believe it's you," he said, propping his hands on slim hips and giving me a thorough study that I felt over every single inch of my twenty-eight-year-old body. He shook his head in disbelief.

"Hi, Matthew," I managed. Oh, look! I sounded semi-normal. Yay.

In my head, I counted four intense, agonizing seconds of quiet while we just looked. Ten years were gone, poof, nothing in those four seconds. Maybe I felt eighteen again standing in front of him, but holy shit, I'd missed this guy.

He held his arms out; his voice a deep rumble when he spoke. "Get over here."

I exhaled a laugh and walked to him, wrapping my arms around his waist, sighing shakily when his thick, muscular arms folded around me.

Engulfed. I felt engulfed by the sheer size and heat of him.

Matthew set his chin on the top of my head and laughed like he couldn't believe this was happening. Join the club, man. I closed my eyes and allowed myself one deep inhale. If this was my window to be wildly unprofessional and smell one of the players, then I was taking my moment, damn it.

He smelled like woods and soap and clean man. Holy balls, Matthew Hawkins smelled *good*. And he felt good. Strong and solid and hot and hard. And he was hugging me like he meant it. Probably because he did.

"I've missed you," I said into his chest, letting the work-shield down for just a second, just a tiny crack, just to say the words, even if they were so quiet that I hoped he didn't hear me.

But he did.

"Missed you too, Slim," he said back.

I was so officially off-the-charts screwed.

CHAPTER 4
MATTHEW

WASHINGTON WOLVES

I eased my hands up to Ava's shoulders and set her back so I could look at her again.

"Damn," I said out loud. She blushed, slugging me in the shoulder, which made me laugh. "Slim, you grew up."

Ava rolled her eyes and gestured to a pair of wide gray chairs across from her desk. It was clear that she was used to sitting opposite football players because those chairs would accommodate even the largest tackle.

It was definitely unprofessional to stare at a member of the front office of my new team, so I stole another quick glance as she sat behind her desk and crossed her legs.

Damn was right.

There was nothing gangly about Ava. Nothing that she needed to grow into anymore. Those bright green eyes, cat-like and unerringly astute, sat over high cheekbones and heart-shaped pink lips. Her hair was curled and long, and the dark shade of brown reminded me of cinnamon and caramel.

In a word, beautiful.

Ava Baker was a very beautiful woman.

"Matthew Hawkins," she said with a slow shake of her head, all confidence now that a neatly decorated desk separated us. "You grew up too."

My head tipped back as I laughed again. Her smile was sly and small, so very Ava.

"Do you still suck at poker?" I asked her with a grin.

Her eyes narrowed playfully. "I was sixteen, and I'd never played before. How good was I supposed to be?"

One weekend during the off-season, I'd been at the Baker house, and Ava saw me shuffling a deck of cards. When I asked her if she wanted to learn how to play, she'd scrambled to the table so fast, she almost tripped.

She was terrible. Her face, at least back then, gave everything away.

Not anymore.

"You picked it up quickly enough. Didn't you hustle me and three other guys for like a hundred bucks once?"

"A hundred and fifty," she corrected and tucked that sly smile even farther up her cheeks.

I hummed, fighting the urge to laugh. "That's right."

"I was surprised to hear your name yesterday," she admitted. Her head tilted to the side as she regarded me seriously. "Didn't you ride off into the sunset already? Last I heard, they erected a statue of you in some town square down on the bayou."

Narrowing my eyes at the Southern twang she infused into those last few words, I used the pause to untie my suddenly clumsy tongue. Her smile grew because she damn well knew she'd unsettled me with this grown-up version of her. There were no shallow niceties. We just jumped headfirst into this new reality.

Suddenly, I had a deep appreciation for her because revisiting that past would be no fun for either of us.

I shrugged lightly. "I think it's a pretty good likeness. They gave me the key to the city and everything."

She rolled her lips between her teeth so she didn't laugh. "Yet here you are."

I nodded. "Here I am."

The jokes were done because her face smoothed out. "Not that

I'm complaining, because it *is* good to see you, and you're about to make my job really easy with this story. But I am surprised. Don't you deserve to finally relax?"

Relax? I thought. Give a guy like me time to relax, and I didn't do well. There was always work to be done. Something that I could make better. Be better. Some part of myself that I could improve. Some cause that I could throw myself into. I got bored when I tried to read. Movies were predictable, and TV was even worse.

Inactivity made me uncomfortable in my own skin. Some form of the old saying, idle hands were the devil's playground.

This time, my smile was wry, a scraping discomfort at the core of what she was asking for. "You been paying attention, Slim?"

Ava held up her hands and started ticking things off on her long, thin fingers, free of any jewelry. No wedding ring.

"Five division championships. Three-time MVP. Four-time defensive player of the year. Man of the year. Most tackles in a single season of any player in NFL history."

The chair creaked when I shifted my weight. She didn't continue, but the fact that she had been paying attention was a slide of warmth under my skin, something comfortable and sweet.

"Two things you can't list," I said quietly.

She nodded slowly. "Conference champion, Super Bowl champion."

Briefly, I lifted my brows in concession. Most new players wouldn't have this kind of meeting with PR. They'd be going over talking points for the interviews already set up for them. I was getting a counseling session from the little sister of the first woman to create a chink in the armor.

The girl I watched football with during bye weeks.

The girl I taught to play poker and how to throw the perfect spiral.

"Those are the two you can't list," I agreed easily, trying to keep a smile on my face, my attention on her and the subject at hand.

The truth was that I could spend my entire life in the weight room, the film room, the practice field, and one play, one player could still step in and rip away the one thing I wanted most.

To prove I was the best.

Every pundit would argue that all the individual things I'd achieved meant nothing without the ring. It was hard to drown out the voices that said with every injury and surgery I would have an even more impossible path to prove them wrong.

And I wanted, more than anything I'd *ever* wanted, to prove them wrong.

Like I'd spoken those words out loud, Ava nodded.

"Good," she said decisively.

"Good?"

She leaned back in her chair and twirled a piece of that maple syrup brown hair in her fingers, watching my face carefully. "Yeah. Whatever was going through your head just now? I want you to keep it there for every question, every answer, every snap of every picture for the next week."

I crossed my arms over my chest and saw her grass green eyes flick down, then back up again. "Why?" I asked her.

Ava leaned forward and tapped her brightly manicured nails on the lacquered top of her desk, the click-clack almost musical. "Because I want them to see that fire in your eyes. I want everyone to see that the reason you're here, with this team over any other, is because we're the ones who will win." She pointed at my face. "That. That's it. I want every single one of them to sit up and pay attention to the Washington Wolves. Because of you."

When I could take a full breath, I lifted my chin and gave her an appreciative smile. "Holy shit, Ava."

She blinked. "What?"

I braced my forearms on my spread knees and leaned forward like she was. "You're really, really good at your job, aren't you?"

She laughed under her breath and held my eyes. "Yeah, I am."

No shame and no artifice. No false humility or brushing off my compliment. If her family was anything like they used to be, Ava wasn't used to getting compliments, and I'd always hated that.

And here she was, in a high-pressure job with a lot of money at stake and a level of competitiveness that would never abate, totally comfortable in her own skills.

The skill of selling the exact story she needed to.

"And you're going to shove me right in the middle of the media circus because of it."

"You're damn right." Ava licked her lips, visibly gearing up for a battle by squaring her shoulders. "Will that be a problem?"

"You know it won't be," I muttered, trying to swallow my smile. "But I like seeing you ready to fight me about it. You're feistier than you used to be, Slim."

There was that blush again. Just a sweep of pink over the tops of her cheekbones. "I wouldn't have fought you."

One eyebrow lifted up.

She lifted one right back. "Because it wouldn't have been a fight at all. In my years here, I can count on one hand the number of players who didn't do every single piece of media that I asked of them."

I took a deep breath and thought through the roster, things I'd heard and seen over my years in the league. I could toss out a few names and guess. Luke Pierson, prior to his relationship with Allie Sutton, was known for not wanting to deal with the media, as was one of the defensive captains, Logan Ward. Ward was a longtime safety, one of the leaders of the team, but he was notorious for giving almost comically awkward interviews in the locker room because he refused to answer so many questions.

He'd been made into memes and gifs that had been passed around my former locker room because, half the time, we wished we could do the same thing to nosy journalists.

I never would, though. I'd learned early on that the media could be as much of a tool as watching film. Keep them on your good side, and they'd send almost any message you wanted. Ava knew that too.

In my silence, she let out a slow and even exhale. "Listen, I love my job. I love this team, from the players to the coaches to the front office. I've been here since college, and I've never wanted to do anything else. Regardless of how we knew each other before, it's irrelevant to what I think you can help us achieve on the field. It's a non-issue for me, and I hope it is for you too."

There was her version of dipping her toe in without actually having to say the words out loud. My eyes drifted around her office, and I was not surprised when I found no pictures of her family adorning the walls. No smiling sister selfies in cute little frames. No trace of them at all.

And it was unsurprising because people like the Bakers didn't really change. Most people who couldn't be honest with themselves were the same. It was certainly the case with my parents. They'd never change how they defined the other person unless they learned how to admit their own shortcomings.

"Ava," I said carefully, "I hope you're not taking my silence as me not being cooperative."

Now it was her turn to shift in her seat. "Well, I'm not sure how I should take it." She blinked slowly, her eyes searching mine. "I don't really know this Matthew, do I? There might have been a time when I could guess at your reactions, such as when you were the guy teaching me cards and forcing me to watch *Rudy*, but ... it's been ten years since I've seen you. We've both been through a lot in that time."

My laughter had a cynical edge to it, even to my ears, and judging by the look in her eyes, she heard it as well. I wanted to ask her if she'd been married and divorced too, but I bit the tip of my tongue because it was none of my business. Ava seemed too beautiful to be single, but in this industry, physical beauty was commonplace. The average.

"No, I suppose you don't know this version of me." I blew out a breath, struggling to get out of my own head and stay present in the conversation. She deserved my attention, even if she'd been a stranger before walking into this office. "In truth, coming here has been a harder transition than I expected. Mentally," I clarified. "Once I really get down to work, I think it'll feel more natural, but this holding place ... this in-between, where I'm not quite part of the team yet, it's taking some getting used to."

She gave me a sympathetic smile. "Have you been able to explore Seattle at all?"

I shrugged. "Not really. I've been unpacking the past couple of days. My furniture finally showed up, so I'm not sleeping on a mattress on the floor anymore."

Her laugh was bright and easy, her smile broad and unaffected. "Well, if you want a tour guide ..."

The words trailed off, and I found myself relaxing again. "You can recommend one?"

Ava rolled her eyes and pulled something from her desk drawer before handing it to me. Her business card. "There's my number."

One eyebrow lifted slowly while I waited for her to clarify. She narrowed her eyes again, just playful slits of green showing between long eyelashes that I probably shouldn't have even noticed.

"In case you want me to show you around Seattle," she said after a prolonged pulse of quiet.

Grinning, I tucked the card in the pocket of my pants. "You offer that to all the new players?"

After a deep, tortured sigh, she pulled her chair flush against her desk. "Shut up. Now, let's get to work."

"Yes, ma'am," I said with a salute that earned me another blush and a shake of her head. After I settled back in my seat, I laughed and lifted my chin at the massive bowl on the corner of her desk. "Still keep chocolate within arm's reach at all times?"

"As do all intelligent people who enjoy being happy."

I grinned.

Suddenly, Washington seemed like a much more enjoyable place than it had when I woke that morning.

"Okay," she said, switching back into business mode. "Let's start with ESPN."

CHAPTER 5
AVA

I n the harsh light of day—aka outside my office and the potent Matthew Hawkins bubble that seemed to mute reality—I groaned every single time I thought about how I'd slid my card across my desk.

There's my number, I'd said like a complete tool.

Groan.

Ten minutes in his presence reduced me to a bumbling teenager all over again. Ten minutes of Matthew Hawkins—full name required because his body and aura were so big and over-whelming that I couldn't possibly think of him with only one name —and I was one heartbeat away from giggling and twirling my hair.

I'd slipped into work mode before that could happen because it was the only conceivable way I could save myself at that point. The dude was a pro at handling the media, so his first two inter-views went flawlessly. Naturally, that eased a little bit of my anxiety over whether I made a complete fool out of myself.

Until I got his text.

Unknown number: Your offer still on the table? I need some-thing to do.

My smile was as quick and big as a lightning bolt, but I killed that mofo real fast. Professional mode.

Me: May I ask who this is? Because that text could be construed in a lot of ways that I don't want to contemplate.

Unknown number: Fair enough, Slim. Is your offer to show me Seattle still on the table?

Unknown number: Take pity on me, please. I'm completely unpacked, and if I sit here any longer, I might start reorganizing my kitchen cabinets. Alphabetize my spice rack or something.

Very carefully, like it might explode if I touched it wrong, I set my phone down and took a deep, steadying breath. *Matthew Hawkins was not asking me out on a date*, I reminded myself firmly. He was new in town. We knew each other from before. There was less than one percent reason for my heart to be thrashing inside my chest the way it was.

But that less than one percent was loud. He was getting to know the other players even though it was the off-season. Surely, he knew one of them well enough to ask if they could do this. But he'd reached out to me.

In the mirror hanging above my kitchen table, I caught a glimpse of myself. My cheeks were flushed, and my bottom lip was pinned between my teeth. Eyes bright and—*groan*—full of anticipation.

No, no, no, this would not do.

Glancing around the room, I sought out a solution to my own stupid brain. And there, on the corner of my table, on top of a stack of bills, was my answer. I picked up my Canon XA11 as an idea developed. And such a good idea it was.

This time, my smile was slow, unfolding like a low rumble of thunder.

I'd only used my new toy a couple of times—at team events and some community outreach functions where I wanted candid footage to use for social media. It would be overkill for today, but it would allow me to meet him without any risk of giggling or hair twirling. I could suit up—metaphorically speaking—to be Professional Ava, PR Ava, and not the Ava who gets nervous at seeing Matthew.

I typed out my answer methodically, already feeling more settled in my idea. Anytime I could control the narrative of how something played out, I felt eight hundred times better. I felt like I was behind the steering wheel.

Me: Don't break into the spice rack just yet. I've got an idea, but make sure you're wearing a Wolves T-shirt.

While the dots bounced on the screen, I saved his number and entered him into my contacts.

Matthew Hawkins: Yes, ma'am. Want me to pick you up?

"Yeah right, buddy," I muttered. "Next thing I know, you'll be opening my car door and then we'd have a real problem on our hands."

Me: Where do you live? Maybe I'll pick YOU up.

He didn't answer right away, and I chewed furiously on my bottom lip. More than likely, Matthew lived in one of the wealthy suburbs outside Seattle, closer to the main Wolves facilities in some sprawling home that could accommodate his huge frame. Personally, I was right in the heart of downtown. I loved the views and the city bustle. I loved the flow of people as they commuted, coming to and from their homes with bright bundles of flowers from the market or fresh fish that had been caught an hour earlier.

My apartment wasn't huge, but it wasn't tiny. I made enough that I didn't need a roommate, save for the bright blueish-purple betta fish named Frankie that made his home on my kitchen counter. Matthew probably had a massive drooling dog.

I'd actively refrained from stalking his social media beyond the last year or so of his Instagram, which seemed to be his preferred medium. Talk about restraint, people. I should win a freaking award for not diving back to see if he still had pictures of his ex posted to his feed, all in the name of searching for a pet or something.

When he was with Ashley, he always talked about getting a German Shepherd.

When he was with Ashley ...

That train of thought would serve no good as I headed into spending a chunk of hours with him.

Control the narrative, I reminded myself. It was one of my capstones at work. If you controlled the narrative, you could influence the outcome. That particular thread would stay un-pulled until further notice because there was no outcome I liked when I thought about their relationship for too long.

My phone chimed, and I did my best calm person impression, slowly zipping my camera into its black case. And look at that, I walked slowly back over to my phone and even allowed a deep breath before glancing at the screen.

Matthew Hawkins: I'm in that new building on Hawthorne.

Okay, so not a sprawling home out in the suburbs. He was about six blocks away from where I lived, though the buildings got much bigger and shinier and nicer in the span of those six blocks. It was one of the things I loved about living in the city. You could cross the street and find yourself in a completely different culture; some imaginary line that popped up years and years ago had held over time.

Growing up in the privileged gated neighborhood in Northern California, I had felt sanitized and stripped down to something clean and boring in comparison. Knowing that Matthew was living downtown gave me a small thrill, like he was part of the same club that enjoyed the noise and the crowds and the busy streets.

Me: I'll meet you at the corner of Hawthorne and Eighth in fifteen minutes.

"There." I nodded decisively. "Meeting halfway between our buildings is super professional."

My phone chimed again.

Matthew Hawkins: It's a date.

"Oh screw you, Hawkins," I said under my breath. If it wouldn't have been childish to reply with NO IT IS NOT, I would've done it. Just to hold on to the last few shreds of my sanity.

I spent the next seven minutes not obsessing over what I was wearing (white shorts and an army green top that maybe made my green eyes look even greener) or whether I had enough makeup on (mascara, a touch of blush, and good ole ChapStick) or if my hair could use some love (a semi-messy topknot that said *I don't want to look like I'm trying too hard, but this also took me fifteen minutes and ten bobby pins to achieve*).

Satisfied that if someone snapped our picture, I wouldn't look like a hobo, I slung the camera bag over my shoulder and locked my apartment door behind me. The elevator chugged slowly to the fourth floor, and I prayed this wouldn't be the day it would get stuck.

The day was beautiful when I walked out of the small lobby of my building, so I pulled my sunglasses out of my bag and slid them onto my face. People who thought Seattle was all rain and gloom had clearly never been here. Summer in this city was gorgeous, bright, and hot and full of things to do.

Today, Matthew was going to get a crash course in Seattle 101.

I jogged through a crosswalk before the light turned red and caught a glimpse of him waiting for me at the corner. He wore a black hat, and mirrored aviator lenses covered his eyes. A flimsy disguise if he was trying to stay incognito, but I suppose that was my fault since I asked him to wear a Wolves shirt.

His massive frame donning any sort of team merchandise was practically an invitation to be recognized. It would be fine, though. I'd been out in public with enough of the players to know that most of the fans were respectful and polite. Still, it made me smile to see him tuck his head down into his chest when two guys in suits passed him, whispering excitedly. His hands were jammed into his pockets, and his chest expanded on a deep breath.

That chest.

There should be a shrine somewhere to Matthew Hawkins's upper body. An exhibit in a museum with bright lights and placards discussing why the curve of his shoulders was perfectly proportionate to the arcs of muscle underneath his shirt, the bend of his biceps that stretched the limits of his shirt.

The sigh was out of my mouth before I could stop it.

"Damn it," I whispered. I could do this. I was a pro-fesh-i-nuhl.

Just as I was reminding myself of that, Matthew lifted his head and saw me approaching.

If I thought there should be a shrine to his upper body, then I refused to consider what should be erected in honor of the smile he gave me.

"Slim," he said in that low, deep voice, and *swoosh*, my stomach flipped over on itself like a traitorous little gymnast. "You playing tourist today too?"

"Huh?" My smooth reply was just a punch of sound from my graceless lips. Seriously, it was like I became a different person around this guy. It was so ridiculous and needed to stop yesterday.

He pointed at the camera, and I touched it with a laugh. We moved away from the street and out of the flow of people so I could unzip the case. When I pulled it out, I saw the lift of his eyebrows behind his glasses.

"That's some serious hardware," he commented.

I clutched the camera to my chest briefly, letting out a girly sigh. "It's my new obsession, and we're going to put it to good use today."

"Yeah?"

Gesturing down the street, I nodded. "Yeah. Matthew Hawkins sees Seattle. If it's okay with you, I want to shoot some stuff for Facebook and Instagram. Thought we could go to Pike's Market and get them to throw some fish at your head or something."

His laugh was loud and came from so deep within that monstrous chest that I felt it somewhere behind my ribs, an answering echo of sound that brought a smile to my lips.

"You're the boss," he said quietly as we started walking side by side.

We simply walked the first couple of blocks, an easy quiet between us as the city hummed in place of conversation.

Matthew broke the silence first. "I googled you last night."

That's when I tripped.

Matthew's hand shot out and grabbed my elbow, big and warm and covered in calluses against my skin, steadying me easily as I tried to channel a little Taylor Swift to cover my embarrassment. *Shake it off, sh-sh-sh-shake it off.*

Once I gathered my composure, I gave him a tiny smile, and his hand dropped from my elbow.

"Find anything interesting?" I asked as we waited to cross the street.

His glasses hid his eyes, and his mouth wasn't giving anything away, but the slight crinkling in his skin on the tops of his cheeks made me feel like he was trying not to smile at me.

"If I *tell* you everything I found, what would we talk about?"

I laughed. "Fair enough."

His shoulder nudged mine when the crosswalk sign lit up. "You take a lot of pictures of your fish."

And just like that, I felt like a gawky sixteen-year-old kid again, watching other people from down the hall, or around the corner, or from behind the front door.

It made me want to yank that steel back in place, centimeter by centimeter, but I fought through that jangling feeling in my stomach.

If it were anyone but him, my face wouldn't have felt hot with mortification, like I'd been caught doing something silly. My life was my job. I'd worked my ass off for years to get to where I was now. To be respected in my position, I had to earn the trust of the people I worked with and the players I interacted with every single day. That wasn't easy, especially with the sacrifices I'd made personally—not going out when most women my age were and not wasting my weekends on pointless dates because I was organizing community events and watching the games from the sidelines.

"Frankie is the baddest fish on the block," I answered lightly. "Plus, he's a conscientious roommate. Never keeps me up at night, doesn't interrupt when I'm bitching about my day, doesn't judge when I finish off a bottle of wine on a Tuesday night. How many humans could you say that about that? None that I can think of."

Matthew smiled, but it was clear he heard something in my answer, the something I most likely didn't want him to hear.

It might have been the subtext that I'd fairly screamed out, *there's nothing wrong with not having a boyfriend since college, okay? I don't want to talk about it.*

"There's nothing wrong with taking pictures of your fish, Slim."

Yeah, he heard it.

"I know that." This time my answer wasn't light. It held a sharp edge. His hand touched my elbow again, just a light brush of his fingers, but it was enough to stop our walking. He faced me, pulling his sunglasses off his face. There they were. The full force of those eyes was potent AF, and I couldn't stare for too long.

There was something about the way his lashes framed the warm hazel, and facing the sun like he was, I could see some amber and yellow on the edges. I'd seen those eyes look fierce, almost savage, on game day pieces when he was about to barrel through the offensive line to try to take down the opposing quarterback.

They weren't savage now. Fierce? Maybe a little.

"It's fine," I told him, holding up a hand when he started to speak. "Ignore me."

As those eyes narrowed slightly, someone bumped into me from behind, forcing me a step closer to Matthew on the sidewalk. He angled himself so that his back was to the flow of people, keeping me out of the way.

Of course, he stepped into the flow of people to keep me out of the way when I was getting snippy and defensive and guarded.

"I also found that you double majored at USC, got your masters at Arizona while working here, and in that locker room, you're respected as hell. Half of them are terrified of you, actually."

My laugh came out as a soft breath, and I squinted up at the building next to us. "That's not true."

I was being modest. It was totally true.

Judging by the smirk on Matthew's face, he knew that I knew it. "I don't know why you changed your mind about going into medicine, but I'm glad you did."

As I swallowed, trying to figure out how I was supposed to say I hadn't gone into medicine because I literally couldn't stomach being compared to Ashley and found lacking in one more aspect of my life, he nudged me again.

"I'm proud of you, Slim. It's not easy to find the thing you were meant to do."

As I stared up at him, I realized something. Matthew wasn't intentionally saying the kinds of things that would make a woman less in control fall in love with him. He was just being ... him.

Thank the good Lord I was not a flailing mess of emotions because I certainly wasn't at risk for that, I reminded myself firmly without the slightest worry that I was mentally protesting too much.

Still. Even if I wasn't at risk, I knew the kind of man I was dealing with. The unicorn kind.

Why Ashley cheated on him, I'd never know. If it was possible for me to ask her and get an honest answer without wanting to rip her hair out of her head, then maybe I would've done it. Why his wife divorced him after five years, I'd never know. But clearly, she was batshit crazy, too.

Professional, I screamed in my head. No swoony eyes. No sighing. No being a love-sick little girl.

So I forced down my swallow and straightened my shoulders. "Thanks. But don't think flattering me will get you out of having the fish thrown at your head."

When we started walking, I held my camera in my hands as though it would protect me from the sheer force of his personality. His steps were about twice as long as mine, which he adjusted so I wouldn't have to run in order to keep up.

"Wouldn't dream of it," he said.

CHAPTER 6
MATTHEW

WASHINGTON WOLVES

There was a lot about playing football that I loved. Some things didn't happen on the field, but most of them did. When I lined up, cleats digging into the ground, fingers pressed against the grass or turf, I loved watching the eyes of the quarterback. Loved watching his body language and hearing the words barked out at their offense. Because the slightest thing could tip off what they were going to do when that ball snapped from their center's hands into their own.

Those little tells—combined with whatever film I'd watched all week—helped me decide which way to spin or whether I should drop my shoulder and plow into the tackle so he couldn't shove me out of the way of a running back.

So far, Ava had given me nothing to guess her next move. Her face was covered with the camera too much for me to see any sort of tics or tells. After she forced me to take some pictures in front of the iconic fluorescent sign for my Instagram, we slowly made our way down the sprawling covered corridor of Pike's Market.

"We've spent years seeing you fall in love with Louisiana," she'd said when we arrived about an hour earlier. "Let your new fans, and your old ones, see Seattle through your eyes."

"Am I falling in love with Seattle today?" I teased.

Instead of answering, she lifted the Canon with ease, watching me through the display as I snapped pictures with my phone. Massive bins of flowers in every color and shape imaginable; fish, octopus, and shrimp laying on packed ice; meats and cheeses behind glass cases.

She dropped the camera long enough to approve which shots to put on my personal feed.

"No, use the one where you're looking down the street," she advised, looking briefly over my shoulder while I scrolled through my camera roll. "The lighting is better than when you're looking straight at the camera."

When I saluted her briskly, she snorted under her breath.

"And don't forget to hashtag," she added.

I gave her a sardonic look, which made her glance at me over the edge of her little shield. "I won't."

Just as I'd hit the button to post it, a young boy approached us wearing a shy smile on his face and the large hand of his dad on his shoulder. He looked even more nervous than his son.

"Mr. Hawkins?" the little boy asked, showing me a gap in his front teeth when he smiled.

I crouched down and held my hand out to him. "Well, Mr. Hawkins is my dad, but you can call me Matthew if you want."

He giggled, slipping his hand into mine.

"I've watched you since your days at Stanford," his dad said in a rush, also holding out his hand for me to shake, which I did. "Big fan, both of us are."

"What's your name?" I asked as I stood.

"This is Malachi, and I'm Robert."

Ava was filming as we chatted, only lowering her camera long enough to ask if they wanted her to take a picture of the three of us.

Robert shoved his phone in her hands before the words were out of her mouth. I watched her face while she adjusted her stance to fit us all in the frame. Her smile was amused, and her eyes only flicked to me briefly before she snapped a couple of shots.

When the two kept moving through the market, I got a question out before she could lift the camera again.

"Do you come down here often?"

Her hands froze in the act of unhooking the camera strap, and the inane nature of my question made me laugh. Her too.

"Sorry," I said, gesturing for her to walk in front of me. "That sounded way more natural in my head."

"Do I come to Pike's Market often?" she clarified, her eyes glinting with humor.

"Yes." I felt a punch of pride because, for the first time since we arrived, she wasn't hiding her face from me. Sure, I understood her wanting to do her job, but I imagined just a bit more reciprocal conversation than what I'd gotten so far. "You'll have to give me all the tips of living downtown."

She smiled. "Every couple of weeks, probably. I don't love to cook, so it's not for all this gorgeous food," she admitted with a slight grimace, "but the flowers are the best. And there's a place across the street that makes cheese curds so good, you'll cry."

"Flowers and cheese, eh? I figured you'd go for chocolate, not curds."

Ava laughed. "Oh, I manage to find that everywhere I go, don't you worry."

A memory had me chuckling under my breath. She glanced at me out of the corner of her eye, and from the way she bit the side of her lip, I could tell she wanted to ask. I leaned toward her. "I vaguely remember someone slipping a king-size Hershey bar into my duffel bag once with a note that said it would help me be strong for our game against Cal."

Ava groaned and covered her face with one hand. "I can't believe you remember that."

"How old were you?"

She blew out a slow breath and shook her head. "Maybe fifteen."

"So thoughtful," I teased, nudging her with my shoulder again.

"We beat Cal that year too. Maybe we lost my junior year because someone didn't give me a chocolate bar."

"I snagged money from my dad's wallet to buy you that," she said conspiratorially. I was laughing, but after a second her face smoothed out. "He didn't notice. No surprise there, I suppose."

A frown pulled down the corners of my lips when we were forced to break apart because a large family walked through the market. No, no surprise there. As often as I'd been there during those years, sometimes it seemed like I was the only one who paid attention to her.

I stopped walking to hand a vendor a wad of cash for a small bouquet of red and orange blooms that caught my eye. The small Asian woman behind the counter wrapped them deftly in white paper and handed them to me with a smile and a nod.

"What?" I asked when Ava gave me a curious look.

Her mouth opened, then closed. She shook her head as I tucked the flowers under my arm. "Nothing," she said finally. "Just ... observing."

"You used to do that a lot."

Ava's dark eyebrows lifted briefly in concession, and her smile was wry. "I suppose I did."

When my memories of Ava as a slightly gawky, hovering-on-the-edges-of-the-room teenager juxtaposed with the woman in front of me , it made for a blurry reality. I remembered her being curious and quiet, and sweet but reserved—probably out of necessity. Ashley had always been the one in the spotlight, leaving no room for anyone else.

Even now, although she directed so much within the Wolves organization, Ava was the one on the sidelines and not center stage. I wondered how much of her upbringing influenced that.

Either way, it almost felt like a challenge to see what this Ava was like when she no longer hid behind her job.

She was the quarterback, her camera the O-line in front of her, and I couldn't tell which direction she was going to move in. For a man like me, competitive to the very marrow in my bones, it was a challenge I couldn't ignore.

"Are you really going to make them throw fish at my head?" I asked when her face made it clear she didn't want to dwell on her observational skills. It was something in the set of her jaw, I realized. When I wasn't pushing her on anything related to the past, it relaxed a bit.

"Oh, come on," she said, nudging me with her shoulder. "It's a Seattle tradition. They're famous for it."

Warily, I watched men wearing aprons and big rubber gloves heft a fish over the heads of two giggling girls. "Yeah, but I'm six five," I replied, giving her the side-eye. "If I get a face full of salmon, you'll owe me big time, Baker."

Ava tipped her head back and laughed.

She was readying her camera to catch every horrifying second, talking at the same time with one of the guys behind the counter, who assured me that they were professionals, when Ava's phone went off.

With one finger held up, she moved to the side and answered it. "Ava Baker."

She cut me a look that I didn't understand.

"Uh-huh." With a twist of her slim wrist, she stared hard at her watch. "Yeah, we can do that. I'm shooting a piece with Hawkins right now, so that's no problem." She nodded. "Absolutely. Thanks for thinking of us."

She disconnected the call and shook her head at the fish guys, who groaned dramatically.

"We're going to have to cut your tourist day short," she said.

Ava tucked her phone back into the camera bag and gave me a small smile. I couldn't read whether it was disappointed or not.

"Sick of me already?"

She barked out a laugh. "Don't fish for compliments; it's not attractive." She moved to the side so people could walk past us. The pun, considering where we were standing, made me chuckle.

"That was *SportsCenter*," she explained. "They had someone

drop out for a broadcast tonight, and they want to do a short interview with you and Logan Ward via satellite. They're highlighting defenses right now, and with the traction you got for the NFL Network piece, they want to do one of their own." She glanced down at her watch again. "But we need to have you showered, shaved, changed, and back at the office in about"—she tsked —"two hours. Can you manage that?"

I rubbed at my jaw, and her eyes tracked the movement. "A shave too?"

Her eyes narrowed, and I laughed.

"Yeah, I can manage that."

She exhaled, clearly relieved. "Good. You're the easy part, though. Let's grab an Uber to save time. I'll call Logan on the way. That will be the hard part."

"Yeah?"

Ava hummed. "Remember how you said half the guys were terrified of me?"

I nodded.

"He's not one of them."

Her face was smooth as she said that, with no hint of anger or annoyance, but the tightness in her eyes was enough that I reached for the wrapped flowers under my arm and held them out to her.

"Here," I told her.

Now her face went blank as she took them from me, her mouth opening and closing again. "You didn't get these for me, though," she said, but her lips tugged up in a smile regardless.

Hadn't I?

I shrugged. "You'll enjoy them more than I will. Besides, I know you'll get home and eat some chocolate. You might as well add another indulgence to the end of your day."

Ava's cheeks pinked slightly, but she kept her face aimed away from me.

Maybe it was a strange impulse to give her the flowers, but it didn't feel wrong. And I was a big believer in following those instincts.

It made her smile, and that made me feel good. That was enough.

The Uber pulled up in front of us at the curb, the driver's eyes bugging out of his head when he saw me open the door for Ava. I smiled politely, waiting for her long, tan legs to disappear before I attempted to get in after her without banging my head on the edge of the door. My seat belt clicked into place, and we still hadn't moved. When I looked up, the driver was staring unabashedly in the rearview mirror.

Ava sighed. "You can get a selfie with him and an autograph if you get us there in less than ten minutes."

"Deal," he answered, and the tires squealed as we took off.

———

"I hate wearing ties."

This from Logan Ward, one hour and fifty minutes after Ava got the phone call.

We were sitting in a large room, surrounded by lights and people wearing headsets, holding clipboards and makeup brushes, with two massive cameras pointing in our direction. He fidgeted uncomfortably in his seat, no tie in sight. I dropped my hand from mine and glanced over at him.

Before I could speak, Ava appeared from the darkness created by all the bright lights aimed at us. "I know you hate ties, Logan. Everyone on the *team* knows you hate ties."

"Not everyone," he grumbled, narrowing his eyes at mine.

Most players had been welcoming. Most guys had sought me out in the building to say hi or sent me a text welcoming me to the team, but not Logan. I'd been the captain for all but my rookie year at my old team. The cursory handshake and curt "Welcome to Washington" he gave me on my first day hadn't sat well with me. And here we were, doing an interview that Ava politely demanded of us, even though those three words were all he'd spoken to me.

Maybe he wasn't terrified of Ava, but he'd still shown up.

Her phone call with him had been quick and her voice fierce. *Ward, I don't care if you're bleeding out in the emergency room right now. Tell them to stitch your ass up, because you will be in nice clothes, in the studio, in two hours. Do you understand me?*

Whatever he said had made her close her eyes and breathe slowly for ten counts, then she said *fine* and hung up. When would I stop noticing how different she was? How changed she was?

Standing in front of me, batting my hand away from the knot of my tie, Ava was the only bright thing in the entire room. Both Logan and I were wearing dark colors. The room was all shades of black, white, and silver as we waited for the interviewer to show up on the video feed.

Her dress was some vivid reddish pink that probably had a fancy name, and her heels were skyscraper tall and bright yellow. It probably shouldn't have looked good, but it did. While she reached her hand out to fix the knot of my tie and lean back to study it with a critical eye, I still struggled to reconcile this Ava with the Ava I'd known so long ago. That Ava wore T-shirts and jean shorts. This Ava was sleek and polished, all solid punches of color and subtle sexiness that made my skin feel two sizes too small.

Especially when she raised her face to mine and the lighting around us made the green of her eyes look exactly the same shade as fresh cut grass. It was the same color as a football field, one of the only places I truly felt at home.

My eyebrows pulled in as if the fact I'd even noticed was strange. She made one more pull to the edge of my tie and nodded.

"Thanks," I told her in a rough voice when she stepped back.

"Can't have a crooked tie on camera." Her glance at Logan was loaded with annoyance, and I bit back a smile.

"That would be awful," he muttered. "Why am I here again?"

My eyes flicked back and forth between them, and I fought the instinct to smack the back of his head as I would've with my former teammates. But Ava's eyes narrowed on him, and I sat back in my chair.

Ava let out a slow, controlled breath. "Remember when the guy from KIRO asked you about whether you planned to retire this year, and instead of answering, you stared at him for a full thirty seconds before walking away?"

"Yeah," Logan answered warily.

"And I had to spend thirty minutes reaming out your ass from here to Tokyo because it started a campaign on Twitter of how the front office should *force* you to retire because you were such a raging asshole to Seattle's most beloved sports reporter?"

Logan cleared his throat.

"That pleasant incident aside," she continued, "it's because you're one of the captains, and if you bailed on another interview, I've planned forty-seven new ways to dispose of your body, Ward."

My laughter was instant, especially when Logan simply let out a slow, controlled sigh of his own. Apparently, this was nothing new between them. I had to remind myself that Ava had been dealing with Logan, and men just like him, for years. It was impossible to be around players and their egos for that long without developing a thick skin. She caught my eye and winked. Apparently, Ava's skin was like Teflon.

Another thing that was new.

Over the years I spent with Ashley, every time I saw her or her parents toss some thoughtless comment in Ava's direction about how she didn't fit in or how she was different than her sister, there was a visible wound in her eyes and a downturn of her mouth.

This Ava seemed impervious, and I added it to the list of things I wondered about her. When had that shield slammed down? It must have been sometime after Ashley and I broke up.

An assistant walked over to us and started asking Logan a few questions, so Ava directed her attention fully in my direction.

Those eyes. It would take me all day, but I kept wanting to think of names for the shade of green they were.

"Need anything? I can't imagine this will take too long. They only need to fill about five minutes, so I think they'll just ask you both a couple of questions. Nothing too specific. Nothing you haven't covered already."

I shook my head. "It'll be fine."

Ava gave me a smile and a slow shake of her head. "If only everyone on the team made my job this easy, Matthew Hawkins. You're going to make it look like I actually know what I'm doing."

"You fishing for compliments, Slim?" I teased.

She didn't answer, only lifted one dark eyebrow.

The words came out of my mouth before I could stop them. "I've gotta tell you, I'm having a hard time getting used to this version of you."

Her entire body froze, so subtly that I might not have noticed it if I wasn't paying such close attention.

"What version?" she whispered. "I'm still me."

"You are still you," I assured her, cutting my eyes over to Logan to make sure he wasn't listening. I shook my head slightly when the words didn't come as easily as I wanted. "You have the same humor, the same smarts ..."

When my voice trailed off, she curled her lips up in a bemused smile. "Seems like someone isn't sure what to say."

I laughed. "I just wish I hadn't said it here," I told her, gesturing around the room. I took a deep breath and held her gaze. "Grown-up Ava has been a pleasant surprise, that's all."

Her eyes took on a glow; the kind of happy, pleased glow that did strange things to her face. Her skin lit up like a light bulb went on somewhere in her body that I couldn't see.

I wanted to say more. I wanted to tell her more about what I saw in her just to keep that glow going. Ava should look like that all the time. And just as I opened my mouth to tell her that, her phone went off in her hand, and both of our eyes went to it naturally.

Iron shutters going down over her face couldn't have had a more instantaneous effect. She stared at the screen just long enough that I saw the first few words of the text.

Ashley: I can't believe you ...

If I could have equated the instant pulse of silence between us to something, it would have been that old footage of a nuclear bomb going off. The plume of smoke billowing into the sky, mushrooming larger and larger until it obscured everything around it.

Even though she angled the phone away before I could see anything else, she didn't pull her eyes off the words. It didn't even matter what must have come after the few words I saw. Maybe Ashley was being nice. I can't believe you haven't called me this week. Or I can't believe you didn't tell me you cut your hair. I can't believe you haven't watched this show yet. There were a million things it could have been.

But I knew Ashley, or I used to. The type of self-absorbed person she was wouldn't just melt away magically. And even if I'd wondered, the look on Ava's face told me everything I needed to know.

The Teflon I'd wondered about earlier wasn't some seamless armor around her. If there was even the smallest hole, the tiniest puncture, then her sister had direct access to it. Because that look in her eyes was exactly what I'd seen so many years ago. Ashley knew exactly what to say to make her sister feel small. Feel less.

Not for the first time, I wish I'd never asked Ashley Baker out on that first date. The dumb college kid I was then had overlooked so many things about her because she was beautiful and smart and popular. Because the wealth of her family was dazzling. Because she made me feel interesting. Until none of that was enough. Until the ugliness underneath her beauty began to show more and more.

Maybe I'd suffered for a while because of Ashley, but the person standing in front of me had put up with her for a lifetime.

"Ava," I said quietly, lifting my hand to touch her.

She stepped backward. Logan shifted in his seat, glancing down at my hand.

Ava cleared her throat. Face blank, internal light now cold and dark, her lips in a hollow, plastic version of a smile. "Play nice, boys. They'll have the video feed ready to go in about two minutes.

Logan, I know you hate answering questions, but please pretend you want to be here, okay?"

I gave him a hard look. Logan never glanced at me once, but he must have seen enough in Ava's carefully blank face that he simply nodded. No smartass answer, no long-suffering sigh. Just a nod.

My shoulders relaxed, and I had to breathe through the sudden hot surge of protectiveness I'd felt toward Ava. It was clear she didn't need a protector with any of the guys on the team, but it didn't negate how instant, how visceral it had felt.

But even if I'd wanted to dwell on it, I couldn't. We were given a countdown, and the video feed to the *SportsCenter* studio in New York filled the screen in front of us. Logan and I smiled, answering questions easily as though we were friends. As if the previous fifteen minutes hadn't happened at all.

Once the camera cut off, I waited as patiently as possible for an assistant to take the microphone pack and unhook me from the wires they needed for sound. Once I was clear, I stood from my seat so fast, it fell backward, but it was too late.

Ava was already gone.

My instinct, the one I listened to without hesitation earlier, had my mind spinning and spinning. Maybe she was used to observing, to staying along the side and directing what happened in the spotlight—and maybe she was that without the influence of her family—but I still liked Ava, and I had enjoyed spending time with her.

It was enough for me to want to learn more about the person she was now. Outside of the team, outside of her family.

I wanted to figure her out. And I knew exactly how to do it.

CHAPTER 7
AVA

Let's get one thing straight. I'm no coward. Whatever word might come to mind at the memory of me all but fleeing down the hallway after that interview—chicken shit, wuss, scaredy-cat, wimp, etcetera—did not apply to me. Okay? Okay.

I just ... didn't feel like having that conversation with Matthew just yet. The one where we talk about the irony that my sister—his faithless ex-fiancée—managed to wedge her way into a moment between us. Because that conversation he initiated three days ago was, without a doubt, a moment.

In those three days, I'd relived his words at least eighty thousand times. In between my vigorous kickboxing classes where I did *not* imagine Ashley's face on the bag, in between the endless work I'd thrown myself into, and in between mouthfuls of Ben and Jerry's while I binged on the least romantic things I could find on Netflix (true crime documentaries, if you must know).

Up until that untimely text from Ashley, the one where she couldn't believe I hadn't sent in my RSVP—even though it didn't matter because she and I both knew I'd be showing up alone and I was procrastinating just to piss them off—Matthew had been giving me serious, thoughtful eyes. The kind of eyes where you knew he was trying to puzzle you out, like a man puzzled out a woman he found interesting. Those kinds of eyes.

Up until that damn text.

He tried to call me once, but I let the call go to voicemail, then sent him a quick text that he did great in the interview, but I had a lot of work to do, and I'd see him around. Because it was Matthew, he didn't push me on my very non-cowardly exit, my very non-chickenshit text, and my very non-wussy absence for the past three days.

The absence that was coming to a very abrupt end as I drove out to Allie and Luke's home on Lake Washington for a "Welcome to the team" barbecue. Since she wanted some of the longtime front office staff to attend, I didn't have much of a choice.

Not that I would've skipped, because I am no freaking coward.

As I took the exit to their house, I tried to settle the fluttery nerves in my stomach with a slow and steady breath, but it ended up being a wasted attempt.

Just as I let the air out and felt the jumble in my head clear, my phone rang, the Bluetooth system in my car startling me as the sound echoed through all the speakers. And of course, it was my mother, whose timing was about as uncanny as Ashley's.

My thumb hovered over the button on my steering wheel that would send the call to voicemail. But I was no coward, *okay*?

"Hi, Mom," I said in a cheerful voice, so obviously fake that even I cringed at the sound of it.

"Ava, you're ignoring us."

Us? Oh, great. I was being tag-teamed. And sure enough, in the background, there she was.

"Mom, she just doesn't understand the kind of stress an event of this magnitude entails. We can't really blame her."

At the sound of Ashley's voice, smooth as silk, throaty as a phone sex operator, *blah, blah, blah,* I ground my teeth together. "Hi, Ashley."

"Oh, you *do* remember you have a sister."

"Couldn't forget you even if I wanted to," I muttered.

"What was that?" my mom asked.

"Nothing," I said. "I'm five minutes out from a work function. What's up?"

Ashley snickered under her breath. She was a doctor, following my father's footsteps of becoming an anesthesiologist, so to say that they didn't respect my job or my career field of PR, in general, was like saying math wasn't very fun.

Translation—massive understatement.

My mom sighed as if I'd somehow inconvenienced her by placing a time limit on this conversation. "I'm going to assume your RSVP card is lost in the mail, and even though your sister thinks we should only count you as one, I'm going to be generous and plan on you having a plus-one."

I rubbed my forehead. So generous. The one serious relationship I'd had in college was no one they ever met because I didn't hate him. My family usually operated under the belief that I was celibate or gay. I wasn't sure, but I didn't really care.

"Okay," I said wearily. "What's the next thing?"

Ashley's voice got louder, so she must have gotten closer to the speaker. "Just make sure you're not wearing white, ivory, cream or any variation close to my dress."

"Hmm, I have a black dress that will do perfectly."

"Or black," Ashley snapped. "I won't have my sister showing up like she's going to a funeral."

I grinned.

"Although," she continued, "black is slimming, so maybe that's a good choice for you."

My smile dropped.

"Ashley," my mom interrupted. Even as I held back the *biiiiitch* that I wanted to let fly, I felt my eyebrows pop up at my mom's unlikely defense. "Don't let her bait you. You're better than that."

And never mind.

"Got it," I said loudly. "No white, eggshell, cream, ecru, or ivory, and no black. Anything else?"

"I think that's it, Ava," my mom said. Ashley mumbled something in the background, and my smile briefly returned that I'd made her mumble in the first place. Normally, my sister only spoke when she was sure everyone in the room could hear the precious golden nuggets of sound coming from between her flawless lips.

"K, bye then." My thumb punched the button to end the call before they could. My heart was still hammering as I jerked the wheel of my car into an empty spot on the cul-de-sac where Luke and Allie's massive home was located. They used to be neighbors, but when they got engaged, they hired some hoity-toity architect to connect their two homes, completely updating the exterior so it was one huge seamless house.

He'd added tall shrubs that obscured a black iron security fence that surrounded the gray and white home. The gate was open, but one of the Wolves' security team was leaning up against it, making sure everyone who showed up was supposed to be there.

"Miss Baker," he greeted with a nod.

"Hey, Charlie." Desperately, I tried to stretch my lips into a normal smile, but it must not have worked because he gave me a confused look. "Did they start without me?"

"I'm sure they wouldn't dream of it," he assured me.

As I walked around to the backyard and down some flagstone steps, I smoothed a hand down the front of my fuchsia sundress. I hated, hated that one ridiculous comment from Ashley could cause my mood to sour so quickly.

Black is slimming.

What a twat. She only said it because I was just barely smaller than she was and that never failed to piss her off. Any chance she got, Ashley made comments about my weight like it would magically conjure an extra twenty pounds on me.

Nope, definitely would not imagine her face on the bag the next time I practiced my roundhouse kicks.

As I turned the corner, laughter and easy chatter floated just above the music playing from the speakers mounted underneath the second story deck that ran along the back of their house. The

smell of smoked meat made my mouth water, and I inhaled greed-
ily. It was just enough to break the stupid choke hold Ashley held
on my brain.

Allie was standing next to one of our new offensive coordinators as I approached, and she smiled to excuse herself.

Her eyes missed nothing, scanning my face with obvious
concern. "You okay?"

I waved it off. "I'll be fine. Nothing that some brisket can't fix."

Speaking of eyes that missed nothing, I did a quick scan of the
yard. No Matthew yet. Allie cleared her throat knowingly. "He's
not here yet, but I know he's planning on coming."

"I'm sure I don't know what you're referring to," I replied
coolly.

Allie was quiet for a moment, then nodded. "No, it's fine. We
can play this game if you want."

Her friend Paige, who'd become a regular attendee of Washington games with Allie in her owner's box, approached us with a
wide smile on her face and a giant glass of wine clutched in her
hands.

"Ooh, what game?" she asked.

Standing in front of these two women, both more beautiful
than was even right, should've made me feel worse after the dig
from my sister. But it didn't. They were both so nice and so kind,
which almost made their looks even more unfair. Paige was a bona
fide model. Like New York Fashion Week, cover of magazines
model.

Not that you'd know it now. Her red hair was up in a messy
bun, and her face was clear of any makeup. Not that she needed
makeup. Ugh. I really wanted to hate her for it.

Allie lifted her chin in my direction at Paige's question. "The
game where Ava pretends she doesn't have a giant lady boner for
Matthew Hawkins."

"Ohhhh, that game."

I glared at Allie.

Paige shivered. "Cannot blame you. They did a profile on him on NFL Network the other day, and his arms ..." Her voice trailed off, her eyes taking on a dreamy quality that made me feel a touch violent. I knew how big his arms were. I'd touched his arms. I'd had those arms around my *body*.

I was one breath away from reminding Miss Pretty Pretty Model of that when Allie started cackling.

"Oh my gosh, your face, Ava." She wiped under her eyes. "You look like you're ready to stab someone."

"I do not."

Paige grinned at me over the rim of her wine glass. "You so do. Should I keep going, or are you ready for me to stop?"

I sniffed haughtily, and they both dissolved into giggles.

Their hysterics were starting to draw attention, so I smacked Allie on the arm. "Okay, that's enough," I hissed. "Fine. You assholes want me to admit it?"

She nodded earnestly. "Yes please."

Paige bounced on the balls of her feet. "Oh, we do love a good workplace romance, don't we, Allie?"

Of course, she was referring to Allie's love story with Luke Pierson, our veteran quarterback.

"There's no romance when it's one-sided," I reminded them. "He doesn't look at me that way."

"You sure about that?" Paige mumbled, her eyes pinned over my shoulder.

"Ava." Damn him and his voice. I felt it everywhere. My skin. My lips. On each individual strand of hair that lifted on my arms. Riiiiight between my legs. His voice was its own force of nature, for crying out loud.

It didn't even make sense. I went ten years without hearing that voice say my name. Ten years. Almost four thousand days. And now after only three days without, my body was reacting like he'd clipped a generator to my nervous system. It was such a strangely powerful reaction that I paused before turning to look at him, afraid of what he might see on my face.

Allie's eyes were ping-ponging between us, and Paige was

smiling at me with such wicked intent that I feared what might come out of her mouth next.

Just as I turned to look at him, one of his hands cupped my elbow. My eyes fell shut, and I blew out a slow exhale.

"Hey, Matthew," I said.

His face was edged with concern. I could see it in the set of his jaw and the look in his eyes. If you didn't know him, you'd probably confuse it with intensity or some other word that wasn't quite right.

He noticed. He noticed my very cowardly exit. He noticed my chickenshit text. He noticed it all.

And I knew that he knew that I noticed it. Which made sense in my head, I promise.

Paige cleared her throat. Loudly.

Matthew blinked over to the women behind me and smiled politely. "Allie, thanks for inviting me."

"Of course." She gestured at Paige. "This is my friend, Paige Adams. She's not part of the team in any way, shape, or form, but I can't seem to get rid of her."

While he shook her hand, I couldn't help but notice that he'd yet to drop the one curled around my elbow.

"I hope I didn't interrupt," he said, edging just an inch or two closer to me.

I couldn't look at his face. I just couldn't. Not here.

In the back of my head, I was well aware that I could control the narrative all day long, but trying to control whatever it was I was feeling around him was a different matter entirely.

Either way, I mentally grabbed the reins and gave myself a firm jerk back to sanity.

"Not at all," Paige insisted. "We were just about to invite Ava out for some drinks tomorrow night."

"We were?" Allie asked out of the side of her mouth. Paige gave her a loaded look. "Oh, yes, we were."

It was enough of a distraction, and God bless them for covering. Glancing over at Matthew, I found his eyes right on my face.

Are we okay?

I could read it loud and clear. Maybe the words weren't exactly what he was thinking, but I smiled at him as if they were anyway.

We're fine.

His face relaxed, and he nodded slightly. "Do you live downtown too, Paige?" he asked, once he'd turned his attention back in their direction.

Before she could answer, Luke walked up to us and shook Matthew's hand, carefully balancing a plate piled high with smoked meat. "I can't wait to hear the answer to this question." He glanced meaningfully at Paige. "Go on, Paige, tell Matthew where you live."

Like a game show host, Paige used the hand holding her wine glass to gesture to the massive home behind us. "But why would I move downtown when you have eighty extra bedrooms, all ripe for the taking?"

Allie smothered a laugh, and Matthew smiled broadly. Luke's disgruntled expression made me bite down on my own grin.

"Eighty is a stretch," he said.

Paige pointed at him. "I live in the half that was Allie's, so it's up to her to kick me out." She glanced at Matthew and me, rolling her pretty eyes. "He pretends he hates it, but you won't see him complaining when he steals my smoothie recipes, or they have a free live-in babysitter for Faith."

Luke sighed. "Matthew, feel free to eat however much you want while you're here because any leftovers today will just cement Paige's desire to stay under my roof that much longer."

"It's true," Paige said. "Speaking of which, I'm ready to eat. Anyone else?"

Allie raised her hand, leaning up to give Luke a peck on the cheek. He winked at her as she walked away. "Matthew, how about you?" Luke asked.

He scratched the back of his neck. "Ahh, in a minute. I actually need to have a word with Ava real quick."

If Luke was surprised, he covered it well. "No problem. I'll leave you to it."

"Just making sure she'll give me a passing grade on the interview I did a couple of days ago," he clarified unnecessarily. I knew Luke couldn't care less whether Matthew wanted to compare grocery lists or proposition me in his backyard.

When we were alone—or as close as we could be with thirty other people milling around the backyard—Matthew gave me a small smile. "You ran out of there pretty fast the other day."

"Did I?"

My faux-innocent tone had him grinning.

"It was Frankie," I said on a sigh. "If he doesn't eat by a certain time, he gets really cranky, and trust me, you do not want to see that."

"A cranky Frankie?" Matthew tsked. "No, I probably don't."

I bit down on my lips but lost the battle when I saw the way his eyes gleamed with humor. I shoved his shoulder, and he laughed loudly.

"What did you want to talk to me about?" I asked.

"Are your plans with Paige and Allie tomorrow set in stone?"

I eyed him speculatively. Hell no, they weren't, but I wasn't letting him know that just yet. "Why?"

Matthew glanced around us, tucking his hands into the pockets of his khaki shorts before answering me. "I've got someplace I need my official tour guide to show me."

"Isn't the *tour guide* supposed to plan what we see?"

His eyes warmed. "You'll love it, don't worry."

I crossed my arms. "Maybe you shouldn't sound so certain about what I'll love or not. You're still getting used to this version of me, remember?"

"Maybe I shouldn't," Matthew agreed, his eyes holding mine steady. "But I don't think you'll turn me down."

I'll let you in on a secret. Normally, I found cockiness to be incredibly unattractive. But facing him the way I was and hearing him say that, I wouldn't turn him down, so I started reworking my definition of what I did or didn't find attractive even though it had been forever since I'd been in this position with a man.

Cocky? No.

Sexy as hell confidence? Yes, please.

"Okay," I told him quietly. "Tomorrow then."

He grinned, a dimple appearing briefly in his left cheek. "Tomorrow then."

And off he went, like he hadn't just overturned the entire trajectory of my day with one brief conversation.

I was so busy turning the interaction over in my head that I didn't hear Paige approach.

"Girl," Paige said, then whistled quietly. "Ain't nothing about that one-sided."

I pressed a hand over my stomach, and I could feel the thud of my heart like it had dropped a foot inside my body.

"Shut up," I told her with zero heat. "Where'd you get that wine?"

CHAPTER 8
MATTHEW

"I will cut you if you try it. Seriously."

I was laughing so hard I had to brace my hands on my knees. Ava leaned up against the brick wall of the building we'd just left, waiting me out, completely unamused.

"You're really not going to share?" I asked when I could talk again, eyeing her prized possession and trying to figure out the likelihood that I could snatch it out of her hands.

Pretty high, considering how many strip sacks I had last year. Plus, I was almost a foot taller than her.

Ava gave me a look so cold, so deadly serious as she clutched the chocolate bar to her chest that I think my balls shriveled up a little bit. "Hell no, I'm not going to share. This is the greatest thing I've ever put in my mouth."

Did she ...

I froze. She froze.

Her lips rolled between her teeth, and her cheeks flushed an instant, bright pink.

My mouth opened, and she held up a hand to silence me.

"I will give you a *small* piece of this chocolate if you absolutely promise to forget what I just said."

Pushing my tongue into the side of my cheek so I wouldn't lose it again, I nodded slowly. "Fair trade."

Ava flattened herself fully against the red and white brick of Theo Chocolate Factory. With careful fingers, she undid the blue wrapping. Inside the crisp folded paper, I saw the edges of the first piece.

How did the woman describe it again? Homemade graham cracker crust, vanilla-infused caramel, and a cloud of marsh-mallow covered in dark chocolate with an alderwood-smoked milk chocolate flourish.

Also known as the best thing to ever be inside Ava's mouth.

Very slowly and very deliberately, Ava pulled one of the three pieces from the wrapping and presented it to me.

"One bite," she said.

"I don't get the whole thing?" Wearing my best wounded expression, I leaned against the building next to her, the tops of her shoulders barely reaching the middle of my biceps.

Her eyes narrowed slightly, and I couldn't stop my smile. "One bite."

She set the chocolate in my hand. Taking the time to study it carefully, I couldn't help but marvel at the fact I was doing this in the first place. Not eating the chocolate. I had as much of a sweet tooth as the next guy, and sweets were one of my few indulgences in the off-season.

I marveled at the fact I'd spent the time racking my brain to find something I could do for her. To show her that I still knew her, even if I wanted to get to know the grown-up version of her at the same time.

I marveled that for those few days she made herself scarce, something more than football and preparing for the season was on my mind. I'd still done my workouts, still prepared as much as I always would have, but I found myself paying attention to other things around me.

There were so many things for us to do around Seattle, but when I tried to find something that Ava would love, that she would know was about her, this was the obvious choice. And the look of delight on her face when I parked my truck in front of the square brick building was worth it.

Ava had been quiet, even visibly nervous when I picked her up outside her building. Maybe I'd shocked her with my offer, but from the moment we arrived, her smile told me I'd chosen correctly.

I'd called ahead, so we got a private tour of the factory. While indulging in samples, we helped them temper melted chocolate on giant marble slabs. With each different thing she saw, each confection she tried, she relaxed more and more.

I was seeing glimpses of the Ava behind the tough work exterior, the side of her honed by years of necessity. There was no camera hiding her face, no barrier of work erected between us, and I was having fun. So was she. Even if she didn't really want to share her Big Daddy, an unfortunate name given what she'd just said.

One bite, she told me. I lifted it to my mouth, and she watched carefully, her pink lips tilted up at the edges.

"You know what they say about big guys."

Her lips curled up even farther. "What?"

I leaned closer until our heads were almost touching. "We take really big bites."

I popped the entire thing in my mouth and chewed vigorously, moaning obnoxiously while she smacked me in the stomach.

"Oh, you ass," she cried.

I laughed around the mouthful of amazing, catching her hand before she could hit me again.

"Best thing I've ever put in my mouth," I said seriously.

That blush was back, even as she rolled her pretty green eyes.

"I can't believe I trusted you."

When I sucked my thumb into my mouth to catch the last bit of chocolate, she watched me with an adorably annoyed expression on her face.

"Your mistake," I told her easily. "I don't eat stuff like this during the season, so if you're going to offer, I'm taking you up on it."

Ava snorted.

When she pushed off the building, I did the same, matching her stride easily as we wandered down the treelined street. It was a cloudy day and a little bit cooler than I'd experienced since I moved here. I took a deep breath of air that smelled faintly of both the salt and ocean from Salmon Bay behind the building and the chocolate from inside it. "That was amazing."

I said it about the experience, but Ava pouted, clearly thinking about her lost chocolate.

"I know," she said sullenly. "Now I've only got two pieces left, and my soul is sad."

Without thinking about it, I chuckled and wrapped my arm around her shoulders as we walked. "You'll survive, Slim."

Ava angled her body toward mine so my arm settled more comfortably around her, and it was impossible not to notice how perfectly she fit there, so I left my arm right where it was. A little old lady smiled at us as we passed her, her eyes larger than normal behind the thick lenses of her pink rimmed glasses. I smiled back.

It wasn't often that I got smiles from strangers that weren't connected to me on the football field. They felt like unexpected and refreshing little pauses in my normal life.

For eleven years, I'd been *Matthew Hawkins*. Thirteen if you factored in the years when my college career really started taking off. When I was married to Lexi, we were recognized everywhere. Even though it was as much about her modeling career as my own, she loved that part of it. Me, not so much. Even when Ava and I went out that first day, I was still in that role. Playing that part of my job.

This was wonderfully, strangely normal.

Ava pulled away from me when a little girl on a bike refused to deviate from her path. "Sorry," she yelled over her shoulder as she rode past us.

My arm fell back by my side. "Where are we going?"

Ava shrugged. "I don't know. I thought we could just wander a bit." She glanced over at me quickly. "Unless you need to get back?"

Get back to what? I wanted to say. I had nothing waiting for me at my apartment. I might have teased Ava about posting pictures of her fish, but at least she had that. Normally, it didn't bother me. If I wasn't working out or watching film or studying the next game, I was sleeping. The single-minded focus that I applied to my career was something Lexi hated, but the things she wanted to do in order to distract me were all things I hated. Going out to loud clubs or big parties with big name people. Lexi was a sweet girl, but she wanted more flash in her life than I could give her.

Flash was quick and bright and had the ability to wow you for a moment, but there was no meat to it. No substance. Flash was trick plays that were about luck, not skill or preparation. I didn't want flash in my career, and I didn't want it in my personal life either. But I'd taken that desire and ignored the fact I had a personal life at all.

And today, I didn't want to do that anymore.

For a time, I'd allowed the dazzling display of wealth and parties and beauty to blind me. In the years since Lexi and I got divorced, I had to face the hard truth of how much my ego had driven my poor relationship choices. In college, Ashley felt like the perfect definition of what I thought I was looking for. During my early years in the NFL, it was impossible not to feel the pressure of the lifestyle and what was expected of us, and it fed the part of me that Ashley had punctured. My pride.

Lexi soothed that for a time until that shallow reasoning couldn't hold up under the weight of real life.

I didn't want to put my head down and keep barreling forward. I didn't want to rush home to a dark apartment where the only thing that waited for me was a big empty bed. I wanted to walk down this quiet street on a cloudy evening and explore with Ava.

"Let's wander," I told her.

She hid her pleased smile by turning her head, but I caught the edges of it, and it brought a smile of my own.

We passed a few shops, Ava pointing out funny novelty items behind the spotless glass windows. One young kid approached us for a selfie, and after I took one with him, I made sure to sign his hat too. When we turned a corner, Ava looked in both directions before heading north. The first building we passed was a short gray building with a wide, empty deck, save for a picnic table and a few tables. Ava walked up the stairs, and I followed, the sounds of Arctic Monkeys coming from the opened door.

"So if you're allowed to have the occasional piece of someone else's chocolate during the off-season," she said, "do you allow yourself to have a drink or two?"

I glanced inside the door, which was open since the air was mild. It was a small place with old-fashioned globe lights hanging over the bar and a basic dining room table occupying the rest of the space. Wooden floors stretched the length of the room, and behind the bar were three simple rows of bottles stacked haphazardly next to each other. Copper tiles lined the ceilings, and at capacity, maybe fifty people could fit in the entire place.

It wasn't like any bar I'd ever been in, and with Ava standing there, a beautiful woman asking me to go have a drink or two with her, I knew I was exactly where I needed to be.

I swept my arm toward the door. "After you."

The bartender, a hipster with a magnificent beard and the coolest suspenders I'd ever seen, didn't glance at me twice when I ordered two old-fashioneds and some pork and veggie dumplings. Either he wasn't a football fan, or he didn't give two shits who came into his bar. Either way suited me just fine.

With deft movements, he mixed our drinks and slid them in my direction.

"I'll bring the dumplings around when they're done if you guys want to pick a seat," he said, tapping the bar before going back into the kitchen.

Ava wandered through a square opening beyond some heavy

green curtains to an area I hadn't seen when we first looked in. There were about four empty tables, and she chose the one tucked back in the corner, ensuring us the most privacy.

I handed her the low-ball glass, and she smiled up at me.

"I hope an old-fashioned is okay," I told her, settling in the seat opposite her. The table was small, so when I braced my elbows on the surface, I all but dwarfed the entire thing.

Instead of answering, Ava took a slow sip and hummed appreciatively. Then she shivered. "Oh, that's delicious."

"Better than the chocolate?"

She took another sip of her drink. "I'm not ready to talk about that chocolate with you, traitor."

"You'll forgive me eventually."

Ava snickered but didn't argue.

Feeling lighter than I had in months, I took slow sips of my drink. The companionable silence we sat in—buoyed by the good music and privacy I did not take for granted and the warm rush from the alcohol—left me in a strange sort of weightlessness.

"What's the worst part about being with a new team?" Ava asked, setting down her empty glass. She leaned back in her seat, motioning for two more from the bartender, then gave me her full attention once again.

My eyebrows rose high on my forehead at her question. I sat back heavily, holding her steady gaze while I thought of how to answer.

"I defined myself as part of that city, that community for so long. I never imagined playing in another jersey, so I never thought I'd be the new guy again, the guy who had to prove himself." I swallowed heavily. "It felt pretty unbalanced those first few days."

She nodded. "What changed?"

A waitress delivered our drinks, and Ava smiled up at her. We both sipped quietly.

"What changed?" I repeated, tasting the words before I answered. Maybe the drink was loosening my tongue because I rarely drank, and I already felt the pleasant swimming in my head. "I think it was you."

Surprise had her mouth going slack and her eyes widening. "Me?"

"You." I smiled. "That surprises you?"

She sputtered slightly over her answer, and I watched the pink blush steal up her neck and across her face. "Well, yeah. It's not like I've done much."

"Are you kidding?" I shook my head. "Slim, I don't think you know how rare it is to be around someone who doesn't require you to wear a mask or keep up the façade that the rest of the world wants to see. You're the only person here who gives me that."

It was clear she had no freaking clue how to respond to that, and honestly, I didn't either.

"I-I'm glad I could help," she replied, quiet and sincere.

Ava composed herself with another deep drink, and I took one of my own.

Cocooned like we were, after a pleasant afternoon, I gave her a long look and decided to see if she'd allow me to pull back the curtain a little bit. There were things I wanted to know, wanted to figure out, and her self-contained nature made me more determined to get her to open up a little bit.

"Can I ask you something personal?"

She inhaled slowly, eyes wide. "Should I be nervous?"

I shook my head. "Nope. We're just talking. You know you can ask me anything too."

Ava's fingers tapped nervously on the table, and because I couldn't stop myself, I laid my hand on top of them. She gave me an embarrassed smile and held them still.

"My relationship history is pretty much," I started, then stopped with a grimace, "public record. But I'm curious about something. What about you? How are you still …?"

Her answering smile was lopsided. "Still single? Maybe I'm impossible to put up with. Or crazy. Or both."

"Come on," I said, leaning back in my chair. My hands slid off hers when I did, and she stared down at them for a minute before answering. "We're all a little impossible and crazy sometimes. No juicy ex stories to share over whiskey?"

Ava's eyebrows bent in briefly. "Not really. Not since college. I stay so busy with work, and I love my job. It's been ... enough."

Enough. What a safe, invulnerable word for such a smart, beautiful, and interesting woman to use. That no one had met her and felt this same urge to unearth the pieces of her that she didn't show the world seemed unbelievable. It seemed ...

"That seems impossible," I said under my breath, and even though I hadn't intended to say it out loud, she heard me. Her cheeks flushed, and she glanced away quickly.

A burst of laughter from the other room sliced through the quiet moment, and our eyes met. She'd felt the neat severing of an unexpectedly weighted moment too, the transition into normal conversation.

From there, it was easy. Laughter came from our own corner, trading stories of things she'd seen and done in her job, and I told her stories from my years in New Orleans. At one point, she clapped a hand over her mouth so she didn't spew her drink over our tiny little table, crowded by my arms as I leaned toward her. Those eyes pinched shut, and given that I was finishing my third drink, I had to fight the urge to lean closer and use my big, clumsy fingers to open them again just so I could see the bright color against her dark, long lashes.

Ava dropped her hand and took a deep breath. "And how long did it take to get the glitter out of your car?"

My eyes saw her lips moving, but I couldn't hear what she said over the rush of noise in my own head. Then I was studying the shape of her lips as they formed the words. Then they spread in a sweet smile, and I realized that I was staring at Ava Baker's mouth.

"Sorry," I mumbled and felt my cheeks heat. "It's just getting loud in here."

She hummed but didn't answer. Probably because it wasn't loud at all. Probably because I was a little buzzed, and I was staring at her mouth, trying to decide what color pink her lips reminded me of.

And her nose. It was straight and small and had the tiniest tilt up at the end.

Plus, there was that freckle she had on her right cheek. How had I never noticed that before?

"Matthew?" she said, clearly amused but also clearly embarrassed by my pointed perusal.

I sat back and did one more slow sweep of her face with eyes that felt clear and a brain that felt fuzzy.

But the fuzziness of my brain, happy and weightless and content in this little bracket of space we were enjoying, held no comparison to my stupid, sluggish tongue. Because instead of telling her how beautiful I found her, I heard myself say something completely different.

"You don't look anything like your sister."

CHAPTER 9
AVA

If Matthew had balled up his substantial fists, reared back his massive arm, and socked me in the stomach, he wouldn't have surprised me more.

I heard the gust of air leave my mouth like a punch, heavy between us, and he sat back, face morphing into some pained, horrible expression as he realized what he said. Realized how it sounded.

"Ava," he said quickly, blinking rapidly and leaning into the middle of the table. "Th-that's not what I meant to say. I'm such an ass. I'm so sorry."

I tried to smile, but my face was so hot and prickly, my skin icy cold, that my muscles locked into some iron cage of whatever they'd looked like the moment he said it.

His hands curled around mine where they were frozen on the surface of the table. They were more than warm. Matthew's hands on mine felt like someone wrapped the sun over a block of ice. Basically, I didn't stand a chance.

"It's fine, Matthew." I sucked in some much-needed air. "I've gone my whole life knowing the transcendent beauty of Ashley pretty much outshines everyone around her. Ashley is what would happen if Blake Lively and Margot Robbie had a baby and then Charlize Theron dumped some of her DNA in there just to make sure she was the most angelic being ever to walk the earth."

Ohhhhh the bitterness was not as absent from my tone as I thought it would be. The words sounded sharp. Like someone poured syrup over ice, the result was something hard and cracked and uncomfortable. Something impossible to ingest.

Lucky for him, Matthew didn't look at me with pity in those warm hazel eyes. If he'd looked at me with pity, my exit would've been so fast I would've left track marks in this nice little bar.

He licked his bottom lip before he spoke again, weighing his words carefully this time. *Maybe* he should've done that about four minutes ago.

His hands tightened over my clenched fists. And what happened to ice under the relentless heat of the sun? It melted, like a little hussy who'd never held hands before. My pointer finger tangled with his, and he exhaled slowly.

"I'm an idiot," he started. I laughed under my breath but made no argument because his words still stung like tiny nettles. "And I won't blow smoke up your ass by denying that your sister was a beautiful woman."

One of my eyebrows popped up. "Was?"

His mountainous shoulders lifted in a casual shrug that belied the intense expression on his face. "I haven't seen her in ten years. Maybe she's ugly now."

This time, I laughed out loud. The ache in my chest started to subside, beat by beat by beat of my heart.

"She's not ugly," I told him.

"It doesn't matter whether she is or isn't." His eyes bored into mine. No, the ache was gone, but in its place was this tumbling hot ball of emotion at the way he was looking at me. Matthew Hawkins was looking at me as though he was recording every part of my face. Not cataloging it as he had been earlier but committing it to his memory. "What I *meant* to say was that you are incredibly beautiful, Ava. It has nothing to do with who you're related to, or how I might've known you a handful of years ago. I'm just glad to be sitting across from you right now."

Well, shit. That hot ball of emotion? That was my heart, melting in an ooey, gooey mess down to the soles of my really cute shoes. The man brought me to a chocolate factory, which was bad enough. Now, I was wholeheartedly tipsy, sitting across from him when he tells me shit like that. What did he expect? I was only human. A female human who had a raging crush on him years ago.

This was a recipe for an unmitigated disaster that could only end with soul-crushing embarrassment on my part.

"I'm not going to cry," I said. Which was weird because the thought hadn't even crossed my mind until I blinked, and my eyes felt itchy and hot. His lips stretched in a smile. "But if I was sober, and even mildly PMS-ey, I'd be crying."

"You only cry when you're sober?" For some reason, he looked delighted with this tidbit of information.

I nodded seriously. "Yes. I'm a very happy drunk under most circumstances." Then I tilted my head to the side as I considered that statement. "Unless you give me red wine. Red wine makes me really, really emotional."

"Noted," he said with a gravity that made me giggle.

Great, now I was giggling, and his fingers were still touching my fingers, and I think we needed to get out of there before I gave in to my impulse to taste his skin with my tongue. Everywhere.

"I'll probably never give you red wine then," Matthew continued as I imagined what the tendon in his neck might taste like.

"No?" I asked after I blinked out of my fantasy. He'd taste like sex. And strength. And a man who could bench press four of me without breaking a sweat, and I really needed to think of something else. Was it getting hot in here?

He squeezed my hands before letting go and sitting back in his chair. "No. Why would I ever want to do anything that might make you cry? It would break my heart."

I stood quickly, and he blinked up at me in surprise. "We need to go."

Matthew answered slowly. "Okay. Are you feeling all right?"

With a shaking hand, I pushed some hair out of my face and nodded. "Yeah, just those drinks hit me, I think."

He laughed, tossing some money down onto the table as he stood. "Me too. I haven't drank that much in a couple of years."

Mistake number one- I walked too close to him as we left the bar, so when I nudged him with my shoulder to give him shit about that, it made for a natural nestling situation up against his enormous chest.

Mistake number two- I forgot about the steps at the end of the deck.

Mistake number three- wearing heels.

My ankle wobbled as we took the first step, and my other foot landed awkwardly. I gasped when I felt the snap of my heel when it hit the pavement at a strange angle.

Matthew's arm snatched me around the waist before I went face first onto the sidewalk.

"Son of a bitch," I groaned as I limped on the concrete.

"Are you okay?"

I blinked down at my feet, one still arched up three-and-three-quarters inches higher than the other. My poor, poor Jessica Simpson Eveena sandals. You were the perfect shade of fluorescent yellow. You did nothing to deserve this.

Matthew burst out laughing, and I groaned when I realized I'd said it out loud. His arm wrapped around my shoulders, given that I was nestled into his side. My lip pushed out in a ridiculous pout, and he clucked his tongue.

"It'll be okay. Were they really expensive or something?"

"No, but the cost is not the point. The point is that I loved them. The *point* is that now I have to be that person, limping home like a drunk ass college girl who doesn't know how to hold her liquor."

In the fading light around us, the sky turning a dark denim

blue as the sun disappeared, Matthew smiled down at me in a way that made me feel like a melted chocolate bar.

"How about I promise to get you home safely? No limping involved."

I narrowed my eyes up, up, up at his handsome face. When did he get so tall?

Oh yeah, when I broke my damn shoe.

"You can't drive," I told him accusingly.

"I know."

Then he lifted his arm, and shouted, "Hey, right here."

A bright yellow minivan cab jerked to a stop at the curb about forty feet past us. "That's so far away," I whispered, my head swimming, and my ankle throbbing, and the entire side of my body pressed perfectly against his. When did my arm slide around his waist?

I did not even care when because underneath my hands, I could feel muscles. All the muscles. So, so many of them. Hot, shifting, strong Matthew muscles.

"Here we go," he said, my only warning as he dipped, banding one arm underneath my knees and one behind my back to sweep me up into his arms like I was freaking sack of grain.

"Matthew," I squealed between breathless laughter. But did I protest?

Sure did not.

My arms linked around his neck immediately. I may have even bounced my feet in a happy rhythm as he walked us to the waiting cab.

"Is this better?" he asked, his face only inches from mine. Meeting his eyes, I could smell the sweetness of his breath. The ambient yellow light from the top of the cab made his chiseled face look harder and more intense than usual.

The air was thick around us as I nodded. His eyes dropped to my mouth, and I licked my lips.

"Thank you," I whispered.

He never looked away from me as he opened the sliding van door to the cab. Once it was open far enough for him to climb in, I fully expected him to set me down, but he just ... didn't. A testament to his strength and the control he had over his incredible body, Matthew ducked into the cab and settled into the first captain's chair.

"Where to?" the cab driver asked in a bored tone.

I rattled off my address, briefly breaking the weird, vibrating eye contact thing we had going on.

As the cab took off, I had to take a cleansing breath and admit that I was sitting on Matthew Hawkins's lap with his arms banded around me, unmoving and unyielding.

"You could put me down," I said quietly, tilting my mouth toward his ear, like it was a secret I didn't want anyone else to hear.

His eyes burned gold in the darkened interior of the cab. "I could."

Shifting slightly so I could see him better, I took a deep breath and let my fingers wander along the back of his head. Under my skin, his short hairs felt soft and prickly as I dragged my fingertips up and down in slow patterns.

The arm that been under my knees was across my lap now, and his hand opened wide along the expanse of my bare thigh.

There was no more sun and ice. No separation of what he was and what I was, or some stark dividing line between us.

It was just all heat. Whatever had been in him seeped into me, into my veins and through every pulse of blood through my body. Tiny movements that could be ignored in almost any other situation. But there was no music. No talking. The driver didn't count because he was focused elsewhere.

It was just him and me in the sweetly stretching silence.

His fingers curling into my skin as his hand moved slowly down to my knee and back up. His breath picked up speed, and I could feel it against my open lips.

My back arching into the expanse of his chest, my breasts

brushing against the front of his shirt as it moved with his deep inhales, short exhales.

My fingers pressing harder against the curve of his skull like I could force him closer to me. But he held firm, his eyes searing into mine with some unspoken thought.

There's a line, and we're about to cross it.

That was what I saw in his face. It wasn't really a question. No *should we?*

The inevitability of it might have been made easier with the sweet slide of alcohol in our veins. But I wasn't drunk. And neither was he.

And I knew what I wanted. Time to see if he wanted the same.

"Matthew," I whispered, inching my mouth closer to his and tightening my arms around his neck. His arms tightened around me.

Closer.

Closer.

My lips brushed against his when I spoke again. My entire body was a throbbing mass of need. "If any part of you doesn't want to kiss me right now, then—"

He shut me up by crushing his lips to mine. A slant of his head and a groan from deep in his chest had me opening my lips so I could touch his tongue with mine. His swept into my mouth, wet and still cool from the ice in his drink, dominating the kiss before I could take a full breath.

His lips were firm, and holy shit, this man knew how to kiss. His big hand gripped the curve of my ass as I pressed myself tighter and tighter against his chest. If there'd been room on the chair, I'd be straddling his lap like it was my job.

This was more, so much more than anything I could have imagined.

Sucking, biting kisses. Sweet sipping of my lips before he'd flip the switch again and drag my bottom lip between his teeth, pulling a whimper from me that sounded desperate.

Matthew Hawkins could kiss.

He was kissing *me*.

And he thought it was impossible that I was single.

I licked at the edge of his teeth, moaning when he sucked the tip of my tongue into his mouth. My fingernails dug into his head, and he grunted into my mouth, breaking away so he could suck on my neck.

"You taste so good," he muttered against my pulse.

With a ferocity that surprised me, I gripped the sides of his face with both hands and found his mouth again. Just the sound of his deep, deep voice saying that had me feeling frenzied and jittery, a junkie seeking a fix, a brief hit to calm my nerves.

I worked my lips against his as my hips rocked. One of his big hands slid up my back, tangled in my hair, and worked the strands into a tight fist. The sound that left me at the barely restrained passion in that hold echoed through the van.

"No sex," the cabbie shouted, turning in our direction. "I mean it. I'll drop you off right here if you can't keep your pants zipped."

Against my mouth, Matthew smiled. I licked across the line of his bottom lip, and he puffed air out of his nose.

"You're not making this easy," he whispered.

Now it was my turn to smile. Ugh, tipsy cab make-out sessions were the best. "So"—I cleared my throat delicately—"am I making it hard then?"

He tickled my side, and I started laughing, only stopping when he slid a hand up my side to cup my breast with one massive hand. His palm covered me and moved in slow, taunting circles. Arching my back into that caress, I wanted it to be more, harder, and with fewer clothes.

"Ahem," the cabbie cleared his throat obnoxiously, and I pulled back. Familiar buildings made me blink out of whatever stupor Matthew's hands and lips on my body caused.

Before he could move, because hello, I was on his lap, I reached in my purse and shoved some cash at the driver. He sighed when I leaned forward to open the door and try to hop out. Matthew's hand stayed on my back as I exited, his big body close behind.

Even though people still walked through the streets, it was dark enough in front of my building that no one looked at him twice. I took one limping step, and he went to pick me up again.

I held out a hand. "Don't you dare."

Matthew slowly lifted one eyebrow. "You don't want me to carry you like I did before?"

"No way."

He shrugged. Then dropped quickly to heave me up over his shoulder in a fireman's carry. I shrieked with laughter as he sauntered into my building, stopping only when the second set of doors wouldn't budge.

"It won't work without my card or someone buzzing you up," I said between giggles. He swatted me on the ass, so I pinched him on his. Homahlord, the ass on that man should be in a museum. Digging through my purse as best as I could while hanging upside down, I reached around him to wave my key card in front of the scanner. The light turned green, and Matthew opened the door.

Once we were in the elevator, I squirmed to get down.

"What floor?" he asked, tightening the arm behind my thighs.

"I can't remember," I told him. "All the blood is rushing to my head."

He sighed, turning me toward the panel. I punched the four, and the elevator churned upward.

Admittedly, I was pretty rusty at the whole dating thing, but what was the expectation when you were both buzzed, had already done some tongue tangling, and he was carrying you over his shoulder up to your apartment?

To me? I translated this as I was really, really glad I wore a cute bra and underwear.

The bell dinged on the fourth floor, and I smacked him on the back. "Seriously, I can walk now, you big ape."

When he tipped me over onto my feet, the hallway spun dangerously, which was how I found myself gripping his biceps while I waited for my head to right itself.

Then I squeezed, feeling the roll of tight muscles under my fingers. So big. So, so big.

I opened my eyes, and my hands slid up his biceps and over the boulders that made up his pecs. His smile dropped, his face turned tight with heat as I held his eyes with my own.

His hand moved up to my face to push my hair off my forehead.

"You tell me what happens next, Slim."

My eyes fell shut at the use of my nickname, something that suddenly seemed precious and secret and ours. Yes, there was alcohol in our bloodstreams, maybe just enough that we weren't second-guessing what was happening between us.

All I knew was that I wanted him. And if this was the one night I got him, then I didn't want to waste it.

My hand dropped from his chest to the silver belt buckle underneath his shirt, and I curled my fingers behind the hard metal.

I started walking toward my apartment, hand hooked in that belt, and maybe I sort of brushed the almost-unbelievable hardness underneath it.

Okay, fine. It was on purpose. But at his sharp inhale, I smiled.

I fumbled with the key as he buried his nose in my hair, wrapping his arms around my hips and pulling me back against him.

Before I let us into my apartment, I turned and pressed my back against the door, staring up at him with wide eyes and a heart that he could probably break with the wrong words.

"If you don't want to come in," I told him quietly, "you need to say it now. I won't be pissed, and I won't hold it against you."

Matthew lifted one hand to cup around the back of my neck, then he leaned down to press a deep, searching kiss against my waiting mouth. I found myself up on tiptoes to get more, more, more of him; my hands unable to touch enough of what I wanted.

His skin on mine.

The heavy weight of him over my body.

To know what he tasted like in the places the world couldn't see.

That was what I wanted.

And I held my breath while I waited for him to answer, to see if he felt the same.

When he pulled back, he held my eyes. "I want to come in."

My lips curled into a satisfied smile. "Good answer."

Behind my back, I turned the knob. We swung around, my apartment a blur as he bent to lift me, pressing me against the inside of the door this time. My legs split from the strength of his hands, and I wrapped them around his narrow hips.

He was so strong. With no more effort than me opening the door, he held me against the hard wood as his tongue twined with my own. I ran my hands over his chest, feeling his heart hammering underneath my palm, my spread fingers.

In his arms, with his hands on me and his lips moving over mine, I felt the slow build of pleasure cover every inch of me. It turned me into a writhing, whimpering mass of bones and blood and skin. A creature that needed more of everything he was giving me.

More of his skin. His lips. His mouth. His hands. His body.

I pushed him back and took a deep breath. Matthew's lips were red from my kisses, and I felt a grin spread over my flushed face.

"What?" he asked, as breathless as I was.

"Room. Bed."

"Right."

He straightened and walked down the one hallway in my small apartment. One hand stayed firmly on my ass, and the other slid up my spine as he carried me with ease.

"Nice place."

I trapped the tip of my tongue between my teeth while I smiled at him, and his eyes tracked the movement with heat and fire. "You're not even looking at it."

"I know."

My room was mostly in shadow, and I briefly wondered if it

would be obvious if I told him to wait so I could flip the light switch.

I didn't want shadows. I didn't just want a glimpse of his masterpiece of a body. I wanted Technicolor. I wanted to know what my hands looked like against his skin in stark detail.

And somewhere in the back of my mind, in the vainest, most selfish part of me, I wanted Matthew to want the same. I wanted him to look down at me as he moved between my legs and see every inch of me.

When he paused and reached behind him, one brief movement lighting up the room in harsh, beautiful light, I had to wonder if I spoke out loud.

That was impossible, though, because my lips were busy licking, sucking, kissing along the hard edge of his granite-carved jawline.

"I want to see you," he whispered against my skin, and I shivered even though his heat was practically incendiary. "I want to see so much more."

Matthew tossed me back onto the bed, and I laughed as I bounced. His answering grin was sweet and boyish, and it made my heart turn over in my chest. Because as he stared at my smiling mouth, his smile turned predatory as he pulled his shirt off and tossed it on the floor.

"I could watch that on a loop every single day and never get bored," I said and then clapped a hand to my mouth when his hand paused over his belt buckle.

His teeth flashed white in his mouth when he laughed, and those massive hands got back to work on his belt. Good boy.

I narrowed my eyes, not wanting to be the only one causing skin-induced mayhem and fumbled words. I sat up, kicked off my sandals, and slowly came up to my knees on the bed.

Matthew's hands paused on his zipper when I crossed my arms and gradually pulled my shirt over my head.

His Adam's apple bobbed slowly as his throat worked on a thick swallow. His eyes burned, never wavering from the nude lace bra covering my chest. Never had my B cup girls caused me so much pride, but Matthew looked right at them and licked his lips, the movement slow and almost lewd as he finished unzipping his pants.

When my hands went to my shorts, he shook his head.

"What?" I asked.

"I'll do the rest if you don't mind." His voice should have come with a warning label. When it reached that timbre, a neon sign should flash over his head. *Proceed with caution. Panties may spontaneously combust.*

He prowled over me, thick arms bracketing either side of my head, his pants hanging open. Desperately, I tried not to gawk at everything he had going on, and he had *a lot.*

I'd never been looked at that way before, the way Matthew was looking at me.

Like he wanted to eat me alive.

The way he held himself over me, a cursedly large amount of space between his chest and mine, made all the curves and lines over his chest, arms, and shoulders pop out in sharp relief. It almost seemed impossible that one body could hold so much strength.

"Are you showing off?" I whispered, nodding my chin at his pseudo-push-up over my body.

He shook his head, lowering his body over mine with aching and teasing slowness. When his chest touched mine, I sighed, wrapping my arms around his shoulders so I could slick my lips along his. He pushed back up, and I whimpered.

"Now I'm going to show off," he said with a wicked grin. He propped his full weight on one arm and used the other to track the space of skin from underneath my bra to the gaping waistband on my shorts. He turned his fingers over and pushed down between my legs; his hand trapped between my skin and the lace of my underwear.

Slowly, sweetly, he explored, working me into a writhing mass of impatience with his thick fingers. First one, then two. I clutched at his neck until he lowered again, but instead of taking my mouth the way I wanted him to, he sucked on the lace of my bra over my breast until the lace was wet and completely transparent.

With some profound sense of relief, I finally realized this wouldn't be some fumbling, tearing, biting, alcohol-induced coupling. This was luxurious, in the way he slid his fingers and lips and tongue over me and in. My hands spread over his back, my fingernails trailed the pops of muscles until he hissed against my breast.

We flipped over, and I straddled his lap while I pulled off my bra.

Neither of us seemed desperate to rush this, which added a thick pulse of significance that I hadn't expected.

As I rolled my hips over his hardness, he pushed my hair out of my face so he could find my lips with a penetrating, almost punishing kiss. His hands gripped my sides, sliding up to cup my breasts with his wide, warm hands. His thumbs rolled in tight circles, and I had to break away from his mouth just to breathe through the crashing wave of what that did to my body.

"Matthew," I moaned, and he flipped us again, briefly sitting up between my legs to divest me of my shorts and rid himself of his. He froze as he settled between my legs, which immediately clamped around his thighs lest he think he was going *anywhere*.

He closed his eyes when I did. "Do you ... I don't have anything with me."

It took a second to figure out what those words meant because hey, it had been a while since I'd shared a bed with anyone, let alone anyone I wanted to see me without panties on.

I stared up at him, waiting for him to open his eyes. Licking my lips, I jumped off the proverbial cliff with what I said next.

"I'm on birth control," I whispered. "It's ... been a long time for me."

His hand cupped the side of my face, thumb brushing the bottom edge of my lip. "Me too."

I swallowed as I watched him think. I knew. I was sure. For fear of pushing him one way or the other, I stayed perfectly still underneath his massive frame. He dwarfed me, in every possible sense. In fact, I wasn't entirely sure he wouldn't break me. Or my bed. Either one.

But holy shit, that was a risk I was willing to take.

The moment he made his decision, no more than a breath later, I saw the change in his bright, fiery amber eyes. He used his hand to push my leg up toward my chest, and with one smooth, long slide, he thrust in.

The breath of air that left my mouth was part sigh, part *I'll never feel anything as good as this*, and part *hallelujah* chorus in my head.

Until he did it again with his forehead braced against mine.

His arms wrapped tightly around my back, and my legs clamped around his back, my ankles locked firmly.

I was going nowhere, folks.

He kissed me deeply as he moved, and my tongue slid slippery against his as I moved in the same rhythm. Pushing when he pulled, rolling when he came back in. His back turned damp with sweat, my chest did the same.

I felt the warm gathering of pressure slip down my spine and into my hips, down to my toes as they curled against the tangled sheets. Throwing my head back, I braced my hands on the headboard of my bed while we exorcized whatever had been building between us.

He made one hard move, the quick snap of his hips, and I broke, wave after wave of sweet, light-bursting relief.

Matthew clutched me to him with bruising strength, his hands curled up around my shoulders as he followed, my name on his lips as he did.

His big body slumped against me, his breath hitting the side of my neck as though he'd just ran a marathon. My arms wrapped around him tightly, and I ran my fingers along the impossibly soft line of his hair where it met the skin of his neck.

After a minute, he lifted his head and stared down at me.

Stay, I wished fervently in my head but was afraid to ask him out loud. Maybe this was it. Maybe this was my one time to know what he felt like. I couldn't read what was in his eyes as they moved over my face.

"You got enough room in this bed for me tonight?" he finally asked.

I smiled. "Yeah."

He settled on his side with a deep groan, dragging me over so that my head was on his chest and my legs intertwined with his. "Good."

I grinned into the sweat-salted skin over his heart, pressing a tiny kiss there. Good was one word for it. Briefly, I climbed out of bed to clean myself up and grab us both bottles of water. He was dozing off as I waltzed back into my bedroom naked, but his eyes opened just enough to watch me.

His lips curved slightly as I slid back under the sheet covering him from the waist down.

I was tempted to drag it down with my pinky, just to make sure I hadn't imagined what was down there because ho boy, he was proportionate. But he looked so tired, so content as he held his arm out, and I couldn't break the mood. I nestled into his side and sighed.

"G'night, Slim," he whispered against the crown of my head, dropping a sweet kiss against my hair.

I laid there for at least an hour as he breathed deeply, his hand curled over my bare hip. Hoping he'd still be there in the morning, I weighed the possibilities that might come up with the sun. *Tonight,* I thought as I touched his warm, soft skin, *tonight, he was here with me.*

CHAPTER 10
MATTHEW

WASHINGTON
WOLVES

Since my divorce, I could count on one hand the times I'd woken up in bed with a woman. On this particular morning, when I peeled my eyes open to see Ava sprawled next to me, her hair an absolute disaster of tangles and her arms flung out toward me, I almost started laughing out loud.

I didn't do one-night stands.

I certainly didn't do one-night stands with someone who I not only respected but genuinely liked, and who I also happened to work with.

The possibility of awkwardness, of heartache, was high with Ava.

But as I turned on my side to watch her sleep, I already knew I'd risk it simply because it felt really damn good to be with her. Because I wanted to know more.

It wasn't my pride driving me or some false ideal I was striving for, ignoring warning signs of where things might go wrong. This was something I could trust, this instinct to lean more deeply into her, into what I felt when I was around her.

Once in the night, I'd woken to her hands stroking down my stomach. Everything after was a lazy, slow blur. I turned her on her side, wrapping my chest against her back, then lifted her leg over mine and pushed back inside her. Neither of us spoke a word. Just small movements because of our position, her mouth finding mine as she looked over her shoulder, my hands sliding down her stomach and between her legs.

It wasn't long. It wasn't sweaty.

It was ... perfect. All I knew was that waking to her hands on me felt good. It was all I needed to know right now.

Ava took a deep breath and burrowed her face into the pillow. She didn't wake, settling back into her rhythmic breathing almost instantly.

Carefully, I slid from the bed without waking her and found my boxer briefs on the floor. I pulled them on as I walked down the hallway, finally able to get a look at her place.

It was small and tidy with hardwood floors and cool tones in her paint and furniture. As bright as her clothes were at work, her decorating style seemed to be the opposite. Everything was mostly white and gray with pops of lavender and light blue in pillows and blankets and ottomans in front of the long gray couch that faced her television.

After using the bathroom, I found her kitchen and searched through the cupboards until I found coffee. Her machine was pretty basic, so I started a pot while I tried to figure out how this morning might play out when she woke. How I wanted it to play out.

We worked together, which complicated things. A bad sign, for sure. Especially for two people who'd never mixed business with pleasure.

We'd had sex twice. That was a good sign. She didn't strike me as a casual sex type any more than I was. Especially since we had history.

I had to swallow past that thought. Ava and I had history. Something we'd actively avoided talking about thus far, and with good reason.

My hands braced on the counter while the coffee dripped hot and fragrant into the carafe. So what if it was ten years ago? I'd slept with both of the Baker girls, and that made a rock sink into my gut because I didn't like how defensive that made me feel about what had happened with Ava last night.

I'd put my relationship with Ashley behind me. That door was firmly shut. Because I had the unerring opinion that if I hadn't met Ava when she was a scrawny, sweet fourteen-year-old girl, I would've absolutely been attracted to Ava Baker, Senior PR Manager for the Washington Wolves.

I would've seen her and thought she was beautiful. I would've talked to her and thought she was smart and funny. Sharp as the edge of a knife and confident as hell. You had to be to put up with fifty-plus football players all the time.

That was the bottom line. I would've wanted her regardless. Maybe it wouldn't have happened as fast. Maybe I would've asked her out after getting to know her for a few months.

But knowing that was enough for me to be willing to try this if she wanted the same.

I turned and leaned against the counter as the coffee brewed. On her small dining table, I saw a flash of deep blue in a large, round glass tank.

Smiling, I bent down and caught my first glimpse of Frankie the fish. He was beautiful with hues of iridescent blues and purples as he wound around a bright green plant that was growing around a clay pot she'd put at the bottom of the tank.

"If only fishes could talk, huh?" I asked him. "You probably hear all the good stuff from her."

Next to the tank, I saw a container of fish food, so I opened it and dropped a pinch onto the surface of the water. Immediately, he darted up in a swirl of long, waving fins and started pecking at the food.

I watched him eat as I poured two mugs of coffee. He was an interesting little clue to her personality.

She had a pet, even if it was one step above a pet rock as far as the companionship he offered. But his tank was immaculate, large for just one fish, and had a place in the middle of her one eating space.

I wanted to know more. Each clue made me want to unwrap the next and savor it like a piece of one of her chocolates until moving onto the next. No rush, with no expectation.

As I walked back down the hallway, I just had to hope she'd let me figure it out. Figure her out.

Before I reached the door, I heard the creak of the bed and a deep sigh. I smiled.

But my smile dropped when I caught a glimpse of her. She was sitting up in bed with the sheet tucked tightly under her armpits and a frown covering her sleep-lined face, staring down at where I'd been sleeping just fifteen minutes earlier.

Frowning was not a good thing.

But once I noticed the frown, I noticed the droop in her shoulders too.

I cleared my throat, and she jumped, clutching a hand to the bunched-up sheet covering her body.

"Holy shit," she breathed, laughing a nervous laugh as I walked into the room. "You scared me."

"Sorry." I lifted up the mugs. "Thought we could use these."

Ava tucked some messy hair behind her ear, her green eyes tracking quickly down my naked chest and then away like she'd been caught doing something wrong.

"Thank you." She accepted the mug as I handed it to her, and I sipped cautiously out of mine as I perched on the end of the bed.

"Did you sleep well?" I asked.

"Are we crazy for doing this?" she asked at the same time.

We both froze.

My heart churned uncomfortably, and I hoped my face was even as I glanced at her over the edge of the coffee mug. "I don't know. Are we?"

Ava pushed a hand through her tangled hair, sending the wavy masses over one naked, smooth shoulder. "I know it didn't *feel* crazy." She looked up at me from beneath her lashes, checking my reaction.

"It didn't," I agreed easily. "It felt amazing."

Her cheeks pinked, and I saw her bite down on her smile before it spread.

What I wanted to do was ditch the coffee, climb back over her, and taste every inch of her body again. More than once. By the color covering her cheekbones, Ava seemed to be thinking the same thing, but she didn't verbalize it. Neither did I.

When she didn't say anything else, I cleared my throat and stood to set the coffee on the dresser. "But we work together."

She nodded slowly. "We do."

Another sip of her coffee. I wanted her to set it aside too. I wanted ... I wasn't even sure anymore if what I wanted wasn't completely selfish.

"And"—she licked her lips, finally setting the mug down on the bedside table—"you were ..."

Then she held up a hand.

"What?" I asked.

"I need clothes on for this." She scrunched up her nose. "Can you maybe grab the shirt on the floor for me?"

I smiled, reaching down to swipe the wrinkled tank she'd had on the day before. Instead of tossing it to her, I walked over to the bed, fully aware that her eyes were sliding down over my chest and my stomach to the front of my boxer briefs that would very soon not be able to hide how I felt about her.

She took it from my outstretched hand and swallowed audibly. Taking her cue, I leaned over to grab my shorts and pull them on. By the time I finished pulling up the zipper, I had caught a glimpse of brown hair, one breast and then whoosh, she was covered, pulling the shirt down over her waist.

I wondered what she was about to say. *And you were ...*

Engaged to her sister?

Only sticking around for two years, based on my contract?

Divorced?

It could've been anything.

But I had the sense, after just these snippets of time with her, that it wasn't about those things. That Ava had her guard up, high and tight, like a boxer protecting his face at all times.

"If you're worried about the team," I said, "I can keep my mouth shut."

She tilted her head. "Worried about the team?"

I shrugged. "The guys giving you shit."

Ava smiled a little. "Actually, I'd be more worried about them giving *you* shit. I've been around longer, you know. Might not earn you any teammate brownie points if they know you banged me into oblivion after only two weeks. No one else has even managed to score a date."

Had someone asked?

I physically bit down on the tip of my tongue so the question didn't pop out. It wasn't my business even though I felt a quick, bright flare of jealousy paint my brain green.

Her words caught up with my caveman thoughts, and I laughed under my breath. *If they knew you banged me into oblivion.* Damn right. I think my chest actually puffed out.

She must have seen it because she dissolved into laughter.

"Oh my gosh, you should see your face." She threw a pillow, and I caught it. "You arrogant ass."

"Do you need me to toss you a compliment too?" One eyebrow lifted on my forehead. "Because I could think of a few words to describe last night."

Ava rubbed her lips together but didn't stop me. Her eyes danced with laughter as I strolled toward her on the bed.

"Hot. Tight. Perfect."

I stopped, leaning down to plant my fists on either side of her legs, still covered by the rumpled sheet. Her face was almost fully pink. I wanted to suck her lips into my mouth, first the heart-shaped top, then the fuller bottom.

"Okay then," she whispered, tilting her chin up. Just a fraction of an inch. It wasn't a blatant invitation, but I took it as one, dipping down to sip on her top lip.

A puff of air from her nose hit my face, and her tongue swept along my bottom lip.

"Delicious," I added when I pulled away. "But I'll do whatever you need me to right now, no matter how many words I could use for what happened between us."

Indecision crossed her finely angled face, causing the slightest wrinkle in her normally smooth forehead. Unable to resist, I drew my thumb along the line until it disappeared.

"I think," she started slowly, "we just think for the next couple of days. Think about what this ... might mean. Or what we want it to mean before we jump in."

The disappointment felt an awful lot like a game that you lost at the last minute while sitting on the sidelines. Out of my control and nothing I could've done to change the outcome.

Pushing Ava was nothing I'd even contemplate doing right now. Maybe she just wanted to see what it was like with me. See if the obvious attraction between us would flare quickly and then fade.

I stood and cupped her chin with my thumb, rubbing softly at the tiny dimple she had there. "Okay. I can do that."

She didn't smile like I expected her to. Ava simply watched my face, and with her face free of makeup, making her look younger, I caught a brief glimpse of her as a teenager. It was like seeing a ghost, and I stepped back before I could get sucked into the *Ashley/Ava/Matthew is a creeper* vortex again.

Maybe thinking wouldn't be a bad thing. Thinking was something I could do.

"Do you want me to whip up some breakfast?" I asked with a casual smile. Or at least I hoped it was casual. "I didn't poke around your cupboards too much, but I can make a mean omelet."

She laughed and ducked her head. "You don't need to do that."

Okay then. Of course, I didn't *need* to. But that didn't mean I didn't want to.

I pulled on my T-shirt. "Frankie can vouch for my culinary skills. He devoured those flakes pretty quick."

Her smile was bigger this time. "You met my famous pet, huh?"

"He's handsome. Not all men can pull off that shade of blue."

Ava rolled her eyes but still laughed. "Thanks."

The word—preceded by a slight, loaded pause—felt weighted in significance. So was the way she held my eyes when she said it. I wasn't sure what she was thanking me for, but I took a chance, leaned down, and kissed her on the top of the head.

"Anytime, Slim." I tucked my phone in my pants and lifted my hand. "I'll let myself out."

She gestured awkwardly to her lap. "Good, because I'm not wearing underwear."

I was still laughing when I walked out the door.

Yeah, everything about this felt good. It was enough that I knew I wouldn't need to do much thinking. I already wanted more.

CHAPTER 11
AVA

WASHINGTON WOLVES

"**W**hat can I get you ladies to drink?"

Allie and Paige immediately piped up, prosecco for one and gin and tonic for the other.

I sighed and looked up at the smiling waitress with puppy dog eyes. "Just water for now, please."

"Gross," Paige muttered as the waitress walked away.

"What's gross about water?"

She lifted her eyebrows like I was stupid. "It's girls' night. You don't drink water on girls' night."

Allie stifled a grin but didn't say anything. A group of swaggering college boys slowed to an obviously sluggish pace as they passed our table, one of them making a kissy face at Paige.

I rolled my eyes.

Of course, they would. I was sitting at a table with two of the most beautiful women in the entire world.

Paige gave him an assessing look, crooking her finger to beckon him closer. Allie raised one perfectly manicured eyebrow.

The kid swallowed, his bravado faltering when she actually responded. Couldn't blame him.

"H-Hey," he said when he was at our table. Smooth. Really smooth.

"What's your name?" Paige asked, eyes big and round in her porcelain face. Her expression was guileless, but I knew her well enough that this poor little baby boy was about to have his balls shrunken in like a bucket of ice down his pants.

His friends whistled and hooted, Allie sighed quietly, and I watched with my chin perched in my hand.

"Uh, it's, uh, Cade."

"Uh-Cade? Or just Cade?"

God bless him, he puffed out his chest and stood tall. "Cade."

Paige held out her hand, and he shook it. Softly, tentatively, like a little baby kitten. She pursed her lips when he dropped it back to his side. I could feel a laugh bubbling up my throat, but I swallowed it down. Yes, girls' night was a good idea. The perfect distraction when I spent all day cleaning my apartment obsessively after practically shoving Matthew out the door.

"Cade," she said, leaning forward on the table. His eyes darted down to her chest and then back up to her face. "I could be married, I could be gay, or I could be single but so anti-men that just that one uninvited gesture from you could send me into a homicidal rage, and you just wouldn't know until it was too late."

He glanced at me, and I shrugged one shoulder. His eyes moved nervously back to Paige. "Okay?"

"I'm going to give you a bit of advice," she whispered. "If you find a woman attractive and are interested in getting to know more about her, just walk up like a man who knows what he wants. Tell her your name and ask her what hers is. Don't make shit-heel kissy faces and assume that will do anything except make you look like a chump who's still waiting for his chest hair to grow in."

Poor Cade. The color drained from his face except for two bright red spots on his baby face.

"Got it," he said and turned to walk back to his snickering friends.

Paige cleared her throat. "Hang on." She motioned to our waitress, who hurried over. He shuffled to the side to allow her some room. "I'd like to buy Cade his next round because he's going to take this as a valuable life lesson, one that will help him immensely in his future."

"Sure thing," she said, giving Cade a pitying glance.

"Thanks," he muttered and followed the waitress back to his friends, who were now chortling with glee.

"I hate college boys," Paige said under her breath.

"Aww, he had the cojones to come over here," Allie told her. "That's gotta count for something."

"Plus," I interjected, "not all college boys are assholes."

Naturally, as it had all day, my mind skittered back to Matthew. Matthew in my bed. Matthew bringing me coffee wearing black boxer briefs. Glory, glory, hallelujah, I'd remember that image as I took my final breaths on earth. Then to Matthew when I first knew him, polite and kind, understanding of the shittiness of my parents when most guys wouldn't have paid any attention to me. No, Matthew hadn't been that kind of college boy.

He was the guy who made sure I had a Hawkins shirt to wear when Stanford played in a bowl game his junior year, and our whole family attended because his parents couldn't make it.

He was the guy who asked me how school was.

If I wanted to play catch in the backyard.

"And she's back in outer space," Allie said, snapping her fingers in front of my face.

I sighed before taking a long drink of my water.

"Sorry."

Paige gave me a curious look. "Geez, what happened with you and Hawkins?"

I choked on a piece of ice, coughing obnoxiously until the people behind her turned to see if I was okay. I waved them off.

Allie chuckled. "I love this. The only time I've ever seen this woman remotely frazzled was the day he showed up. Until Matthew Hawkins walked down that hallway to her office, she was the unflappable one." She wiped a fake tear from her eye, and I flipped her my middle finger. "It's the most beautiful thing I've ever seen."

"I'm not frazzled," I argued, wiping a chunk of ice off the side of my face like an absolutely frazzled woman.

She patted my hand in the most condescending way possible. "Mmkay."

"So what is it about this guy?" Paige asked. "Besides the obvious."

With twitchy, restless fingers, I started shredding a napkin as my thoughts whirled furiously in my head. Without making eye contact, I gave them a brief rundown of what happened yesterday. They awwed about the chocolate factory, then fell into hushed silence when I told them about the drinks and the cab ride back to my place. Allie only squealed once when I mumbled something like, *and then we had two epic rounds of sex in my bed, the end.*

"So what's the problem?" Paige asked.

I sighed heavily, scooping up the tiny pieces of white paper and forming a little mountain next to my water. "I don't even know what happened. I don't even know how to do this anymore." Dropping my head into my hands, I could barely look at them as I struggled to define what my problem had been. "One minute, I'm falling asleep praying he'll still be there in the morning because I wanted him to be there in the morning. But once he brought me coffee, I started thinking about how insane we must be to even think about attempting this. Whatever *this* is."

"Ava, honey, I don't think it's insane," Allie said gently.

"Yeah?" My eyebrows popped up on my head as I lifted my fingers to tick off all the reasons why. "I've never ever crossed that line with one of the players, and he's only been here for a couple of weeks. He's got a short-term contract and a life in New Orleans he's been building for a decade. He was engaged to my sister, for crying out loud, the sister I cannot stand, so what am I supposed to do when I show up at my parents' house for Christmas? Surprise! Here's that guy who was once going to marry your favorite daughter until she cheated on him, and now I'm banging him. Can you please pass the mashed potatoes?" I smacked the table, and they jumped. "Except we don't have mashed potatoes at

Christmas because *heaven forbid* Ashley put a single gram of carbs in her body lest she bloat. Yeah, let's just imagine that happy family gathering."

Like gorgeous twin images in front of me, their mouths hung open and their eyes were wide in their faces. So I'd ranted a bit.

I sank my head into my hands again and stared unblinkingly at the black surface of the table. "For some reason, I could ignore all those things until he walked back into my bedroom. And I didn't want to let any of that get to me, but here I am. Not with him because we're both supposed to be thinking about what we want next."

"I'm so sorry, Ava," Allie said. "None of this is easy."

Paige snorted. "Sure, it is."

I lifted my head, narrowing my eyes at her. "How so?"

"First off, cart before horse much? You spent one night with him. Christmas isn't for another six months, and so what if he has a history with your family? Your family sounds like a bunch of assholes. Why would you base your life happiness off them? Why are you even overthinking it this much? You like him. He likes you. The sex was good. I say keep doing it while it is and while you still like each other. The end."

She made it sound so easy. Partially because those were all completely rational thoughts. Those had a way of sounding easy.

"The end," I repeated slowly, watching a line of condensation trickle down the side of my glass. "It's my job to overthink, you know? It's my job to consider every angle of how things could go wrong or sound bad to the audience, whoever that might be. It's hard to shut that off in my personal life. Not that I've had much practice since college," I mumbled. "Which is also part of the problem. I'm dating defunct."

"Do you think Matthew is the type to overthink this too?" Allie asked.

All I could do was lift my shoulders in a helpless shrug. "He could be. I know him but not in this way. I don't really know what relationship Matthew is like."

"And he doesn't know what relationship Ava is like," Allie pointed out.

"True." I took a sip of my water. "*I* don't know what relationship Ava is like anymore. She hasn't shown her face for a few years."

"So can't you guys just ... play it casual? If it's working, keep seeing each other, but don't put all this family pressure on it right away before you even know if relationship Ava and relationship Matthew make sense together?" Paige asked.

Putting Matthew in any slot labeled casual felt strange at first, but maybe I was looking at this all wrong. There wasn't any reason to have some big serious talk about his past with Ashley, or my family, because they were a non-issue at the moment. They'd only become an issue if I let them, and I had no intention of that happening.

Paige leaned forward. "I'm basically telling you to avoid the drama right now. You're making this so much harder than it needs to be."

She wasn't wrong. I laughed when I caught sight of her pleased expression. "You have an awful lot of advice for someone without a boyfriend."

"Well, shit," Paige said. She slumped in her chair and gave me a sympathetic look. "That's probably why I'm single."

Allie snorted. "You're single because you eat men alive, and most of them run scared as soon as you open your mouth."

She smiled, unrepentant and stunningly scary. "True."

Turning to me, Allie smiled. "Listen, just talk to him. He seems like a reasonable guy, and he's clearly feeling the same magic sex juju that you are."

For the first time all night, I felt those happy flutters. The flutters I got when he hugged me in my office. The flutters I got when he ate my chocolate and grinned at me. The flutters I got when he slid his big hand up my leg and touched his tongue to mine with zero hesitation.

There was no reason to make this harder than it was.

I drummed my fingers on the table and stared at them. "Ladies, I adore you, but I'm going to break a cardinal rule and ditch girls' night."

Paige pouted, but I could tell she wasn't serious. Allie wiggled excitedly in her seat. "Are you going to his place?"

I looked down at my outfit. Casual, cute, but a girls' night outfit. "I'm going to change first." Then gave them a pointed look. "I'm wearing comfy underwear."

"Ahh," they both said in understanding.

"Good luck," Allie called after I blew them a kiss and hopped out of my chair.

By the time I made it back to my apartment, flew through the lobby, and let myself into my place, twenty minutes had passed. My phone had remained silent, but then again, I hadn't texted him either. My plan was all centered around him being home, thinking very sexy, fluttery thoughts about me, and that made me pause before I stripped my shirt off.

What if his thinking was done before he even got back to his place? It could've been easy for him. Eh, that was fun, but it's too complicated for an already complicated season of my life.

I sank down onto the edge of my bed. I wasn't used to so many insecurities shouting in my head. Damn it, Matthew Hawkins and his perfectness.

No, I thought with a smile. He wasn't perfect. Nobody was. This was my chance to find out what his flaws were.

I grabbed my phone and tapped out a text.

Me: Are you at home?

Almost instantly, three little gray dots bounced on the screen. I bit down on a grin. Yup. Flutters were abundant.

Matthew Hawkins: I'm not. Are you?

Like a dying flower, I wilted. Good thing I hadn't stripped yet. With a sigh, I replied back that I was.

Matthew Hawkins: Good. I'm about to knock on your door.

I shrieked, glancing frantically at my closet, then down at where my comfy underwear was underneath my jeans. At my door, there was a firm knock. Like a general about to head into battle, I stood and marched to the door. Only pausing to take a fortifying breath and smooth my ponytail, I opened the door to find him leaning a shoulder against the doorframe.

He looked so good. So good. Wearing dark jeans on this thick, long legs and a white Wolves T-shirt over his broad chest, he was beyond tempting, and I wanted to lick him from head to toe. Twice. And on his face was a happy smile. Aimed at me.

Mimicking his stance, I leaned my shoulder against the opposite side of the door. "Hi."

"Can I come in?"

I rolled my lips between my teeth and moved back. Before he said a word, I inhaled deeply while he passed. His scent was so potent, I wasn't sure my comfy underwear hadn't already completely disintegrated.

I leaned against the closed door. Matthew leaned against the back of my couch, and we smiled at each other like fools.

"Did you do your thinking yet?" he asked.

I nodded slowly. "You?"

Tension snapped, crackled, and popped while teeny explosions went off as his eyes tracked down the length of my body. This wasn't any little flutter. He was incinerating me without laying a single finger on my skin.

"I did." He spread his arms and gripped the back edge of the couch.

Neither of us moved.

"And?" I asked, my voice husky and all sex operator-esque. His eyes darkened, turning into a warm amber color I hadn't seen yet. Oh, I liked his eyes like that. I'd forever think of them as Matthew's sex eyes.

"I know there are reasons we could leave last night as it stands," he said. I licked my lips, suddenly unsure of what might come out of his mouth next. He inhaled deeply, his chest stretching the measly cotton confines of his shirt. "But to me, they're not good enough. I want more, Ava."

Long before it touched my face, I felt the smile down in my belly. That was where all the good smiles started because it warmed my entire body before it ever curled my lips.

"That so?" I asked, slowly walking in his direction. I saw the knuckles on his hands turn white as he gripped the couch frame.

"Yeah."

"Good." I wedged myself between his thighs and smoothed my hands up his chest. Still, he didn't touch me. "Because I came home to change so I could come to you and tell you that I was thinking the same thing."

He didn't smile, but the skin around his eyes crinkled like they did when he was happy. Maybe his smile was starting in his belly too.

Finally, his big hands curled around my hips and pulled me flush against him. He was already hard for me. I was just as ready from only a few seconds of his hands on my body.

He slid his hand from my hip, up my back and down again, playing with the edge of my shirt until I felt his fingers brush my skin. It was meant to be comforting, but it was inciting enough that I closed my eyes against the sudden flare of heat. How had I gone my entire life without feeling like this? One slide of his hands and I was ready to burn my clothes off just to feel more of him.

Grabbing his arms, I pulled them around me even tighter, giving him no choice but to wrap me in a crushing embrace. I pushed my nose into his neck and breathed him in. His hands slid down underneath my pants until he was palming my bottom in both hands.

Wriggling my hips even closer to him, I started thinking of all the places we could start. The couch with me on top. The kitchen table with him behind. Oh! The wall. Yes. I liked that idea.

Then I gasped and pulled back. His hands remained on my flesh, but his face was drawn with concern.

"What?"

I covered my face with one hand and laughed. "Sorry, that was an overreaction." I peeked at him through my spread fingers. "I just

... I'm wearing comfy underwear. I meant to change before I saw you."

He bit back his smile, started moving his hands so that his knuckles brushed against the offending garment. "Yeah?"

I nodded miserably.

"The big cotton kind that covers you from your belly button down?"

I smacked his chest. "Shut up."

His booming laugh was worth my embarrassment, though, even as I dropped my forehead against his shoulder.

"You're the worst," I said into his shirt. He wasn't, though.

Matthew was still smiling as he kissed up the side of my neck and nibbled on the edge of my jaw.

"Slim," he muttered. "Look at me."

I pulled back and glanced at him through my lashes.

"I can't wait to see 'em." He brushed his lips against mine, and I melted, twining my arms around his neck as he tilted his head and deepened the kiss. My tongue wound around his, and his hands gripped me tight until I was writhing against him for relief. He broke away and dragged his nose against mine. "Even if it takes all night to get them off."

I burst into laughter as he swung me into his arms and marched us to my room.

CHAPTER 12
MATTHEW

WASHINGTON WOLVES

W hen I was twelve, I helped my dad roll new insulation in the attic of his house. To this day, it was the worst job I've ever done. It was hot and itchy in uncomfortable tight spaces, and by the time we finished, he slapped me on the back as payment. As a kid, I didn't understand the ins and outs of owning a home. How things like those puffy pink rolls of hell we'd put down would lower his heating bill and save him money when he was still forking over child support to my mom every month.

"You need that stuff, boy. Trust me, there's enough bullshit out there that if you don't insulate from the outside, it'll bleed into the space you want to feel safe and warm."

I didn't fully understand what he meant by that until I started seeing Ava. And after so many years, I understood the deeper layer underneath his fairly obvious statement because we absolutely, unashamedly insulated ourselves.

Today, a couple of days after I first showed up at her place, she beat me from the office and had let herself into my apartment with the key I gave her. I'd told her it was just to make things easier when she gave me a surprised look.

I opened the door and immediately smelled garlic. Lots and

lots of garlic.

Short of plugging my nose, there was no escaping it.

"Slim?" I called out as I tossed my duffel bag on the ground by the door.

"In here!" Her voice came from the kitchen.

When I found her, she was standing in front of the sprawling kitchen island, her hands propped on her hips and a perplexed look on her face. Her hair was up in a messy bun, and over her petite, slightly curved body, she wore one of my aprons that was about six sizes too big for her.

Holy shit, my eyes started to water from the smell.

"Whatcha makin'?" I came up behind her and wrapped my arms around her waist, dropping a kiss on her shoulder where the oversized neck of her shirt had slipped off.

"I was trying to make this pasta dish Allie told me about." She slumped in my arms, and together we stared at the rubbery mess of noodles, and the sauté pan of about fourteen garlic cloves, if I had to count.

"It looks ... great."

Over her shoulder, she gave me a disbelieving look.

"It looks terrible," I amended.

"I know." Ava turned in my arms and wrapped her hands around my waist, burrowing in like she did when she wanted a tight hug. As always, I was happy to comply. She felt so slender in my arms, perfectly tucked underneath my chin. It's where she slept too, curled into my side, her body wrapped under my arm where it naturally folded over her shoulder, and her leg slung over mine.

"I didn't know you cooked," I said carefully, dropping a kiss onto the crown of her head.

"I don't," she said glumly. I laughed, easing back so I could kiss her frowning lips.

"Why'd you want to try tonight?"

She shrugged, circling the tip of her pinky around the top button of my Henley. "It felt like the right thing to do."

I started walking us backward, out of the kitchen, away from the smell. "Yeah?"

Ava nodded, her lips finally starting to turn up at the edges. "Yeah."

"Is it the right thing to do to kill me with garlic?"

Her fingers pinched my side, and I yelped, grabbing her hand so I could bite at her fingertips. Then she grinned because those tasted like garlic.

We opened the windows and the slider overlooking my private patio to let out the stench. Twenty minutes later, I went to grab the food that was delivered to the door, mine with twice as much protein, no carbs, and double the veggies of her dish.

I sat on one of the teak chaise loungers and stretched my legs out, patting my lap so she knew where I wanted her to sit.

She did, facing me with her legs straddling my lap, balancing our plates in front of us.

"This is ridiculous," she said around a bite of my chicken.

"The chicken?"

Ava rolled her eyes, swiping at the side of her mouth. "This. I could sit on my own chair."

"You could."

She didn't move, and I didn't make her. Between bites of food, we talked about our day at work.

"Aww, you made a friend," she teased when I told her Luke invited me out to their place the following weekend.

I shook my head. "He's just being a good captain. But it has been harder than I thought to get to know the rest of the guys. Maybe training camp will help. Really get into our normal schedule."

She nodded, fully aware that off-season still included hours of training and weight lifting and running. It was just usually each guy doing his own thing.

"I love training camp," she said with a sheepish grin. "Almost more than the regular season."

I settled in my chair after I set my empty plate down on the ground. My hands found her hips, sliding leisurely along the tops of her thighs. "Yeah? How come?"

Ava took one more bite and set her plate down too, tangling her fingers in mine and letting me direct the movements of our hands. "I love the fans that come and watch and how the players get to interact with them. Retired players come back and help the rookies, and it's like this strange little reunion. There's a different level of excitement at training camp, you know? Before the stress of the season really kicks in."

I knew exactly what she was talking about. Watching her face while she explained it, though, gave me glimpses of the kid I used to know. The one who asked me about games, who wanted to come to practices.

This ... this was new for me. Someone who loved the game almost as much as I did.

"What?" she asked when I didn't speak. I was still staring at her. My expression must have given some of my thoughts away because she blushed and looked away.

I used my thumb and forefinger to turn her chin back toward me. "I've never been with anyone who got it before."

And because it was Ava, I didn't have to elaborate what that meant. She leaned forward and gave me a hard kiss. "Not even your ex?"

We'd skirted around the subject of her sister, but this wasn't the first time she had asked me about Lexi.

I shook my head. "She liked all the perks that came with football but not the actual day-to-day lifestyle."

"That makes it hard. Because the day to day is what makes the career a successful one."

"Exactly. And I'm not the party animal, red carpet guy. The one who rents a huge yacht on bye week so I can throw a party."

She adopted a grave expression. "I made a poor choice then because that's *totally* my style."

That was how it was with us, I was quickly learning. And it fit. Happiness fit me as easily as it seemed to fit her, and we weren't in any rush to break through what was insulating us from all the bull-shit outside.

After three days of almost perfect evenings, making (attempting to make, on her end) food, giving up and ordering takeout, watching movies, talking football, and having sex just about everywhere in both of our apartments, I felt like it couldn't possibly be like this all the time.

This had to be too good to be true.

"Why not?" she asked when I posed the question to her while she was helping me work out.

Helping me by straddling my upper back while I did push-ups. I paused with my arms extended straight out, groaning when she shifted.

"Well," I said, only slightly out of breath. I'd be damned if a woman who weighed a buck ten managed to make me huff and puff after only a hundred push-ups. "Is this normal for you? That it's this easy?"

"Who you callin' easy, chump?" She pinched my side.

I growled over my shoulder at her, catching a glimpse of her wide smile.

She planted her hands safely on my shoulder blades as I did a few more. "No, this isn't normal for me," she said after a few minutes.

It wasn't the first time we'd waded into any topic of her relationship history. But when I'd asked at the bar, I only got a partial answer, and I felt like there was so much more underneath it, maybe even more than she realized. So I took a beat before peppering her with questions even though that was what I wanted to do.

"How was it different?" I asked as I lowered our bodies to the ground.

She sighed heavily. "Well, the last guy I dated could do *two* hundred push-ups with me on his back, so ..."

Ava squealed when I stood, dumping her onto the ground when I did. I prowled over her as she sprawled laughing on the floor. Her punishment started with her skirt rucked up around her waist, my head ducked underneath, and tongue, lips, and teeth everywhere but where she really wanted me. In the next five minutes, I heard language that would make a man's ears blister, but I refused to give her what she wanted until she was begging and clawing at my back.

I lifted my head from between her legs, and she pinched my ear.

"Ow," I said then bit the side of her inner thigh.

"You're the worst sort of tease, Matthew Hawkins," she groaned. "Go, get back to work."

"Yes, ma'am." I notched two fingers against my temple and saluted her, which earned me a grin.

She laughed when I tickled the inside of her knee, then her sounds changed to quiet whimpers and soft moans as I feasted on her.

When Ava was limp from her release, I carried her inside, something I found I loved to do because of how slight she was, how naturally she fit in my arms. I fell back on the couch with an oof, and she nuzzled into my chest.

"You missed your calling, Hawkins."

"Yeah?"

"Eff football, you could perform cunnilingus for a living and probably make more money."

The couch shook from the force of my deep, booming laughter. I swept her hair away from her face so I could see it better. "And who am I performing for?"

Her eyes flashed. "Me."

That slight bolt of jealousy made her eyes almost unholy green, and I wished I had a picture of her looking just like that. My cheek rested easily on the crown of her head, and I stared down at where my hand curved up over the edge of her thigh.

"I'm going to say something, and you can't make fun of me."

Ava snickered. "Okay."

"That would make a good picture."

She glanced up at me. "What would?"

I nodded down at her legs, my hand, a tangle of skin. "That would."

"You gonna post it on your Instagram with some poetic caption?" she teased, nibbling at the bottom of my jaw.

Normally, I'd find her lips with mine and finish what I'd started on the floor because, underneath her, I was *ready* to finish what we'd started.

Instead, I watched her face carefully as I answered. "What if I did?"

Her smile dropped, and she briefly held my eyes before looking back down at my hand on her leg. Ava was quiet for a long moment before she answered. "Well, your fans would freak the hell out. You haven't posted pictures with a woman since Lexi, and you didn't have much of a social media presence then."

I smirked. Someone just admitted to doing some cyberstalking. "True."

Neither of us spoke, and until that beat of silence, I didn't realize how much I wanted this. I wanted to give the world some hint of what I'd been sharing with her.

I held my breath while she thought because I knew she was sliding naturally into 'PR for the team' mode. Even worse, I could practically see her bring those gloves up in front of her face to protect against some unknown assailant. Hopefully, she didn't think it was me.

"How many followers do you have?" she asked.

Not what I expected, but okay. "Uhh, a couple of million, I think."

She laughed under her breath. "A couple of million, he thinks," she muttered. She gripped my chin and kissed me fiercely. "You have three and a half million followers, Matthew. They will unleash holy hell trying to figure out whose leg your hand is on. They'll see that freckle on my right thigh and start searching until they can match it to someone. Are we ready for that? I don't know that I'm ready to make this harder than it needs to be, you know?"

There was nothing but truth in what she said. Because I'd been not just high profile but also single for so many years, there was always speculation about my love life and even my sexuality after Lexi divorced me. I wanted to stand on the proverbial rooftop and scream to the world that there was the seed of something amazing here, but I also knew she wasn't wrong.

Slowly, Ava moved so she was straddling my legs, and she gripped my face in her small hands. Her thumbs brushed over my lips, and I kissed them as they did.

"Nothing about this relationship is normal for me, Matthew." Her face was so vulnerable, I wanted to bury her in my arms until she felt better, looked happier. And that should have scared me. My desire to make her happy should have scared me, but it didn't.

"And I'm glad for that. I'm *so* happy with what we are right now," she told me, holding my face so I couldn't look away even if I'd wanted to. I smoothed my hands up her back.

Ava leaned forward and touched her lips to mine. A slow glide of her tongue into my mouth had me clasping her tightly against my body, and the way her breasts pressed against my chest had my heart racing.

When she spoke next, it was into the skin of my neck. "It's not about you or questioning whether this is something I still want. It's just ... everything outside of us that makes me feel like I'm not ready. Like it complicates this more than necessary. Does that make sense?"

I closed my eyes and kissed her temple, breathing in the sweet citrusy scent of her shampoo.

"Yeah, it does," I told her. It was the first lie I told myself about Ava, and at that moment, I believed it.

WASHINGTON
WOLVES

"Three days till training camp," someone yelled at the end of the weight room. "We ready?"

A chorus of *hell yeah* and *damn straight* rang out among the clanging of weights, the grunts and yells of the defense sweating out our frustrations and our desires for the upcoming season.

"Need a spot?" one of the safeties, Christiansen, asked as he passed me doing bench presses.

"Thanks," I groaned. He held his hand under the bar as I gritted my teeth, relished the burn in my muscles.

"Come on, old man," he teased. "You've got two more in ya."

"Oh, screw you," I said, but we both damn well knew I was going to do three more since he asked for two. I planted my feet firmly on the ground, and even though my arms felt like they were being licked by fire, and my face was dripping with sweat, I puffed air in my cheeks and finished my third before he helped me fit the metal bar in the holders.

I sat up and stretched, only managing to wince once before I smiled up at him. "Thanks."

"You get laid or something, Hawkins?"

My entire body froze as did about five or six players who were within earshot. "What?"

"Aww, come on, man," Lopez asked from the weight machine to my left. "You've been walking around here grinnin' like a damn fool for the past week."

A sweat towel from the floor served as an excellent way to hide my face as I thought about what to say. I snapped it at Lopez when he started elbowing Christiansen. "Can't a guy just be in a good mood?"

Someone coughed obnoxiously, and I glared as effectively as possible to the small audience that'd gathered. Stupid Christiansen. And it wasn't annoying because I didn't want to tell them. I wished I could. But this was probably the one place where I understood Ava's hesitance.

"If I did get laid," I said as I stood from the weight bench, "I wouldn't tell you assholes."

Laughter answered that one, which started a few stories from the single guys of their own weekend conquests.

I shook my head, shoving at Christiansen as we walked back toward the locker room.

"Dick."

He laughed. "Sorry. You've just been pretty quiet since you got here. I was the new guy two years ago when I got traded from Arizona. It ain't easy all the time."

"No, it's not," I agreed. We stopped so he could refill his water bottle.

The door to the weight room pushed open, and Logan Ward strolled in.

"Afternoon," he said, lifting his chin at both of us.

"Ward," Lopez bellowed from the machine. "You need to start doing what Hawkins is doin'. Maybe you'll lighten up too."

Logan glanced at me and then back at Lopez.

Lopez shook his head. "He's not even gonna ask."

"Why would I need to lighten up?" Logan asked, looking genuinely confused.

The entire weight room cracked up, and even I managed a smile. Maybe he wasn't a complete asshole, just ... serious. Or maybe he was an asshole. Who knew.

"You need to get laid, Ward," Christiansen said, shoving at Logan's back. "Why do you think Hawkins is all smiles and heart eyes the past couple of weeks?"

Logan narrowed his eyes at me but didn't say anything.

I held up my hands. "Don't look at me. I have nothing to do with this."

He sighed, a consternated look on his hardened face. Logan had been in the league longer than just about anyone on the team, except maybe Luke Pierson, so he probably got sick of stuff like this really easily.

"Back to work, guys. Shit like this won't win us any games."

I had to lift my eyebrows in concession because he was right. But a little camaraderie didn't hurt either. Except everyone seemed to take his gruffness with ease, a few jokes in his direction. I followed Christiansen out of the weight room and stopped to grab my duffel.

"You gonna grab a shower, man?" he asked, stripping his shirt off and tossing it on the floor.

"At home."

He nodded. "See you tomorrow."

I lifted my hand and started toward Ava's office. It was only three, so I knew she was still in the building somewhere. Just that morning when I'd crawled out of her bed, she mumbled something about a meeting that would run until six, and to wait so we could have dinner together.

Every day, I saw her.

Every night for the past ten days, we'd slept in the same bed, either hers or mine.

And every time she kissed me, wrapped her arms around me, and burrowed her face into my chest, I fell further. Every time we watched *Pardon the Interruption*, and she argued vehemently with something Wilbon or Kornheiser said, I felt a pinch in my heart. Every time I was inside her, I knew I'd never felt anything so good.

And every time I tried to tiptoe over the invisible line in the sand, the one where we talked about the future or anything of substance in our pasts, she deftly avoided the subject.

I understood her wariness. To a point. And to a point, I knew why she was so cagey. Coming from a guy who'd been cheated on and divorced, I *more* than understood taking things slow. But it didn't make it easier. Not now that I'd finally found someone I could trust, someone who made me want to fall headfirst into this feeling.

As I walked down the hallway, I felt the frustration of keeping this amazing feeling buried. My skin felt jittery and tight as I passed someone, giving them a polite smile. I just pretended I was another player going to find another employee.

Her door was barely ajar, but I could see the soft glow from her desk lamp. Rapping my knuckles on it before I walked in, she held up her finger as she finished a phone call.

She winked at me when I shut the door quietly.

"Yeah, we can make that happen," she said. Darting forward, she snagged a red notepad and scrawled something on the first page. "Uh-huh. Just make sure you email me the questions first. We don't want any surprises, do we?" She laughed. "Okay. Thanks."

Her phone hit the desk with a clatter, and she groaned as she stretched back in her desk chair.

"Busy day?" I asked her with a grin.

"Just the stupid kind of busy." She stood from the chair and came to where I was leaning against a filing cabinet, conveniently out of sight of the small window in her door. When I'd seen her that morning, she'd been rumpled and sleepy in a simple blue tank with matching shorts.

Now she was sleek Ava again, her hair pulled back in a tight knot and a bright yellow dress covering the body I loved so much.

My hands found her waist, and I drew her close to me. Her grin was naughty, and I very much liked the look of it.

"You're all sweaty," she whispered. But she tilted her chin up, so it didn't bother her too much.

I kissed her, pouring all my frustration into her lips, grabbing her ass with hands that might dirty her dress, but she pressed into me instantly. I sucked her tongue into my mouth, and she whimpered before pulling back.

Ava rolled her forehead against my chest. "Lifting weights got you all worked up, huh?"

"You've got me worked up," I told her, wishing I could work my fingers into her hair, mess it up, tangle it around my fingers and pull it into a tight fist just so I could have a primal outlet for this feeling.

Worked up.

Tied into knots.

Desperate to claw away at the armor she still clung stubbornly to, and I couldn't understand why. So badly, I wanted to wrench it away, have her show me the soft underbelly that I knew was there, and the irritation of not being able to kick-started a furious rhythm in my blood. Ava must have felt it in the flex of my fingers, the tremor of my body.

She didn't say anything; she just pulled in a slow, ragged breath. Everything I needed to know, I heard in that choppy inhalation. She wanted me too. She knew it was probably stupid to do this in her office, but she wanted me too.

Ava wrapped her fists in the neck of my shirt and dragged my mouth down to hers again. I groaned, turning us so her back was against the filing cabinet, and I could lift her higher. Her legs wrapped around my waist as I ground into her. Suddenly, I was thankful for two things—her dress and my gym shorts.

She pushed at the latter, and I yanked at the former, shoving up her dress and only taking enough time to tug her underwear to the side with impatient fingers.

Just as I was lined up and about to thrust in, she shoved a hand at my chest.

"Wait."

My hand cupped her breast, and she dropped her head back. I moved my hips forward just barely, enough that we both stopped breathing at what a tease it was.

"Is my door locked?" she whispered.

I stopped.

"Shit," I groaned. "No."

With a growl building in the back of my throat, I helped her drop her feet to the floor as I pulled my shorts up.

"Patience, big boy," she said, tapping my chest and walking on unsteady legs to press the button on her doorknob that would ensure our privacy. My hands were still gripping the filing cabinet when her phone rang.

"No," she whined. I glanced at her over my shoulder, almost laughing at the look on her face. "I just ... I have to make sure it's not Cameron. I'm waiting on something time-sensitive before I meet with him later."

At the name of our team president, I hung my head. "No problem."

When she picked up her phone and greeted him, I let out a deep breath. Guess there would be no fun to be had in the office. I turned and gave her a wry smile when she pouted.

As she spoke to Cameron, I wandered around her office, noting the brightly framed quotes, her diploma, and a picture of her and Allie from the playoffs the year before.

They both looked beautiful with wide smiles and excited eyes after a win, but my gaze stayed locked on Ava. Her cheek was pressed to Allie's, her lips the same scarlet red as the team's colors, and a look of such genuine happiness on her face that I wanted to rub at the spot over my heart.

How many people in the world got to do a job that brought such happiness?

I was one of the few, and most players felt the same. But

looking at her face, I knew Ava was among that number. I had no right to it, but I felt so much pride staring at that picture, trying to reconcile her with the girl who wanted to learn poker, the girl who used to watch football with her dad and me on Sunday afternoons.

My eyes drifted down and caught on something on top a pile of papers.

I pushed aside the edge of a heavy cream envelope and seeing the name Ashley Baker-Hughes went off like a bomb in my chest. Since my back was to Ava, she didn't see me pick up the paper with a surprisingly steady hand. Nothing could kill a hard-on faster than seeing your ex-fiancee's name five minutes after you about to screw her sister senseless.

The honor of your presence
Is required at the reaffirmation of the
Wedding vows of
Adam Hughes and Ashley Baker-Hughes

There was more, a date and time, not too far in the future, and the location. Orcas Island. I knew Adam Hughes. Very well, actually.

"Oh shit," Ava whispered from beside me. She reached forward to take the invitation from me, and I let her.

"Sorry, that's what I get for snooping."

She shook her head. "You weren't snooping. I'm the one who left it out."

Everything felt tangled and weird in my chest. Of course, she'd kept this from me. We'd avoided the subject of Ashley like she was a plague that could descend on our happy bubble.

Yet I felt that familiar frustration build at the fact that I still hadn't known about it.

"Adam," she started, then cleared her throat, "he's, uh ..."

"The guy she cheated on me with," I finished. I smiled a little even though it was forced because I could tell how uncomfortable she was. "Yeah, I know. I didn't know him personally, just that he was a rich frat boy who fit her standards better."

Ava snorted. "He's a horse's ass is what he is. They're so stuffy, I could choke after five minutes around them."

That made me laugh under my breath. Suddenly, the frustration I'd felt at keeping this under wraps felt petulant and selfish. I wasn't the one who had to deal with Ashley or her parents. Ava was. And apparently, she had to deal with them soon.

"Are you going?" I gestured to the invite, still clutched in her hand.

She nodded slowly. "Yeah. I'm sorry I didn't tell you."

I waved that off because I understood why. Sort of. "It's fine, really."

"I wish I could bring you," she said, her voice trailing off. Then she shrugged her shoulders.

"Pretty much impossible."

"Yeah."

We both sighed. I took her hands, tossing the invite onto the floor. I didn't want anything of her family between us, literally or figuratively. Ava clutched my fingers tightly like I was a lifeline, and I reeled her in for a hug. She breathed out a sigh of relief.

"There's literally nothing on this earth I hate talking about more than my family."

I smiled into the top of her head, but it felt forced too. I wanted her to want to discuss her family with me. Even as I understood her reasoning, or tried to, it felt like one more part of her I wasn't allowed to figure out until she was ready to drop the curtain.

What if I asked her? What if I invited her to share that stuff with me because I cared, and she still said no?

I swallowed before I spoke. "Then we won't talk about it."

"Okay." Her voice was small, and I kissed her hair. "I've just gotta get through that one day, huh?"

I nodded, and her arms tightened around me. "However you need to."

Ava exhaled and tilted her chin up to me. "I can do that."

My hand cupped the side of her face, and she nuzzled into my palm.

"After that's over, we've got plenty of time to figure this whole thing out, okay?"

This time, I think we both knew that I was saying it simply to make us feel better. But she kissed me, I kissed her back, and we left Ashley lying on the floor.

CHAPTER 14
AVA

WASHINGTON
WOLVES

There was just something about waking up naked in your man's bed.

Because Matthew was a huge man, his bed was in proportion. I could starfish my body, stretch my arms and legs out, and not touch the edges of the California king mattress covered by Egyptian cotton sheets in a decadent shade of gray.

I pressed my face into the memory foam pillow and grinned, fighting the urge to curl my toes and giggle. If I thought too hard about the fact he was the one screwing me senseless

every

single

day,

I'd lose my mind from sheer girly bliss. It was almost impossible to believe he was even real. The only shortcoming I could find was his absolute refusal to keep any form of processed carbohydrate in his house. In fact, even healthy gross carbs weren't there. No eighteen-grain bread or crackers with giant chunks.

Lots of meat. Lots of fruit. Lots of veggies. The occasional chocolate bar that he'd stash for me in the cupboard.

But I guess I couldn't complain about his eating habits either, I thought as my legs burned in protest when I stretched my body out. That. Body.

I almost had to fan myself. He was one of those men who worked his ass off for the body he had, and he knew how to use it.

I sat up and grinned. Yes, he did. For two weeks now, no shit, every single day, I was learning just how well he knew how to use it.

I flopped back on the bed and sighed. A note sat on the nightstand next to my pillow, and I picked it up.

Unless you made other plans, be back here at 7, wear that red dress you showed me in your closet. - M
PS- I think you reinjured my back last night. I'm too old for those kinds of positions.

I laughed, tracing my thumb along his perfectly square, neat writing. Who was he kidding? He could toss me around like a Cirque du Soleil performer and not break a sweat.

For the rest of the morning, I practically glided. I showered and got ready at his place, then made it to work early and greeted everyone I passed like I was Suzie freakin' Sunshine, throwing veritable glitter bombs of happiness everywhere I went.

Maybe I wasn't dating defunct after all.

Honestly, I *was* happy before he showed up. I loved my job, I had friends, and kept busy. But this ... it felt like a cloud burst open and dumped an entire bucket of bliss on me. I was sitting at my desk thinking about that when my phone rang.

Ashley.

"Even you can't ruin my mood today, dear sister," I said cheerily, hitting the decline button with particular cheer.

She sure tried, though. Over the next two hours, she called two more times, finally leaving a voicemail on the third attempt. For a solid ten seconds, I wondered why she wasn't leaving me the hell alone, but whatever it was could wait twenty-four hours until I was back home after whatever Matthew had planned for us.

A knock on my office door broke me out of my thoughts. The receptionist from the front desk grinned at me.

"What's up?" I asked her.

From behind her back, she produced a perfectly lovely bouquet. And not just any flowers. My favorite flowers.

Tied together with a white ribbon was a bright spray of ranunculus in pinks, oranges, yellows, and whites. A few glossy green leaves framed the outside, and I actually laid a hand on my chest when I stood to take them.

"They're so beautiful," I breathed.

She nodded. "Girl, whatever you did to deserve those, keep doing it."

I laughed, not sure what to say. Because I wasn't even positive I knew who they were from even though I hoped. Oh, I hoped.

The square white envelope tucked into the side of the flowers had me grinning in anticipation. I'd never had flowers delivered to me before. Not from anyone.

When I finally read the note, typed out in impersonal ink, I burst out laughing.

After careful consideration, I changed my mind about the positions. Even if it sidelined me, I'd risk any injury for you.

It was ridiculous and sweet, and I imagined him calling the florist, repeating that message, and my face burned hot. Ugh, why wasn't it seven already? I wanted to see him, touch him, kiss him.

Obsession. I believed they called this phase of the relationship obsession.

Feeling impulsive, I picked up my phone and dialed his number. His voicemail picked up, the generic voice letting him know his number wasn't available.

Keeping my voice low, and my back toward the slightly open door, I left my very first sex message.

"When I see you tonight, I'm going to thank you in ways that you can't even imagine, mister. That red dress you wanted me to wear? It won't stay on for long because if you don't use those hands to rip it off me, to hold me down on that big table of yours, then I'm not going to be very happy." I inhaled slowly, audibly. "Just thinking about how I'm going to use your body tonight, mmm, I can't wait to see you."

"You're having *phone sex* at work?" a snide voice snapped from behind me.

That voice. I pinched my eyes shut as I fumbled with my phone, praying I'd ended the message before he heard her. I took a deep breath, thanking the universe that I looked hot today. I smoothed a hand down the front of my emerald green sheath dress. The small cap sleeves made my toned arms look good, and the small black ribbon around my waist was classy and flattering. My shoes were Louboutin, the one pair I owned, and I knew she'd covet them. And then I ground my teeth together because I was cataloging my appearance to make sure Ashley Baker-Hughes wouldn't find me lacking in any way.

Damn. It.

I turned, leaning against the desk and giving her a confused smile. "Ashley. This is a ... surprise."

She huffed, walking toward me to give me an air kiss next to my cheek. No hugs for us. But even without her arms around me, I caught the slightest hint of her signature scent of Chanel No. 5, and it made me want to choke.

"It wouldn't be one if you ever listened to your messages," she said, casting a disdainful eye around my office. "No window."

I tilted my head. "Do you have windows in the operating room?"

Ashley exhaled. "Don't be ridiculous."

We couldn't be in a room together for ninety seconds without snipping. I rubbed at my forehead. "Sorry, I'm just surprised to see you here. In Washington. In my office."

She shrugged, pushing her heavy fall of golden hair over her shoulder. "I wasn't happy with some of the communication with the venue for the ceremony, and since I wasn't on call the next couple of days, I decided to fly out here myself to talk to the events coordinator to make sure we're on the same page. Adam and I got engaged there, and I need everything to be perfect." She rolled her crystalline blue eyes. "You'd think she'd understand the difference between white and eggshell for the roses I want."

"You'd think."

Her eyes narrowed on the flowers behind me. "Speaking of blooms ..."

Shit.

She waltzed up to the desk and plucked the note from the plastic holder.

"Presumptuous much?" I asked dryly, my heart pounding even though Matthew hadn't signed his name.

Her pink lips, the exact same shape as mine, moved as she read the note. Her eyebrows lifted. "Well then, sounds like someone is mixing business with pleasure."

Because of course, it was perfectly clear an athlete had written that note.

"You can't possibly know that," I said, but my voice lacked conviction.

"*Sidelined*?" She sniffed. "Please. It's cute. Not very original, but cute. But I suppose football players aren't typically known for their brains, are they?"

If I hadn't been completely freaking out, I would've laid into her, but snide comments like that would have to wait for the moment.

I knew Ashley didn't follow football. After her relationship with Matthew went so sour, she refused to watch a single game, college or pro. She hopefully—probably—had zero clue that he still played. That he played for my team. I almost whimpered at the possible ramifications of this little impromptu visit.

"How long have you been dating?" she asked. "Can't be that long if Mom and Dad don't know about it. Though I suppose you held on to what's his name in college for almost a year before he moved on."

What if this was one of those times Matthew randomly dropped by my office? What if he got my message and wanted to find me, lock the door, and finish what we didn't a few days earlier.

"Umm, n-not too long," I stammered. "He's ... we're..."

She rolled her eyes. "I can see why you've impressed him so much. Are you always this articulate?"

Just like that, I felt my spine straighten out with a quick snap, and I opened my mouth to unleash on her when the deep sound of someone clearing his throat made me jump. Logan Ward stood in the doorway to my office, and I almost threw up from relief.

"Sorry," he said gruffly, giving Ashley a brief, uninterested flick of his eyes, "am I interrupting something? I can come back."

"Logan," I answered, flustered beyond belief and heart lurching at the way my sister was glancing back and forth between us with narrowed, suspicious eyes. "No, it's fine."

I walked toward him, pressing my hand to my roiling, unsteady stomach, and he zeroed right in on my hand. Logan had never seen me as anything other than unruffled.

"Are you okay?" he asked, sounding concerned.

Shiiiiiiit.

Because he sounded like a boyfriend.

Ashley hummed behind my back, and I pinched my eyes shut.

Except.

Hang on.

In my wobbly brain, a terrible yet brilliant idea bloomed. I opened my eyes and gave him an apologetic look. *Please*, I mouthed, and his dark eyebrows bent in.

I wasn't stupid. I knew this could backfire if Logan opened his grumpy ass mouth. But he was hot. Actually, Logan was one of the hottest guys on the team, especially because he had that whole grouchy, brooding thing going for him.

"Ashley," I said, keeping my eyes trained on Logan's. "This is Logan Ward. He's ... he's the one who sent me the flowers."

His mouth dropped open, but I glared effectively enough that he snapped his jaw shut.

"Oh," she drawled. "I've never met one of Ava's boyfriends. Not that she's had many," she added under her breath.

"Uhh," he muttered, blinking rapidly, then stepping into my office. "Nice to meet you."

He didn't touch me as he held out a hand to Ashley, for which I was thankful. I just needed her out of here, and Logan was the perfect excuse.

Ashley assessed him slowly as she took his hand in hers, and I knew what she was seeing. Dark hair, scruffy, hard jaw, wide, muscled chest, and tan skin. Really tall, really built, and really hot. For a momentary decoy boyfriend, I could've done worse.

"The pleasure is mine," she told him. And then she smiled at me. Actually, really, not faking it smiled at me. Then she winked. "Nice work," she said out of the corner of her mouth.

W.T.F.

Logan pulled his hand back and cleared his throat.

I wanted to puke all over my shiny black shoes.

"I can come back," Logan said again, giving me a weird, prolonged look.

"No, absolutely not," Ashley all but cooed. "I hope we'll see you at the ceremony, Logan. Ava has never brought anyone around our family before. And you look like a man who would wear a tuxedo well."

"It's black tie?" I asked incredulously. "It's a *vow renewal*, Ashley."

She was unrepentant, shrugging lightly as she lifted one eyebrow. "But it's mine, and this is what Adam and I wanted."

Logan gave me a quick look, and I shook my head. "Umm, Ava and I haven't had a chance to talk about it yet."

Before I knew what was happening, Ashley leaned in to hug me and whispered in my ear. "Ava, he is *gorgeous*. And the way he's looking at you? Holy hell!"

"Uh-huh," I said weakly, patting her on the back and praying desperately that I didn't pass out. I needed her out of this building.

"I better go," Ashley said. "Ava, why don't you meet me for drinks tonight at eight? I'll text you my hotel address. That way I can go over how you can help for the ceremony before I head back home tomorrow evening."

"Uhh," was all I managed.

My sister faced Logan, leaning up to air kiss next to both of his cheeks. He couldn't have looked more uncomfortable if she had pulled a gun on him.

"Logan, it was *so* wonderful to meet you. I hope it's not the last time."

He gave her a tight smile, and we both stood dumbfounded as she waltzed out of my office. I sank into the chair across from my desk and dropped my head in my hands.

"Holy shit," I said under my breath. I almost forgot Ward was in the room with me until he spoke again.

"Ava," Logan grumbled curiously, "what the hell is going on?"

CHAPTER 15
AVA

WASHINGTON WOLVES

Such a good question.

What the hell was going on?

I covered my mouth with still shaky fingers and glanced up at Logan. Arms crossed over his chest, inscrutable-as-always look on his face, guy who just saved my ass Logan.

"That was my sister, Ashley."

No part of his entire body moved, except one dark eyebrow.

Translation: *No shit, Ava.*

I sat up and blew out a slow breath. If I told Logan the entire story, I'd have to spill the beans about Matthew and me; something we hadn't discussed. Logan wasn't friendly, per se, but the guys who knew him respected the hell out of him. Sure, he'd made my job a living hell from day one because he was about as easy to train as a banana, and he wasn't going out of his way to make Matthew comfortable, but he deserved at least a slice of the truth for what he'd just done.

"W-we don't have a great relationship. We never have." My head dropped back, and I stared at the ceiling for a few seconds. "And I'm dating someone new." I gestured weakly at the flowers. He gave them a long, inscrutable look but didn't say anything. "Someone I'm not ready to ... tell her about."

"Why not?"

Hysterical laughter came crawling up my throat, and I swallowed violently to keep it inside. If I'd had to list a hundred people I could've possibly had this conversation with, Logan Ward wouldn't have come close to making the cut.

"Logan?" I asked, holding his gaze as steadily as I ever had. "You know how you hate talking to media, and you give me attitude at every turn when I ask you to do the simplest task that might make my job easier?"

"Uh-huh."

"Well, I'm cashing in all the imaginary tokens that those moments have gained me over the years. Because this is just not a subject I feel like discussing with you."

His dark eyes narrowed a little on my face, but he didn't say anything at first. Then he glanced away, and I got the feeling I'd made him uncomfortable somehow.

"I can't blame you there," he muttered.

Wearily, I stood and made my way back behind my desk, giving the beautiful flowers a lingering glance as I sat. Ashley had left the card face up on my desk, and I reached forward to grab it, not eager for Logan to see what it said.

"I really am sorry. I'm not trying to be difficult," I told him. "It's just ... do you have siblings, Logan?"

"Five."

"What now?"

"I have five siblings."

My mouth dropped open. How did I not know this? "Since *when*?"

He rolled his eyes a little. "Since, I don't know, thirty-three years ago when my brother was born, followed later by my four sisters over a six-year span."

I blinked for about twenty seconds before I was able to talk, and he waited silently the entire time. His lips might have even been curved slightly with amusement at my shocked reaction.

It wasn't atypical for me not to know family histories or who players had in their life because it rarely held any relevance for my job.

"Okay," I said slowly. "Do you get along with them?"

"Not my brother." His tone was even, but his eyes were hard. "I want to punch him in the throat whenever we're in the same room."

That was a feeling that I could understand.

"So you understand my reluctance to discuss her, or why I'm in this shitty position in the first place."

He nodded, then scratched at his jaw. "What ceremony was she talking about? I was only half-listening."

"Oh," I interjected quickly, "just forget she said that. It's nothing."

"Okay." Logan leaned forward and dropped a paper on my desk. "I came to drop off that thing you needed for the interview I don't want to do."

A reluctant smile tugged on my lips. "Thanks."

He started walking out of my office, then stopped and glanced back at me. "Listen, siblings suck sometimes. I don't know your sister, and I don't even really know you that well. But if I can help, let me know."

Surprise had my eyes widening. "Uhh, thanks."

Logan nodded and left my office. The air was sucked out of my lungs like someone had attached a vacuum to my mouth, and I slouched forward until my forehead hit the surface of my desk.

First, I needed to find Matthew and tell him what happened.

Second, I needed to have a little chat with the front desk about how random sister drop-ins were not allowed to walk in unannounced.

The ringing of my phone had my lifting my head, but my whimper of defeat returned when I saw it was my mom. Vaguely, like mists of fog that I couldn't touch, I remembered how happy I'd been that morning. Quite desperately, I wanted to rewind time to waking up in Matthew's bed and clutch that feeling to my now aching chest like it would make all this go away.

"Hi, Mom," I said into the phone.

"You have a *boyfriend*?" she started in a rush.

I pinched the bridge of my nose. "I see you talked to Ashley. Thanks for the heads-up on that visit, by the way."

"You know she likes an entrance," she chided. "Besides, how often does your family get to surprise you?"

Approximately never, which was why I wanted to move away from California in the first place.

"Oh, it was a surprise all right."

"Quite a looker, she tells me. Tall, right? How did you meet? Oh, I suppose you met through the team."

In the past fifteen seconds, my mother just asked me more personal questions about my life than she had in the past two months. I stared glumly at the flowers as she chattered in my ear. Chattered excitedly, even. Not a word about the vow renewal. Not a word about Ashley except what information she'd relayed.

My throat tightened up because I wanted to feel excited about this. I wanted to feel pleasantly overwhelmed that my mom cared so much about the man in my life. But I couldn't because I couldn't foresee a single way to tell them the truth.

"Ava," she said forcefully. "Are you still there?"

I blinked. "Yeah, sorry."

"You're not telling me anything about him."

My hand traced the edge of the card from the flowers, and I screwed my eyes shut, forcing Logan and Ashley and everything else out of my head except Matthew.

"He's ... he's amazing," I told her quietly. "Kind and funny and supportive. We're together all the time outside of work, and I can't imagine ever getting sick of him."

She hummed, a happy little sound I'd never heard from my mom. I was officially in the Twilight Zone. "And he's a player?"

I sniffed, feeling the full weight of my relationship with Matthew in the face of my family for the very first time. It didn't feel good. It felt impossible. And it also felt impossible—now that I knew what it was like with him—not to have him in my life.

Something that was supposed to be fun and good and easy suddenly wasn't easy at all. My staunch refusal to discuss this exact thing went from self-protection to a cage of my own making with no exit in sight.

My eyes burned hot, and I swallowed back unexpected tears. Thankfully, my voice came out steady when I answered. "Uh-huh, he's a player."

"So he does well then, financially."

I almost laughed. Of course, she'd list that as a positive characteristic. "Yeah, he does all right."

If I told her that his two-year contract with Washington was worth twenty-six million dollars, not to mention all his endorsements, she'd stroke out. My dad, Ashley, and Adam Hughes the Third didn't come close to touching what Matthew made, even if they combined their salaries.

"I want to meet him," she said.

"Nope." It was out of my mouth before I could stop it.

"Ava Marie Baker, we've never met a boyfriend of yours, and we will all be in the area for the ceremony. There's no reason we can't."

I'd had too much emotional whiplash already that day to even try to filter myself. I laughed under my breath, unable to believe I was even having this conversation. "You've never asked me about anyone I'm dating. *Ever.* Why do you even want to meet him?"

Thankfully, my mom didn't argue. If she had, I might have thrown my phone against the wall. "Because if he's important to you, then he might be part of this family. If he's making you happy, don't you think we'd be curious about him?"

I exhaled roughly. "No, Mom, I didn't think you would be curious at all. Prior history and all."

She cleared her throat primly. "Well, there's nothing I can do about the past. But if he's still around when we're there, your father and I want to meet him. Minimally, a kind, funny, *supportive* boyfriend would want to come with you to your sister's vow renewal. Right?"

Having your words thrown back at you like weapons was super fun. Especially when I couldn't argue. Frustration had my vocal cords frozen as I tried to steady myself. The last thing I would do was cry on this phone call with my mom. But I wanted to.

Normally, I could reach out and grab the reins, steady myself with ease. Put on the game face for any situation. But my hands were slippery, and my emotions were ping-ponging violently, unable to stick to one single place where I could pin them down.

This was a narrative I couldn't control, and an outcome that I could not predict or influence in any way. Not as I sat in my office and listened to my mom's happy chattering.

It was the only reason I had to explain that desire to cry.

I wanted to cry big, giant, self-pitying, *this freaking sucks* tears because I had no clue what I was supposed to do with any of it.

So when she asked me if a kind, supportive man in my life would want to attend the ceremony with me, all I could do was answer truthfully.

"Right." Because it was true. If our situation was different, if he had no history with me before that first day in my office, Matthew would be by my side for all of it. He'd refuse to let me deal with them alone. I tucked my lips between my teeth and breathed slowly. "Mom, I have a meeting I need to get to. I'll talk to you later."

I disconnected that call before she could say anything else.

All the work I'd done to keep myself and Matthew in a good place emotionally—a place that wasn't under the shadow of my family—was all for nothing. Because, like it or not, they'd ripped that shade off us.

One single, stubborn, rogue tear snuck out of my eye before I could stop it, and I dashed it away quickly. Almost as if it didn't make it very far down my face, then it didn't really happen, and I wasn't rapidly losing control of this situation.

Unfortunately, Matthew walked into my office at the precise

moment I tried to erase it from existence. His face went from happy smile to obvious concern in a heartbeat.

"What's wrong?" he asked, closing and locking the door as soon as he cleared the doorway.

One tear became two. Two became three, and by the time he strode to my desk and hauled me out of my chair, the situation was not pretty in the slightest.

He folded me into his big, big arms while I cried. He didn't even know why I was crying, but he rubbed my back and kissed the top of my head without pressing me. Which, of course, made me cry even harder. This man was too good for me. He was too good to be saddled with someone who couldn't even introduce him as her boyfriend. Because I'd never called him that.

I was aiming for fun, easy, and good, refusing with a stubborn short-sightedness to delve into the hard shit that inevitably faced us. And he was still holding me like it could take all of it away even though he didn't know what *it* was.

"Thank you for the flowers," I said in a thick, tear-choked voice.

When he tilted my chin up, I almost had to look away from the misery etched on his face. "Should I have picked roses instead?"

My laugh was watery, and he used his thumb to wipe moisture off my cheekbones.

"You're killin' me, Slim. Something happened between that voicemail and now, and if it made you cry like this, I kinda want to break something if it would help make you feel better."

I rolled my forehead against his chest and breathed him in. "Ashley happened."

His body froze for just a beat, but then he smoothed a hand down my spine again. "What'd she say?"

My exhale was shaky and long before I looked up at his face again. "She showed up at my office about twenty minutes ago. Right after I got the flowers."

"She's *here*?"

I shook my head. "Not anymore. She left. But Logan walked in while she was here, and then Ashley left, and Logan left, and my mom called and said I need to take my boyfriend to the ceremony because Ashley saw the flowers and heard me leaving the voicemail ..."

"Hey," he interrupted, leaning down so he could hold my gaze steadily with his own. "Take a deep breath for me, okay?"

I did. Then another.

"Why the tears?" he asked.

My fingers picked at the collar of his white T-shirt where a thread was unraveling. "Talking to my mom, I just ... it's the first time I really understood how hard this was going to be."

Matthew nodded. He studied my face, which was probably streaked with mascara and eyeliner. Maybe fully made-up women could cry prettily in the movies, but that never, ever translated to real life.

"She sounded like she cared," I whispered brokenly, and his face softened in understanding. "She sounded like she cared about this man in my life who was making me happy, and I was telling her about you, and then I just ... had to get off the phone and cry like a crazy person because I couldn't think of a way to explain this in a way that would make sense to them."

"I'm so sorry," he murmured.

"Are we insane, Matthew?" I whispered, feeling a small swell of panic that I'd even dared to voice it. "What are we doing? You were engaged to her, and I'm starting to think that we are padded-room insane for thinking that we can find a way around this."

His face went determined in the snap of an inhale. "No way, don't even go there right now."

The hands on my back went from soothing to strong, cupping my shoulders so I couldn't turn away.

"How can I not?" I asked, feeling positively wretched.

"Ava." His eyes seared into mine, and I felt my tears slow, my heart speeding up at what I saw there. "I want to be with you. And I refuse to let them get in the way. I refuse to allow them any sort of power over this thing we're building. Because make no mistake, we've been building something amazing whether we've put it into words or not."

My lip wobbled at his declaration. All I could do was nod because he was right. We'd slipped so easily into our relationship, and labels had nothing to do with it. No conversation would've changed that.

"Beautiful girl," Matthew said in a low, soothing voice. He pulled me into his arms again and spoke against the top of my head. "I wish I could go with you. I wish I could make this easier on you."

"You are right now," I told him. "You're making it better right now."

"I'm not doing anything."

"Shut up," I said into his chest. "Just hold me while I pretend I didn't just lose my shit at work."

"Done." His voice was a quiet murmur against my hair, but I felt it everywhere. Matthew Hawkins had some sort of magic inside him, maybe even a part he wasn't aware of, to be exactly what I needed him to be and say exactly what I needed him to say.

I wished to do even half the same for him.

"Oh shit," I gasped, pulling back and staring at him in horror. "Ashley is making me meet her. You planned our date. My red dress."

He smiled in understanding, despite my stammered, disjointed, grammatically incorrect sentences.

"I'll cancel with her," I said firmly. "She didn't tell me she was coming, so she can't expect me to drop everything."

Matthew cupped the side of my face. "When does she leave?"

"Tomorrow, I think." I sighed. "Not soon enough, at any rate."

He blew out a breath. "Wear the red dress, meet her for one drink, and then come to me when you're done."

"But—"

My words were cut off when he gently kissed me. "It might not feel like it right now, but we will figure this out. I'm glad your mom sounded like she cared because she *should*. She should care about the man who's making you happy."

I smiled up at him. "*You*. You make me happy."

His grin was smug, his hands proprietary as they cupped my bottom over the material of my dress. "Good."

"One drink?" I asked him with a scrunched-up nose.

"One drink and you come to me." He kissed me again, licking lightly at the seam of my lips until I opened for him. "Then I'll make you forget all about this day."

I snuggled back up to him. "Deal."

CHAPTER 16
MATTHEW

While I waited for Ava to show up, I did my best to keep my mind off what had happened earlier in her office. I'd never imagined Ava could be so broken down by one interaction with her sister and one phone call with her mom.

Her tears felt as if someone had punched a ragged hole through my stomach and took all my air, leaving me feeling weak and out of control. That slight shake in her shoulder as she wept in my arms because her selfish mother had shown a modicum of interest in her life had me feeling a rage that I was wholly unaccustomed to.

Rage and a masochistic desire to self-reflect.

Look in a mirror I hadn't looked in for ten years.

I found the box I was looking for shoved into the back corner of my walk-in closet. Most of my college stuff had been unpacked. My jersey was framed, and my trophies and framed pictures were tucked neatly onto the shelves of my office. But one box I'd left untouched for years. Lugging it between homes, I had been unwilling to leave it with my mom, but unwilling to throw it away either.

Bracing my back against the wall, I yanked the box between my legs and pulled open the cardboard flaps. Right on top was a picture of Ashley and me before one of our winter homecomings. One of the last we attended together if I remembered right.

Looking at us together, I felt close to nothing. No painful pinch, no rock in my gut at the thought of her betrayal. But what I did was close my eyes to try to piece Ava into that memory.

She'd always been around. And if I remembered right, while her mom snapped pictures, Ava was watching through the glass of their massive front door. Ashley told her to quit skulking like a freak, and I'd chided her for that. Something I'd paid for later with her snotty silence.

What was clear to me now was that I couldn't conjure a neat definition for why I'd stayed with Ashley. Ava didn't have a choice. She was born into their nonsense, but I had a choice. And I chose wrong. I chose wrong when I bought a tiny speck of a diamond and slipped it onto Ashley's finger. I chose wrong by giving her all those years of my life. Neither of those things could be taken back now or be changed into something more palatable.

The pride I'd felt then in having her by my side seemed childish and shallow now.

I flipped through the pictures, just a stack that had been held together by a rubber band, and found one I didn't remember. It must have been Thanksgiving, and Ava and I were sitting on the couch. She had her knees tucked up against her chest and her arms wrapped around her legs, and she was smiling at me. Ashley was sitting on the floor, looking at a magazine. I was smiling too but not at either one of the sisters.

My thumb brushed over the image of a young Ava. Her hair was lighter then, her body thinner, but her smile was exactly the same. Very carefully, I turned the picture and folded a neat seam through the middle, pressing along the edge with the pad of my thumb until the line was crisp. When I looked at it again, it was just Ava and me. I closed my eyes and set the pictures back in the box.

Just as I was putting it back into its place, my phone rang. I almost dropped it in my haste to see if it was Ava, but my brother's name flashed instead.

"Hey, Mike," I said, finding my spot against the wall again.

"Holy shit, he actually answered."

I rolled my eyes. My younger brother had tried me once earlier in the week, the day we normally caught up, but I'd been in the shower with Ava.

"I was busy, asshole."

"Uh-huh. What's her name?"

I rubbed a hand wearily over my face. There was no point in denying it.

"Ava," I told him. A smile spread across my face just from saying her name, a telltale sign that I was in deep shit when it came to that woman.

"Ooh, I thought I'd have to work harder than that to get anything good out of you. Where'd you meet?"

In front of my very eyes, the veritable fork in the road appeared. Take the coward's way out and say that I met her at work, or lay out the entire messy truth for him.

I sighed, knowing that the second I said her name, I'd tell him the messy truth. Ava had people to talk to this about, Allie and her friend Paige, but I had no one.

"Well," I started slowly, knocking my head back against the wall just once before I launched my little tale. "That's sort of complicated."

By the time I finished, wrapping up with what had happened in her office only a few hours earlier, my little brother whistled under his breath.

"Damn, son."

I nodded. "I know."

In the background, I heard the rustle of papers, and I tried to imagine Mike leaning back in his desk chair. He was a college coach, having never made it into the pros himself but not ready to leave the world of football entirely. The Division II school had a solid record and one national championship under their belt since he took over. Suddenly, I wished I wasn't so chained to my own schedule and had time to watch my brother coach.

"And she's ... uhh, I'm trying to figure out how to say this."

"Just say it, Mike."

He sucked in an audible breath. "She's nothing like her sister, right?"

"No. Not at all." I shook my head and laughed at how unlike her sister Ava was. "She's incredible, man. So damn smart. Beautiful. Funny as hell. And Mike, she'd keep you on your toes if you talked football with her. She ... she makes my head spin a little."

"And she's in a tight spot, being with you."

I didn't answer right away because we both knew it was true.

"What does she say about it?" he asked.

Shifting uncomfortably against the wall, I answered as honestly as I could. "Today was really the first we've talked about it. She, uh, she doesn't like talking about her family."

He hummed. "Guess I can't blame her, but ... it's something you'll have to deal with eventually, right?"

I dropped my head back with a thud. "Yeah."

"Have you tried talking to her about it?" he asked carefully.

"Sort of," I hedged.

"Sort of," Mike repeated slowly, then laughed under his breath. "And you're okay with that?"

No, I thought immediately.

"I trust Ava," I said instead, hearing my defensive tone. "When she's ready to talk about this, she will."

Mike was silent. The kind of silence that was loaded and heavy, but he didn't say anything else for a long moment.

"I'm happy for you, Matty. Even though it's a shitty situation."

At my nickname from when he was about two, I rolled my eyes again. "Thanks. It's not much in the way of advice, though."

"I'm the little brother. I wasn't aware it was my job to give you advice."

"Shut up," I said without any heat. "Come on, you and Beth have been married forever. I've got an ex-fiancée and an ex-wife, so clearly I need some advice when it comes to relationships." Now I sounded like I was on the wrong side of bitter. My voice had an edge to it that I didn't like, but I'd left both of those relationships behind me. The second they were done, I put my head down and got back to work. Got back to what I was good at.

Mike sighed. "I'm not in your position, though. Yeah, I'm married, but Beth isn't Ava. There's not much she doesn't want to discuss with me after so many years, but that took time, you know? I guess if she didn't want to figure out how to fix something that was facing us, I'd probably worry a little bit." He cleared his throat and rushed to add, "But again, that's Beth. I can't say the same for Ava."

"I know they're different. I just ... I wish she'd open up a little bit about that stuff. Right now, it feels like I'm a few steps ahead of her. I just want her to catch up." My brother was about the only person I'd admit this stuff to. My mom would have started planning a wedding and naming her future grandchildren, and my dad would try to convince me that Ava was lying about something and couldn't be trusted. I didn't need the emotional seesaw of their own issues being draped over my relationship.

"Brother, most relationships start with a little imbalance. It doesn't mean something's wrong. And I don't think you should loop that in with whatever is going on with her family."

"I'm not."

"Aren't you?" he asked easily. "Her family isn't the defining characteristic of what you two have."

"It feels like they are," I told him. Earlier that day, she and I were forced to have an honest conversation about the reality of what we were dealing with because of Ashley's visit and her mom's phone call. "It feels like we have to hide because dealing with them won't be easy. I hate that feeling."

"For right now, maybe you are hiding. But at the end of the day, what she's facing is the hard part, not what you're facing. Mom and Dad have their problems, but at least we've got each other, you know? No matter what happens, no matter how much they fight or bicker or make holidays shitty because they're arguing over who gets Christmas morning, you, me, and Tim have each other. She doesn't have that."

I closed my eyes and let that sink in.

On all counts, he was right. Ava wasn't vain and selfish like her sister. She wasn't trying to make me into something I wasn't like Lexi had. And the one place she should have a safety net—her family—was the one place she felt truly alone.

"You're really smart, you know that?"

He snorted. "Yup. That's why they pay me the big bucks, hotshot. How much was your contract for again?"

"Screw you."

While he was laughing, I heard the scrape of a key in the lock, and I bounded up. "Mike, I've gotta go."

"Love you, brother."

"You too."

I tossed my phone on the bed and turned the corner out of my bedroom just in time to see Ava close the door quietly behind her and flip the deadbolt, then taking a deep breath.

She wore the red dress.

The whole thing looked like small strips of fabric wrapped carefully around her body, keeping everything in place, until one of those strips arched up around her neck and held the whole thing up.

A Band-Aid dress? She'd called it something like that.

Whatever it was, my mouth watered the moment I saw her. She turned and leaned against the door when she heard me. There was a slight flush in her cheeks that told me she'd probably had more than one drink, but she was smiling, not crying, so I couldn't be upset in the slightest.

"You look beautiful," I told her quietly.

She smiled. "Will you take it off me?"

"Yes, ma'am." I strode toward her quickly, eager to touch her, hold her, kiss anything and everything.

"Good, because I haven't taken a full breath in three hours."

My hands froze just before I grabbed her hips, and I started laughing. I kissed her forehead and pulled her in for a hug. "That bad?"

"No, the dress is just that tight," she answered seriously. Then she looked away, almost guiltily.

"What is it?" I asked.

Ava licked her lips, holding my gaze as though she was about to make a big confession. I found myself holding my breath as she spoke. "It ... it wasn't horrible."

It took a second for the meaning to sink in, but then I smiled a little. "That's good, though, right?"

She shrugged miserably. "I don't know. I mean, it wasn't fun or anything ... but it wasn't horrible."

Keeping in mind what my brother said, I inhaled slowly. "I'm glad."

"Really?"

I cupped the back of her neck and used my thumb to tilt her stubborn little chin up toward me. "Really."

"Just one day I have to get through."

"Just one day," I agreed.

"Except I promised I'd meet her tomorrow to help with one little thing, then it's only one day," she said quickly. I couldn't help but laugh. She sounded like a kid, rushing through an admission of guilt.

"Do what you need to do, okay?"

Ava flung her arms around my neck, and I clutched her to me. When her lips touched mine, I felt the familiar buzz in my blood. Something she did that felt elemental and vital. Like I needed it to breathe.

Wasn't that what love was? I thought dazedly as my tongue swept against hers.

The presence of it in your life with the right person felt vital. If you didn't have it, your heart wouldn't beat properly, your blood wouldn't move the right way in your veins, and your bones would feel brittle and breakable.

Against her mouth, I felt like I'd explode if I didn't say the words, but I kissed her harder instead.

It was too soon.

Could I love her after only a couple of weeks?

My heart, my head, every part of me knew the answer to that question as I lifted her in my arms.

I did love her. And it clicked something into place, something that allowed me to breathe fully for the first time in thirty-five years.

"Where are we going?" she asked, her lips brushing mine.

"Bath."

"Oooh, we haven't tried that yet."

And tried the bath we did.

While the water was running, my big, clumsy fingers searched for the hook on the zipper of her dress so I could pull it down. Moving slowly, I unveiled one inch at a time of her smooth, tan skin.

I counted her ribs as I pulled the dress open. Underneath it, she was completely bare. The dress slid from her body as she yanked off my shirt and pushed down my shorts and boxer briefs.

Ava bent to test the temperature of the water, and I stood behind her, letting my hands wander over the smooth skin of her back and bottom. She held my hand as she stepped over the edge, settling between my legs once I joined her.

Soapy and slick with water, Ava languished over me, her hands driving me crazy and mine doing the same. She slid her fingertips over my chest, and I counted the bumps in her spine. When I cupped her breasts in my hands, working the suds away from her flawless skin with my fingers, she finally snapped. When she straddled my lap, a wave of water splashed over the edge onto the tile floor, but we ignored it.

I groaned my feelings into the skin of her shoulder as she moved over me with maddening slow circles of her slim hips, hips that I held tightly in my hands. No matter how I tried to increase the pace or mute my mounting feelings with rougher movements, rougher hands, and rougher words, Ava stayed sweet and slow and torturous.

It was a test of my resolve and my will to allow her to continue at that pace.

Give me more, I wanted to yell.

More.

Everything.

Let me fix what they broke.

Trust me with what was inside.

By the time she exploded around me, I had to bite down on her neck to keep from shouting that I loved her, that I wanted her with me forever, that she was it for me. I thrust up hard one last time, and she slumped happily against my chest, her heart hammering in her chest so hard that I could feel it.

She kissed along the edge of my jaw, then found my lips with hers, where we stayed until the water grew cold.

Much later, when she was tucked against me in bed, her breathing deep and even against my chest as she slept, I said the words quietly against the silk of her hair as it tickled my chin.

"I'm in love with you, Ava. But I don't think you're ready to hear it yet."

Only then could I relax enough to fall asleep.

CHAPTER 17
AVA

WASHINGTON WOLVES

Honestly, I don't even know how it happened. Between drink one and two the night before, I agreed to help Ashley. Worse that agreeing to help, I agreed to *shop* with Ashley.

When I left Matthew's place, he'd given me a solemn smile as I walked out the door. It meant I'd miss the first day of training camp, which sucked *ass*, but my presence wasn't completely necessary, so Reggie had no problem with me taking the morning off.

"I don't know. This shade of cream doesn't look like it'll match the roses." Ashley stepped back and peered at the pashmina draped over her arm.

"Does the shawl you *might* wear need to match the roses?" I asked innocently.

She put it back on the shelf and gave me a look. "There's a theme for a reason, Ava. Otherwise, I might as well show up dressed in jeans."

I almost laughed at the horror in her voice, but I stifled it. The last thing we could possibly have was Ashley thinking I found her humorous. We'd been shopping for a couple of hours, and while I still rolled my eyes roughly every seven seconds, I found myself again in the utterly confusing position of not having a horrible time with my big sister.

And that confusion had me asking things I'd normally keep locked up in my head. "I think you need to explain something to me."

Ashley stopped and turned to me with an expectant eyebrow raised.

I started cautiously. "You're so ..." My pause was inopportune because she narrowed her eyes, thinking I was about to insult her. "Put together. Perfectly put together, all the time. But you do a job that has you in scrubs all day long."

Her expression had relaxed, but her voice was wary. "Is there a question buried in there?"

"I'm just trying to reconcile that dichotomy, that's all."

At first, I didn't think she'd answer me. Honestly, I was just proud of myself for not wording it the way I wanted to word it. *You look like a Stepford wife. Your husband probably makes three hundred grand a year on his own, so explain to me why you still work sixty-plus hours a week.*

I can only imagine how well that would've gone over. But I didn't get it. I'd never understood that part of my sister. Bottom line, she didn't make any damn sense to me, and after twenty odd years of wondering what made her tick, I suppose I'd lost my ability to wonder quietly anymore.

"A couple of days ago," Ashley said, leaning up against the table of scarves, not meeting my curious gaze, "I had to perform an epidural. Routine stuff. I do them almost every single day at work. The husband puked on my shoes when he saw the needle. I wiped off what I could because I didn't have an extra pair in my locker, but when I got home, I realized I'd been walking around with that man's vomit on my socks for the remaining ten hours of my shift."

Blech. Not what I asked, but I kept quiet.

"When I'm out of work, I like to look my best because on any given day, I have no idea if I'll be walking in someone's bodily fluids for hours on end." She glanced at me. "Does that help?"

"A little," I answered honestly. "I guess it's just hard for me to imagine Dr. Baker-Hughes. I've never witnessed it myself."

I could imagine Ashley doing a lot of things. Like, be a trophy wife.

Her smile was small, but she was clearly amused. "I was raised knowing I'd do that job. Mom and Dad didn't exactly give me a choice."

The realization that I'd never thought of it that way made me shift uncomfortably. She was right, though. I remember conversations about where Ashley would go to school, where she'd do her residency, where she'd become an attending, and what practice she'd be a part of because it was the path our dad had traveled. She was continuing his legacy.

The part of me that wanted to remind her that at least she got their attention would never go away, but I watched her differently as she meandered through the boutique, looking at earrings and trying on bracelets that didn't match her theme.

We left the store and turned back in the direction of her hotel. My brain was mush, pulverized by the idea that maybe all this time and distance from my sister had left me without the opportunity to understand her better.

Ashley and I moved to the side, out of the way of a large group of tourists snapping pictures.

"And Adam is fine with what you do?"

"What do you mean?"

What I meant was that I knew virtually nothing about my sister's marriage. I'd met Adam once before they got married, and I'd hated him on principle because I'd been firmly Team Matthew. Oh, the irony.

Now I felt like sending him a thank-you note.

"Well, I know Adam does well, but you must make more than him, right?" I looked over at her. Her golden hair was shining even under the overcast Seattle sky, and not a hair was out of place. Her makeup was flawless, and in comparison, I still felt like a little kid playing dress-up when I was around her. "He's okay with that?"

Ashley's scarlet red lips curled up in a smile. "Adam understands familial pressure as well as I do. Our respective careers could be a case study on the effect of nepotism. So yes, he's okay with it. We both work hard, and we enjoy the fruits of that labor in the type of home we live in and our ability to travel anywhere in the world. It's why we chose not to have kids. We enjoy that freedom."

She said it almost defensively. Like she was waiting for me to harp on her for not procreating, for not popping out a little army of flaxen-haired, blue-eyed babies who would have been as spoiled as their parents had been.

Years ago, my mom had given me this giant spiel about why Adam and Ashley didn't have kids. Too busy, too driven, blah, blah, blah. During that conversation, my first and only thought had been, well, at least my kids won't be overlooked by their grandparents because I'll be the only providing another generation.

Except she hadn't asked if I wanted kids. Maybe she didn't care. Or maybe my parents were afflicted with the same lack of awareness that Ashley was and didn't know that their actions had unintended consequences that didn't always reflect well of them.

"And your new beau?" she asked slyly.

Cue awkward laughter. "Wh-what about him?"

"He supports your little job?"

Oh, look! It'd been a solid ten minutes since I rolled my eyes. *My little job.*

I mean, I didn't inject people with drugs for a living or manage whatever money crap Adam did, so naturally, my career was something cute and unnecessary.

"Mm-hmm," I answered between clenched teeth. Only when I breathed deeply and centered my Chi was I able to unlock my jaw and speak actual words. "Our respective careers could be a case study in the effects of absolutely no nepotism whatsoever."

It was Ashley's turn to roll her eyes. At least we were keeping

things even. It was one of the cornerstones of our sisterly relationship.

"He's certainly good looking," she said as we arrive at her hotel.
"I'd probably leave Adam naughty messages too if he looked like
that."

At her teasing tone, I gave her a sharp glance. Was that ... wait
... was my sister displaying even the tiniest amount of envy for
something in my life?

Granted, she had no clue that the certainly good-looking man
was Matthew, but who freaking cared? Not me. I licked along my
bottom lip and felt a dreamy smile curve my lips as I thought
about Matthew in that bathtub.

"Yeah." I sighed. "He's ..." I fanned my face. "I'm a lucky girl,
that's for sure."

His body, wet and glistening as I rode him, was something I'd
never get used to. Not in a million years. He was so big, so strong,
and he dwarfed every sense I possessed the moment he put his
hands on me. All I smelled, tasted, heard, touched, and saw was
Matthew.

"I never imagined you going for the gruff, broody guy, though,"
she said, popping the imaginary lust bubble over my head.

I crossed my arms and gave her a disbelieving look. "You've
thought about my type?"

"Don't read too much into it." She glanced at her watch. "I need
to go freshen up before I head to the airport."

"Okay."

Ashley appraised me frankly, seeming to come to a decision
before she spoke. "Thank for you coming with me today."

"You're welcome." I exhaled slowly. "Thank you for inviting
me."

The only comfort I had was that she looked as unsure about
this entire exchange as I did.

She gave me a quick, awkward hug and disappeared into the
revolving doors.

By the time I made it to work and sat at my desk in a daze,

replaying the strange morning I'd spent with her, I decided that I was officially Jon Snow. I knew nothing.

In two weeks, she'd be back with her husband, my parents, and a small handful of their friends and colleagues in tow, and I'd have to sit in a chair by myself and watch them re-pledge their lives to each other. For such pragmatic people, it was weirdly romantic.

Apparently, my parents and sister were on some sort of agreed-upon schedule. *Ashley, you butter her up and confuse the shit out her, then I'll swoop in with a text or phone call to really knock her off her game.* Because sure enough, I'd barely read through two emails when my phone dinged.

Dad: Can't wait to meet your new man, kiddo. Maybe we can find time for a round of golf with the four of us.

Because I'd played golf approximately never times in my entire life, but I couldn't fault my dad for not knowing that. And *kiddo?* I'd never been called kiddo. Not once.

With a groan, I dropped my head down onto my desk. This was awful. The iron structure I'd built around my family—the idea of them, what they thought of me, and what our relationship looked like—was crumbling like it was made of cotton candy. Sticky sweet but irresistible to look at and play with, then devour.

I felt like gorging on that one text. Staring at it until I felt sick from the excess. The idea that my life held even the tiniest bit of interest to them after all this time. And the moment I showed up with Matthew? Well, I could practically hear the steel beams clang back into place.

"Ava?"

My head snapped up at the sound of Logan's voice. Of course, he would show up again when I was mid-meltdown. At least I wasn't crying.

"What's up?" I schooled my face, but the bend of his eyebrows told me I wasn't fooling anyone.

"Now what?" he asked.

"Now what, what?"

He glanced down the hallway before coming into my office. "I just wanted to make sure you weren't like unconscious or anything."

"Huh?"

The look he gave me was only slightly patronizing. "Your head was down on your desk."

I looked at said desk and blinked. "Oh. Right."

"Are you okay?" he asked like I was slow.

Maybe I was. I was just, you know, in the middle of re-evaluating everything that I'd thought to be true.

I nodded absently. "Just ... still dealing with some of that family crap you walked in on yesterday."

"Ahh."

"Yeah. My parents are losing their minds over wanting to meet you." I pinched my eyes shut. "I mean, the guy I'm seeing who isn't you but who they think is you."

He cleared his throat, and I looked up at him. His face was so damn hard to read. It had always been, and it drove interviewers crazy. Which is why I almost choked on my spit when he said what he said next.

"I can come to that party with you." He held my eyes. "If it helps you."

Blink.

Blink, blink.

"Logan," I said slowly.

But he held up his hand. "I know you're dating someone. I'm not ... I'm not confused about what this is. But I'll help you if you want me to."

My stomach rioted at the thought. My hands felt clammy, and I couldn't help but stare down at my phone, those innocuous little message wreaking absolute havoc in my head and on my heart.

"Just one night I have to get through," I whispered.

"Exactly."

I blinked up at him, surprised he thought I was talking to him.

Logan sighed, running a hand through his dark hair. "I know I haven't made your job easy. Consider this my peace offering."

When I didn't answer, he sighed deeply and glanced away. "Or something. Whatever. You don't have to think of it that way if you don't want to."

At that, I laughed. "Oh, if you think coming with me to one party absolves you of years of torture, you're deranged."

He shook his head but didn't so much as crack a smile. His eyes, though, they were a touch softer; something I'd never, ever seen on him before. "It's a start."

While I mulled the absolute lunacy of doing it, Logan saw the invitation lying on the floor of my office. He leaned over and picked it up.

"This it?" he asked.

I nodded.

Before I knew what he was doing, he pulled his phone out and snapped a pic.

"Why'd you do that?"

One eyebrow arched up. "Now I know where and when this thing is."

Panic had my heart racing. My stomach roiled and twitched. This was a bad idea.

"You look like you're going to puke," he observed dryly.

"I *feel* like I'm going to puke. I feel like this is a no-win situation. I've never ..." I couldn't believe I was admitting this to Logan. *Holy shit.* "I've never had them care this much about anything I do. But bringing you, I don't know if it's a good idea."

His eyes briefly searched my face. "Will your sister be jealous?"

She probably would. I was sure Logan looked like a freaking ten in a tux, but that was beside the point.

I buried my head in my hands. "No, it's fine. There's no way I'm making you do this. My family will get over it."

Matthew's face flashed in my head, the flash of his smile, the way his face creased when he was happy, the look in his eyes before he kissed me, and I had to grit my teeth against a hot wave of tears crawling up my throat.

I'd never be able to explain it to him in a way that made sense. Never.

Not if I brought Logan.

Not if I was doing this because I craved this weird new attention from my family.

He wouldn't understand any of it, and I couldn't blame him.

"You don't sound sure."

Because I'm not, I thought instantly.

Somehow, that felt like a bigger problem than anything else.

"Just ... delete the pic off your phone, Logan." I exhaled shakily, looking up at him even though I knew there were tears in my eyes. "They'll get over it. So will I."

He opened his mouth like he wanted to say something, but then he closed it again, finally giving me a slow nod. Nothing on his face made it seem like he believed me.

I didn't believe me either.

WASHINGTON
WOLVES

"**M**atthew! Matthew, over here! Will you hold my baby for a picture?"

The voices were loud and plentiful. Day three of training camp was wrapping up, and most of the players were milling around the edges of the field to sign posters, hats, signs, and footballs, taking selfies with fans, and chatting with each other.

The current of energy was contagious, and with a big smile, I took someone's offspring in my outstretched hands and posed for a picture with the little girl cradled against my chest.

I turned her around, her gummy smile and big blue eyes were irresistible, and she wore an impossibly tiny Wolves jersey with my number on it. "You are gonna break hearts someday," I told her, handing her back to her mother.

On one side of me, Logan scrawled his signature onto a kid's hat, and he was smiling more than usual. Other defensive players, even some of the Wolves' former players were around, taking pictures and chatting with the coaching staff.

"Good practice today," I said to Logan, cutting my eyes over to him to see how he'd respond.

"It was." He nodded at the little boy, now cradling his signed hat to him as if it was a treasure. "You did good."

My eyebrows lifted in surprise. "Thanks."

Since we'd reached the end of the fans, we both turned toward the field again to head toward the locker room.

"Back bothering you at all?"

"Feels great," I answered honestly. "Disappointed?"

He almost smiled. "No, I'd rather have our players healthy."

We were quiet as we entered the building.

I cleared my throat before I spoke. "You're in a good mood."

"It appears so," he said in a dry voice.

"Training camp has that effect."

Logan hummed, but that was it. Then it was his turn to glance sideways at me. "You married, Hawkins?"

My smile was wry. "Ah, no. I was once, but that was years ago."

He nodded.

Easily the most bizarre conversation with a guy who I felt like I couldn't get to know if my life depended on it. Not that you were always close with teammates. Every year, the locker room had a different feel. Sometimes, you had teammates who knew everything about your life—knew your kids' names, knew when your anniversary was—and some years, it was just small talk. Nothing too personal and no friendships too close. We worked in an industry where faces changed year in and year out; that was one of the givens that we dealt with.

The difference for me was that I'd only been the new guy my rookie year. And now.

"You?" I asked even though I knew he wasn't.

He shook his head.

"Married guys usually give good advice," he said cryptically.

We walked into the quiet locker room. Everyone else was still out on the practice fields.

I stripped off my practice jersey and tossed it on the floor by the long red bench. His was a few down from mine, so I gave him a quick look before sitting down and bracing my elbows on my knees.

"I know you're the captain and I'm the rookie," I joked, "but if you, I don't know, wanted to get something off your chest, there's no one around to judge."

"Besides you?"

I laughed because I could tell by his dry tone that he was kidding. "Yeah, besides me."

He pulled the tape off his elbow and wadded it up. "Lots of guys ask your advice before?"

I thought about the team I'd left, the faces of the guys who I now only interacted with casually on social media and the occasional text giving me shit about when we'd play next. The guys I'd known since they were rookies were now the veterans I'd left behind for this new arm of my career. "Yeah, they did."

His eyes narrowed in on his locker before he turned to face me. "I don't talk about this shit with my teammates, just so you know."

I held up my hands. "I won't say a word to anyone."

Logan let out a heavy breath. "There's ... someone I'd like to get to know better. I like her even though I can't figure out why."

I grinned, reaching down to unlace my cleats. "Sounds like a solid start to any relationship."

He rolled his eyes.

"Is she interested too?" It felt asinine to say to this big dude in this mid-thirties, *does she like you back*?

Logan shifted uncomfortably, scratching the side of his face before he answered. "Well, it sounds like ... she's dating someone else. Don't know how serious it is, though."

"Ahh."

"Yeah."

I tapped my fingers on the side of my leg as I considered my next words carefully. "And she told you she was dating someone?"

He nodded.

"Did you ask her out?"

"Not exactly," he hedged. "This feels fucking weird talking about this. Never mind."

I shrugged. Logan pushed off the bench and paced around the large black L-shaped couch in the middle of the massive room.

I set my cleats down in the bottom of my locker and shook my head. He'd probably kick my ass for saying something, but I couldn't keep my mouth shut either.

"Look, Ward, I'll just say one thing, and then I'll shut up."

He sighed but didn't argue. "What is it?"

"I'm over it now, but I've been the guy who was cheated on, and it sucks, but if you want to get to know her better, at least respect her enough to be honest with her. Maybe the relationship isn't serious. Maybe she's only been on one date, but you won't know unless you ask. Don't dance around why you're doing it."

Even as I said the words, I heard my own hypocrisy in them. Ava had no clue how strong my feelings were for her. Sure, it was a risk to tell her that I was falling in love with her, but if I trusted her, *truly* trusted her with my feelings, then I owed it to her to be honest.

Risking a quick look at him, he had his hands propped on his hips, and he was staring me down with narrowed eyes and a tight jaw to match his defensive stance.

"Take the shot if I'm presented with one," he said. "That's what you're saying?"

I tilted my head to the side. It wasn't exactly what I'd meant, but clearly, it was what he wanted to hear.

"I- I'd never be the other guy," he clarified in my silence. "I'd never make a cheater out of her. Or anyone."

I held my hands up again. "Didn't think you would, man."

The locker room door burst open, and Logan lifted his chin, probably the closest thing I'd get to a thank you. And that was fine by me. Turning back to my locker as the room filled with chatter and big, booming laughter, I let out a deep, relieved breath. With the start of training camp and just that one odd, stilted conversation, I felt more at home in this locker room than I had since I showed up.

My phone buzzed on the top shelf of my cubby, and I grabbed it, grinning when I saw Ava's nickname.

Slim: Did you shower yet?

Me: Nope.

Slim: Good. I want my man dirty so I can clean him up.

I kept my expression even, but it was almost impossible to control the rest of my body. Breathing deeply, I closed my eyes and recited the Pledge of Allegiance in my head.

Me: You're a cruel, cruel woman, doing this to me while I'm a room full of half-naked dudes.

Her immediate response was a wink emoji followed by the shower emoji.

Me: Meet you at my place in an hour?

Slim: Did I mention I'm about to hop in your shower now? I'd hate to get started without you ...

Then that devil woman sent me a picture of just the naked curve of her shoulder where it met her neck and a glimpse of brown hair.

Me: Be there in 20.

I was there in fifteen.

CHAPTER 19
AVA

WASHINGTON WOLVES

Ashley's surprise visit a week earlier had ushered in something that I started thinking of as BAV relationship status and AAV relationship status.

Before Ashley's Visit relationship status was Matthew and me living in a happy bubble of denial that my family existed at all. If we didn't discuss them, we didn't have to deal with it.

After Ashley's Visit was a bit murkier. Probably because my head was a bit murkier.

I wasn't unclear about Matthew.

But I could no longer deny the problem looming on the horizon. Whether we talked about my family or his relationship with Ashley, we'd have to deal with them eventually. Sure, I could get through that one day. Ashley's vow renewal was only a week out, and since I'd successfully shelved Logan's offer of help, I could get through it with a relatively clear conscience.

I say relatively because there was the minor issue of me not telling Matthew that Logan had been even tangentially involved.

There was no reason to worry him, I told myself for the thousandth time. Nothing came of it; it was two little blips of time when he happened to show up. His presence hadn't been planned.

Therefore, there was no reason to make a bigger deal of it than it was.

"You want to keep watching this?" he asked, chest rumbling under my head as we snuggled on the couch.

The giant flat screen mounted on the wall hadn't been holding my attention in the slightest, but I patted his stomach. "Whatever you want is fine."

I closed my eyes and snuggled closer to his side, my arm idly playing with the hem of his T-shirt above the waistband of his sweatpants. Mmm. They were dark gray and hung all nice and low on his narrow hips. They showed things when he walked. Good things.

Before I could follow that trail to another round of sexy times—Lord, we were insatiable—I took a deep breath and just enjoyed the feeling of a lazy Sunday with my guy. Pretty soon, preseason would start, and his weeks would undergo a complete trans-formation.

Every day of the week—even Tuesday, the 'official' day off—would be spent practicing, conditioning, reviewing film, restoring the balance to his body that would be wrecked on the field every Sunday. Days like this would be almost impossible until we reached our bye week, and that wasn't until the sixth week of the season.

"You know what's weird?" he asked.

"Hmm?"

Matthew kissed the top of my head. "I'll miss this when the season gets going."

I couldn't help but laugh, but I pinched his side hard. "And that's *weird?*"

He grabbed my hand and brought it up to his mouth so he could nibble on my fingers. "No, crazy, it's weird that I even have something in my life that makes me feel that way."

My body shifted to the side so I could prop my chin on his chest and stare up at his face. "What do you mean?"

He stared hard at my face for a few seconds. "Because I've never missed anything except football when I'm not playing it."

Well, holy shit. For some women, they'd think that sounded insane. To me? He might as well have proposed marriage.

"Seriously?" I whispered. "Matthew ..."

His smile was lazy and sexy, and I wanted to kiss the shit out of his handsome face. "Seriously."

"Never?"

It wasn't like I was fishing for compliments, but when the guy was married before, and he was telling me that this was the first time he'd ever felt like this, it made a girl wonder, okay? So yes, I was completely fishing for compliments.

He shook his head, weaving his fingers through my hair until he cupped the back of my head. "Never. And that doesn't mean I'm ready to retire." He laughed under his breath. "Retire *again*, I suppose. I still love the game. I can still compete, and I can still be a valuable contribution to the team, but it's always come first. And now I'm lying here thinking, how can I shift my schedule around so I can have time to lie on the couch and watch reruns with my beautiful girl."

My throat was thick with emotion, and I leaned up to kiss him softly. Under my hand, I felt his heart throb steadily.

If someone told me that the muscle beneath the skin—the one that beat with precision and consistency, that kept his beautiful, strong body running—would be able to power an entire city, I would've believed it.

When I pulled back, his face was sharp and intense, his eyes laser focused on mine.

"Ava," he said, "I know we haven't labeled anything, mainly because everything feels so ..."

"Effortless," I supplied.

He nodded. "Yeah. But I want to be able to say that you're mine. I don't want things to feel so easy that I stop making an effort for you every single day. I want to be able to say that I have a girlfriend, a partner who gets all the best parts of me because I get all the best parts of her. That we've committed to something together."

I smiled a little, only biting down on the edges of my lips so I didn't look like a loon. "I like that."

He smiled a little too. "You do?"

Slowly, I nodded. With the help of his hands, I crawled up higher on his chest so he could wrap his arms around me and I could burrow my head in the crook of his neck. It was a perfect moment.

All was happy and bright and rosy and good.

I absolutely refused to let anything ruin the moment. No questions or concerns or conversations that needed to be had.

That was when my phone rang.

I groaned, and Matthew chuckled, dropping a kiss on my temple. "It's okay if you need to get it."

"Who the eff would call during big relationship declarations," I grumbled, trying to sit up gracefully.

My mother. That was who.

It was impossible to hide the screen, and for a second, Matthew and I sat there, staring at her name on the display.

"I don't need to get it," I said. "It's probably not important."

But for the first time, I felt a minor twinge of guilt over sending her to voicemail. As if he sensed it, Matthew rubbed a hand on my back.

"They still hassling you about next weekend?"

While I set the phone back down, I chewed on my bottom lip. "The opposite, actually."

"What do you mean?"

"Yesterday, she called me while I was driving home from work. After she finished updating me on something for next weekend, she asked me something just ... out of the blue. And for about five or six minutes, we talked about stuff that wasn't even remotely related to Ashley."

Matthew was quiet. Watching me talk, he allowed me to sort

through that cloudy mess in my head when it came to my family. But his forehead had a slight crinkle to it, just one line of concern etched into his skin.

"What is it?" I asked.

"Nothing, Slim." He kissed my lips. "Just listening. I'm glad to hear you talk about it."

"Liar."

His mouth lifted on one side in a wry smile. "I promise, I'm not. I can't imagine what it's like for you to see this different side of them. It's hard enough for me to, and I only knew them for a couple of years."

"*Is* it different? Or did I just not notice it?" I finally voiced my biggest fear. Had I spent years boxing my family up and painting them as the bad guys in my life when maybe I was the one creating space between us by throwing my guard up so high that they wouldn't even have a chance to continue hurting me.

"Slim, I was there, remember? They didn't see anything beyond themselves or molding Ashley into exactly what they wanted."

"I know." I sighed. "But shouldn't I allow that people can change? That maybe they're trying to atone for that?"

Matthew turned his body, mirroring mine, to create a man-shaped wall between me and the rest of the room, the rest of the world. He leaned his head on his hand and stared down at me.

"Yeah, people can change, but I also think they have to want to. We have to look at our relationships and know that what they show us, that's the real person. Day in and day out, how they treat you, how they speak to you, and what they expect of you, they're showing you who they are. And you should believe them. When you try to make someone different than what they really are is when you get disappointed."

The words might not have sounded bitter. His face might not have looked it, his eyes weren't hard or cold, and his mouth wasn't set in a hard line. But my heart ached because, while he might act like he didn't still carry any wounds from his relationships, I heard bruises in those words.

I traced his lips, felt the catch of his stubble against the pad of my thumb while I tried to decide whether I was being naïve about my parents and Ashley. Whether I was projecting some familial fantasy onto their actions.

"Can I ask you something?" I said quietly.

He nodded and kissed the tip of my finger.

"Is that what you did with Lexi?"

I knew better than to ask about Ashley. My view of that relationship might not have been front row, just glimpses when they were at our house, but I knew Ashley had shown him who she was even if he hadn't seen it.

Matthew swallowed heavily and exhaled through pursed lips.

"You really want to talk about my ex-wife?"

"No." I smiled. "But yes."

His answering smile mirrored mine. "A little bit, yeah. And she did the same to me. Neither of us lied about who we were, but ... I think we both assumed we could bend the other person to the mold we wanted them to be."

I nodded. "What mold did you want her in?"

While he pondered, I questioned my sanity for a moment. He had been married for five years, and I'd only been with him for a few weeks. Why was I asking these questions? To torture myself by thinking about the blond bombshell he'd legally bound himself to? I'd had one semi-serious relationship in college, and then a six-year drought of my own making. I was doing an excellent job of reminding him that I still—for all intents and purposes—had no freaking clue how to be in a healthy relationship.

"I thought she'd settle down a bit. She was a sweet girl. She wasn't after me for my money because she did well on her own, but she thought I'd join her in the party lifestyle, and I thought I'd ease her out of it because we were happy just being us. Marrying her or someone like her felt like the thing I was supposed to do back then." He shook his head. "And I ignored the signs that it wasn't right because my pride was too big. I still felt like I had something to prove to the world about who I was."

As he spoke, I wasn't sure exactly what to say, so I just kept my hands moving in slow, soothing circles on his back and sides. When I saw my mom's name on my phone, I definitely didn't think it would lead us here.

Matthew sighed heavily, and I marveled at his ability to lay this all out there for me. "There was no big bad in that relationship," he continued. "Just two people who weren't compatible. We weren't honest with ourselves or with each other."

I blinked a few times as I processed that, and he cupped my chin.

"What's going on in that brain of yours?" he asked.

My throat caught in a swallow, and I had to fight that tight feeling of discomfort that cloaked my body anytime my family came up. Like someone took a screw and wrenched my bones in a size, lacing up a corset over my ribs, I wanted to keep the words inside where I wouldn't have anyone to judge my feelings or my thoughts even though rationally, I knew Matthew wouldn't do that to me.

"Honestly, I just wish next week was over. I feel like I'd have more clarity about them. About how to move forward, or if we just stay the same, you know?"

Matthew wrapped his arms around me, and I tucked my legs through his.

"Slim, if they come out of next week and they act the same as they always have, it's their loss. You know that, right?"

"Hell yeah, I know that. I'm awesome."

His whole frame shook with laughter, and it set something at ease in me. This was the one thing in my life that was clear. That was right.

I hugged him tightly, afraid sometimes that I'd reach a point where I genuinely, physically could not allow him away from me. Matthew Hawkins—my personal form of crack, ladies and gentlemen.

When I inhaled his clean, soapy scent, I wanted to trap it in my lungs so I could smell it long after he was back at work. No, I wasn't necessarily looking forward to missing this either when the season started, but knowing he felt the same, knowing that he was as clear about us as I was, made it easy to close my eyes, press my lips against his seeking, searching ones, and forget about anything else for just a little while.

CHAPTER 20
AVA

WASHINGTON WOLVES

"**W**hoa, he is so tall."

The reverent hush in the little girl's voice made me grin. I crouched down next to her on the sideline. Her red hair was braided in precise stripes going down either side of her head and tied at the ends with black ribbons. Her Wolves jersey was freshly pressed, and the black leggings she wore under it were glittery and amazing.

"He's six five," I whispered to her. Matthew was lined up with the defense, wearing the black practice jersey that he'd been assigned that day at training camp. Opposite of him, the offensive players were wearing red jerseys.

"That's like ... three feet taller than me." Her brown eyes were like saucers in her beautiful little freckled face. Standing behind us, her mom grinned at the excitement in her daughter's voice.

Every day at training camp, certain kids were allowed to meet their favorite players. Sometimes it was through charities like Make A Wish or St. Jude's, but today, little Charlotte was next to me on the sidelines because she won a contest through Matthew's foundation, which gave low-income and at-risk youths an opportunity to be involved in extracurricular activities like music, arts, and sports that their parents couldn't otherwise afford.

Charlotte, the go-getter, raised twice as much as her nearest competitor with her Gatorade stand that she set up outside the doors of a local gym. Her reward was a meet and greet with Matthew and a few of the other players at training camp. I stood but kept my hand on her shoulder while we watched them set up the next play.

Coach Klein blew the whistle, and the players lined up. The coordinators shouted out demands and things they wanted to see improved on this series. The fans lining the field quieted down as they'd been trained to do.

Luke Pierson stood behind his center, glanced left and right, then spouted off some gibberish, which set the running back in motion behind him. Matthew visibly dug his cleats in, shifting his body just slightly to the right. I narrowed my eyes, fascinated to be able to watch him play this unabashedly, this close up. Underneath his helmet, I couldn't see his eyes, only the black line of paint covering his cheekbones and the determined tilt to his head.

"Set, hut," Luke bellowed, and Gomez snapped him the ball, dropping his massive weight to stop the surge of the defensive line. Luke stretched his hand out, faking a handoff to the running back, who tucked his arms like he was cradling the ball and darted out to the left. The two defensive players bought it but not Matthew.

He spun around the left tackle just in time to reach a huge, sweaty, muscle-popping arm out, knock the ball from Luke's hands, and scoop it up from the turf when Luke didn't recover it. Matthew ran with the ball clutched against his side, a roar of victory echoing in the air as the fans cheered. Luke was watching him with his hands propped on his hips, helmet shaking back and forth, but I could see a smile on his face.

As if he could really be mad.

What Matthew just did was precisely why Washington forked over millions, maxed our salary cap, and took a chance on a player who had already announced his retirement. Because he was the best.

Watching him run, spin, and tackle—all the things he'd honed his body to be able to do—was incredible. Even if I'd never kissed him, I was fairly sure I'd be halfway in love with him just watching him play the game.

Lucky for me, I did get to kiss him, so it was a moot point. Getting paid to watch him play was just a super, duper *Ava's life is awesome* bonus.

This was what I had to remember in the grand scheme of things. The drama awaiting me in just three days' time was a blip. An anomaly. Aberration. Whatever word my little desktop thesaurus could come up with.

The defensive players ran to Matthew in the end zone, smacking his helmet, smacking his ass, and whooping obnoxiously as he spiked the football. Even Logan made his way over and tapped his knuckles against Matthew's, which made me grin like a fool.

Look! He's making friends! I wanted to yell.

"Is it time for me to meet him?" Charlotte asked, tugging on the hem of my white linen blazer. The watch on my wrist said that practice was just about wrapped up, which meant time for the meet and greets, then giving autographs to the fans, but the coaches were still huddled up with the players, analyzing what had just happened on the field.

"Let's give them about five more minutes, okay?"

She nodded, bouncing on the balls of her feet. Her mom laughed, and I stepped back a touch so I could chat with her. "She's so excited about this. I could barely get her to go to bed last night."

"It's one of my favorite parts of my job," I confessed. "The looks on their faces when they get to meet the person they've admired for so long."

Just like the look on Charlotte's face now. She was gripping the field passes looped around her neck with a black Wolves lanyard in her tiny little hand like they were made of gold. When Matthew glanced over at me, I motioned to the girl by my side, and he nodded. His hair was matted and sweaty now that he'd taken off his helmet, the sun beating down on us with a pleasant heat. Before he jogged over, he grabbed a towel from an assistant and tried to clean himself as much as possible.

Mmm. I wish he hadn't. I wish I could take him in the closest hallway and lick the sweat off his neck.

"Ava?" he asked, eyes gleaming.

"Yes, right." I cleared my throat. "Matthew, I would love to introduce you to Charlotte Kuyper and her mother, Diane. She was the contest winner with your foundation."

He bent down and held his hand out. Suddenly, Charlotte was shy, turning into her mom's legs with bright red cheeks.

Matthew smiled at her, and I wanted to die because of how much kindness was in that smile. "I heard about your Gatorade stand, Charlotte." He tsked, shaking his head slowly. "I wish I'd thought of something like that when I was your age. You're a very clever kid."

From behind her mom's jeans, her big brown eyes appeared fully. "I told the gym owner he could have a percentage of the earnings if he let me stay there after the busiest classes."

Matthew tipped his head back, and the surrounding area boomed with his deep-chested laughter. I was still grinning about it when one of our staff writers jogged up to us with his camera in hand.

"Sorry I'm late," he said, chest heaving.

"No problem. Just make sure to get some footage of them together—candid and staged. Ask Charlotte about her contest and try for some soundbites about Matthew's foundation. I've already got pictures from her mom of the stand outside the gym. We'll send it all down to A/V, and they can piece something together for Fan Friday on Facebook and Instagram."

"You got it."

Nonchalantly, I looked over my shoulder at Matthew, who was listening to Charlotte's excited chatter with a heart-achingly earnest expression on his chiseled, handsome face. Briefly, he glanced up at me. I motioned that I was going to leave and gave him a tiny wink. The only indication he saw it was a brief appearance of the dimple on the left side of his mouth.

Le sigh.

Players were gathered haphazardly on the sidelines, posing for selfies, and I saw one of our favorite retired players from a few years ago giving advice to a rookie running back.

I was too busy smiling at all the preseason football happiness that I almost ran straight into Logan. He held out his hands, steadying my elbows before I bit it on the grass.

"Holy crap, Ward, do you make *any* noise when you walk?" I pushed my hair out of my face, unsuccessfully trying to free some strands where they'd gotten tangled in the sunglasses I'd had perched on my head.

When I was standing straight, he pulled his hands off my arms, a considering look on his sweaty face.

"What?" I said, just a hair over the line of defensive. See, this was what happened when someone you did not know at all had witnessed one of your greatest deep-seated insecurities. You snapped at them for no reason when all they were doing was standing there staring at you.

With the edges of his taped, dirty fingers, Logan scratched the side of his face and continued to study me.

"Ohhhhhkay then, good chatting with you." I went to move past him, and he reached out like he was going to stop me, but his hands didn't land on my skin.

"You okay?" he asked, glancing around, but no one was within earshot. Just standing here made me twitchy. As if I had a blinking neon sign over my head—with sound effects— that proclaimed *I introduced Logan as my boyfriend, and it was stupid, and I wish I'd never done it, but there's nothin' I can do about it now.*

"Why wouldn't I be?" I sighed, crossing my arms and punching a hip out to the side. Like attitude would help me escape this.

"Well, isn't that ... thing ... this weekend?"

I deflated. Well, if he was going to be nice about it, I guess I could put the hip away. "Yeah." I waved a hand. "It's fine. It'll suck, and I'll want to drink to survive it, which is a horrible idea because I am not a good drunk in emotional situations that stress me out, but survive it, I will."

Logan nodded, his eyes staying steady on my face. Did he blink? Ever? The sun was so bright that for the first time in years, under the intense Logan Ward scrutiny I was being subjected to, I noticed that his eyes weren't brown as I'd always thought. They were streaked with green. I blinked away when I saw Matthew straighten after taking some pictures with Charlotte. He'd be done soon, and we already agreed on leaving at the same time so we could have dinner together in a tiny hole in the wall place on the way home. Somewhere no one would recognize him.

"Doesn't sound healthy," Logan said.

If he only freaking knew.

I laughed. Then I laughed some more. His face softened slightly as I gave him a look of amusement. "No, nothing about that entire situation is healthy, trust me. Drinking to cope is the least of my worries."

Matthew started toward us, and I looked away, pulling my cell out of my jacket pocket. "Logan, I've got to go. But ... thanks for checking in."

He must have heard the sincerity in my voice because he gave my face an appraising look before he nodded slowly. "You're welcome."

Logan turned away just before Matthew reached us. They nodded at each other in greeting.

"Good practice, slick," I told him as we started walking toward the building.

"Felt good." He hitched a thumb over his shoulder. "Charlotte was great, huh?"

I wanted to wrap my arm around his waist as we walked and

feel the weight of his arm on my shoulders, but I settled for nudging him with my elbow. "You're such a big ole teddy bear."

Matthew mock-growled, leaning in to whisper in my ear. "Yeah? I'll show you how not true that is later, Slim."

Yup. One aberration aside, nothing about this day or my life sucked. I held on to that thought like it was made of solid gold.

CHAPTER 21
MATTHEW

"**A**va ..."

She didn't hear me. Standing in front of her absolutely wrecked closet, my girl was gnawing on her bottom lip like it was made of her favorite wine.

"The green," she said, ripping something off the hanger and holding it up in front of her while she looked at her reflection in the large standing mirror she had in the corner of her bedroom. "No, not the green. I can't wear underwear with it."

"Well hey now," I muttered, leaning over to pick it up when she tossed it on the pile of seventeen other outfits that had been found lacking. All the clothes were bright, solid colors, something I'd realized was all she wore, with the exception of a few black or white pieces. "I like dresses like that."

But she didn't hear me. Ava shoved shaking hands through her hair and stared blankly at her closet. The suitcase at her feet didn't have much in it because she'd already unloaded her entire makeup collection into a separate bag.

"Slim," I said more firmly this time.

"Do you know that before you showed up, I was the unflappable one. Nothing ruffled me, ever." Her voice had a strange faraway quality, and she kept her hands speared in her hair. "I was like ... like, Teflon."

I tried not to be hurt by what she said, but it was still there. Just a tiny sharp sting, like the pinch of a needle you weren't expecting even though I'd thought of her in exactly the same way so many weeks ago. So I took a deep breath, and the feeling faded.

"Were you?" I asked.

Maybe the pinch wasn't as gone as I thought because a gust of air left her body, and she turned to me with a miserable expression on her beautiful, stressed-the-hell-out face. "Oh, that sounded awful. I'm sorry." Ava pinched her eyes shut. "I mean, it's like I opened myself up to all these feelings the moment I saw you again, and once I did that, everything I was keeping in just came pouring out." She mimicked a puking motion, and I smiled.

"I get it."

She paced at the foot of the bed where I sat, still clutching the green dress in my hands.

"Every day this week, I kept repeating what we'd said, you know? It's one day, it's just one day, but now that it's here, I realize how much I was fooling myself." She deflated right in front of me. When she looked, her eyes were glassy with unshed tears, and it made them glow like emeralds on her face. "I *want* them to prove me wrong this weekend. I want them to revert to their old selves because it makes all this so much easier, and I know you're worried for me. I *know*," she said, laying a hand on her chest.

"Come here." I stood and held my arms out, and she walked straight into them, hugging me so hard that I was actually knocked back a step.

"Maybe I'll just not go," she said into my chest, and I chuckled.

"You're going."

She whined and pulled back, pouting up at me. "No, I think this is a good plan. I'll text Ashley and tell her I came down with like, umm, H1N1 or something. Ooh, or the West Nile virus!"

I held her eyes, and she sighed.

"I knowwwww."

"You know why you're going to go?" I told her. "Because you're going to be the bigger person. Even if they prove themselves awful, or if they don't, you're going to show up regardless. You're going to look beautiful no matter what you wear, and you're going to congratulate them on nine years of wedded bliss." My words were heavy with sarcasm, and it made her smile. "You'll drink the champagne your parents paid a fortune for, wake up to beautiful views of the sound, and then come back here where I'll be waiting."

She nodded. "I thought about that."

"What?"

"That since you kissed me, this will be the farthest apart we've ever been. We work in the same building, and we're together every night. And after camp tomorrow, I don't get to go home with you. I need to take this stupid suitcase filled with too many clothes when I already bought a dress for this thing and get on that stupid ferry, and you won't be on it with me." She smoothed her hands up my chest, and I felt the familiar stirrings, the delicious ache that always came with her touching me. "It'll be weird to be in bed without you. I don't like thinking about it."

"I know," I muttered, leaning my head down toward her face as my hands slid up and down her back, lower with each pass until her ass was cupped firmly in my hands.

Ava breathed out shakily, her fingers curling into my skin until I could feel the sting of her fingernails through my shirt. Her face came up as mine went down, and I slanted my mouth over hers as desperation rose like a swift, hot tide in my blood.

Finally, she was talking to me about this stuff.

Tonight, she was with me.

Tonight, I was the one who was there.

I'd be that one forever if she let me.

My hands were shaking from the intensity of my thoughts as I tore my mouth away from hers and ripped her shirt over her head.

She'd given me some, but I wanted more. I wanted all of it. All of her.

I filled my hands with her breasts, and she all but climbed up me, using her arms around my neck to lock her legs like clamps on my waist.

Awkwardly, I fell backward, but we only took breaks from the deep, endless kisses to rip at each other's clothes with greedy hands. If Ava was feeling half of what I was right now, we wouldn't last two minutes once I was buried deep in her.

Something knit together inside me, stitch by stitch, row by row until my entire body was a solid mass of want and need and desire to claim her as mine for the entire world to see.

"After you get back," I panted against her mouth when she shoved her hand inside the front of my boxer briefs. Her tight grip made me hiss.

"What?" she whispered.

"No more hiding." I bit her bottom lip and tugged. "No more secrecy."

She whimpered when I soothed the spot with my tongue, teasing her with a kiss that I didn't deliver.

I flipped us, leaning up long enough to pull the last piece of clothing off her. Naked before me, Ava was almost blindingly beautiful. Her face was flushed from my words, her body quivering from my touch.

"When you get back," I said gruffly, pressing her knee up toward her chest and looming over her until she was arching her neck for a kiss, "everyone will know you're mine."

Under me, she was mindless, and that was before I snapped my hips forward.

Instantly, violently, with my name on her lips, she exploded.

But I didn't stop. I chased the rolling, coiling, churning sense of furious desire until my body was sweaty, until my legs were burning and my teeth were gritted, until Ava was practically in tears from release after release.

It wasn't enough.

Earlier, I thought we wouldn't last two minutes. But now, I felt the roaring flame so bright and so hot inside me, so primitive, that

I wanted to last all night. I wanted to torture myself for hours, withhold my pleasure if it simply meant that she'd be mine.

If I embedded myself deeply enough—gripped her skin under my hands, kissed her lips, sucked her tongue, and made sure that every second of this was a clear enough definition of what I felt for her—then maybe I'd be able to ensure this feeling forever. For both of us.

I knew I loved her. Could she sense it?

She clutched at my neck, begging for kisses that I was powerless to withhold, and when she sobbed against my lips that she couldn't take anymore, I pressed my forehead to hers and bared my teeth in a low growl while I finally allowed the threshold of pleasure to swamp me.

I fell against her, heedless of my weight over top of her slender body. Apparently, she didn't care because she wrapped shaking arms around my back and held me to her just as tightly as I'd just held her.

"I think ..." She gasped, placing an open-mouth kiss on my sweat-soaked shoulder. "I think I'm dead."

Chuckling, I moved off her but kept my arm slung over her waist. Her face was flushed, and her eyes started fluttering closed. So what if my legs couldn't move. If it put that look on her face, I'd risk paralysis every damn night. "That good, huh?"

She smacked my back. "Don't fish for compliments. It's not cute."

"Okay." But I grinned unrepentantly anyway.

Ava gave me an adoring look and slid out from under my arm so she could go clean up. By the time she crawled back under the covers, clad in my massive T-shirt, I was already dozing. She snuggled up to my side and whispered good night. I kissed her forehead and did the same.

But sleep didn't come.

I watched her as her breathing deepened, as her hands started twitching slightly when she started to dream. As she always did, Ava moved to her back and then flipped to her other side. I played with the ends of her hair, which looked black in the darkened room, and I thought about what she'd said. What she'd rambled about.

Memories of how callous they used to act toward her crowded my head, cuts and snippets of pictures of my relationship with Ashley. How she spoke to me at the end. How she spoke to Ava. The guys giving me shit for getting cheated on, especially with a slimy frat boy. Visions of Ava lying on a big, dark bed by herself, wishing she was somewhere else with people who understood her, who supported her, and who loved her in the way she deserved to be loved.

The way I loved her.

The way she didn't even know about yet. Only she would know, not just by me saying the words but by me showing her.

All the shuffling pictures, some that had really happened and some imagined, coalesced into one idea. One plan. Glancing over at her to make sure she was out, I slid carefully out of the bed until I found her laptop on the kitchen counter.

Frankie swam lazily around his bowl as I pulled up a seat and winced against the harsh light of the screen.

I gave him a look. "Man to man, you'd tell me if this was a bad idea, right?"

In answer, he flicked his majestic fins and turned in the opposite direction.

"Good talk, Frankie, thanks."

I took a deep breath and started searching.

CHAPTER 22
AVA

The morning I was scheduled to leave for the vow renewal dawned bright and clear, and I would know because I laid in bed and watched the light in my bedroom turn from black to soft gray to pale pink to bright, blinding, violent, omen-of-death yellow.

Beside me, Matthew slept heavily, his muscular arm slung over my waist, and his face turned into the pillow. Somewhere deep in my chest cavity, in the vicinity of my lungs, I felt a yawning sense of foreboding about the next forty-eight hours. I had to close my eyes against it. That disconcerting pit in my stomach, one that I couldn't breathe away, that all the meditation or prayer or hot yoga or goat sacrifice would abolish, had me feeling like I was three seconds away from throwing up.

"You need to leave for camp, big boy," I whispered to Matthew. His long, dark eyelashes fluttered up slowly, and his sleepy smile helped the pit in my tummy recede a bit.

During moments like that one, when I watched him wake up, I couldn't help but marvel at how I ended up here.

One day it was making out in the cab and WTF is happening right now to let's unofficially officially live together, and neither of us had seemed to blink.

Maybe that was where the portent of doom was coming from. From the ridiculous sense that two days would somehow alter our relationship. It made me feel better to think that was the case instead of the alternative. The alternative was my bad, icky, terrible feeling was coming from the time I'd spend with my family because of how awful they'd be.

Matthew grumbled and tugged me closer. He placed an absent-minded kiss on my lips before he slipped out of bed, standing and stretching with a great roar of sound from deep in his chest. I smiled and watched him pull his stuff together.

Without having to see it, I knew he grabbed a banana from the basket on my kitchen sink, and he'd stop for a protein-packed green smoothie on his way to camp from his favorite place, which was the same way he always started his early mornings. Once the door to my place slammed shut, I laid in bed longer than I should have.

All morning in the office, I kept my head down and focused on my work. The door to my office stayed conspicuously shut as though I was girding my metaphorical loins for what I was about to do. At camp that afternoon, I kept a smile on my face and did my job, shuffling people where they needed to go, conducting a few interviews, and keeping our VIP guests for the day happy, a rock band that had a connection with our star wide receiver, Johnson.

Matthew caught my eye a few times, giving me secret smiles and tiny winks that no one would notice but making sure I knew he was paying attention to how stressed out I was. By the time camp wrapped up, I knew he needed to go straight into a team meeting.

I stalled in my office as long as I possibly could, but the hands on the clock ticked closer and closer to when I needed to head over to the ferry to catch the last ride for the day. What had dawned as a bright, sunny day had clouded over, dropping the temperature just enough that I kept my jacket on while I walked out to my car.

"Slim," Matthew's voice yelled just as I was unlocking my driver's side door.

I exhaled in relief. "I didn't think I'd see you before I left."

He jogged over to me and slid his hands down my arms. "Sorry, everyone else got let go, but Coach was feeling chatty. I couldn't get away."

I smiled up at him. "No apology needed."

He glanced around, but we were alone in the staff parking lot. "You've got this."

Nodding, I let out a deep breath. That pit was back. And it was loud. It made my whole body hurt. "Okay."

Matthew opened my car door for me and waited until I was settled behind the wheel before he crouched down to give us a brief window of privacy. He leaned up and kissed me sweetly with just a hint of his tongue before he pulled back.

"I'll talk to you soon, okay?" he said, eyes concerned by whatever he saw on my face.

"Yeah," I told him. "It'll be fine."

It would be fine. As I stared into his eyes, warm and soft and chocolatey, I leaned in to kiss him again. Longer this time. And I didn't even care to check if anyone was around. His forehead touched mine before he pulled back and stood.

"Text me when the ferry gets there?"

I nodded. "Will do."

Matthew shut my door for me and stood in the spot while I pulled out.

By the time I got my suitcase, ran a brush through my hair, requested my Uber, and slicked some more lipstick over my lips, I knew I was cutting it close. Since I wasn't bringing my car, it wouldn't be too bad getting on the ferry, especially for the evening run, but my heart thudded uncomfortably all the same, right up until my driver peeled up to the entrance.

"Thanks," I yelled as I slammed the door shut and walked briskly up to the long, covered entryway. The massive white and green boat barely moved in the choppy water of the bay, and I hugged my jacket more tightly to my body as wind from the west swept over me in a gust.

I handed my ticket over to a worker wearing a fluorescent yellow jacket, and she lifted her chin in acknowledgment before moving on to the person behind me. The sun was low in the sky as I made my way through the enclosed deck. The blue chairs and booths bracketed to the floor were mostly empty, and I took a deep breath, the silence punctuated only by the sound of cars sliding into place and the engine on the boat clicking into gear as we started our slow glide across the waters.

Where I'd be stranded. With my family.

I avoided holidays easily because of work. Thanksgiving and Christmas were still incredibly busy times of the year for me unless they fell on a bye week. But even one day for a holiday with a night spent in a hotel had nothing on this little shindig.

Once the ferry left, I was well and truly stuck.

I sank into a seat toward the end of the boat and dumped my purse next to me on the floor.

Just as my eyes were closing so I could rest until we arrived, someone cleared their throat.

Low. The voice was low. And close.

Before I opened my eyes, I took a second because it sounded familiar.

It sounded like someone who was not supposed to be there.

And sure enough, when my eyelids lifted, I started at the bottom, his big feet clad in heavy brown boots, his long legs encased in dark denim, his torso covered in a basic gray shirt, and saw Logan *mother effing I was going to kill him* Ward.

"Logan," I said quietly. "You're standing in front of me right now. I'm not imagining this?"

He dipped his chin. "Hey."

"Hey?" I repeated slowly, my confusion morphing into something bigger and louder.

Logan cleared his throat.

"Wh-what are you doing here?" I whispered.

He must have heard the restrained violence in my tone because he grimaced before looking away. Over his shoulder was a large black duffel and in his other hand, a dry-cleaning bag. You know the ones. They usually held suits. Dresses. Or tuxedos.

"I'm taking a chance that you were full of shit when you said you didn't need help."

"What?" I yelled, standing to my full height, which was still a solid seven inches under his. I didn't care. "Oh no, you march your ass straight off this ferry, mister."

He lifted his eyebrows, then glanced meaningfully at the Seattle skyline in the ever-growing distance. At the pier, the white Ferris wheel moved slowly as if it was waving goodbye.

I sank my head into my hands and breathed deeply, breathed slowly.

The chair next to me was empty, which I regretted now, because Logan lowered his big, stupid frame into it and sighed.

"Listen," he said in his gruff, gravelly voice, "maybe it was a little presumptuous to just show up."

Slowly, oh so slowly, I turned my head and gave him an incredulous stare. "*Maybe?*"

Logan was quiet. Probably because he sensed murder in me.

I straightened, keeping my face forward on the bluish-gray water outside the boat, the white-tipped waves moving along with the gusting wind the farther we got away from shore. "Explain, please. Something that makes more sense than what you just told me."

Logan gave me a sideways look that I saw in my peripheral vision. "Besides just wanting to help?"

"Yup." I knit my fingers together on my lap and clenched them tightly. "You and I are not people who help each other. We barely know each other."

He was quiet for a minute. "That's true," he answered slowly.

"Which is why it doesn't make sense." Did I seriously need to fill in the blanks for him? I mentally tallied how many concussions Logan had suffered since he came to Washington. Two? Three? I couldn't remember. My brain was too preoccupied with the fact that Logan Ward decided to channel his inner white knight with me as his test subject. If I wasn't so freaked out, I might have thought it was sweet. Sweet, in a meathead, clearly didn't take my words at face value kind of way.

We sat in silence for a few long moments, and Logan shifted in my direction enough that I had no choice but to quit my staring contest with the water and glance at him. I tried not to glare, honestly, but I was freaking out that he was on this ferry with me.

The last ferry of the day.

Cue hysterical laughter.

"I may not have the same family issues you do. Whatever your issues are with your sister. But"—he scratched at his jaw and looked incredibly uncomfortable—"sometimes it would be nice not to have to face their bullshit alone, you know?"

My anger fled. Poof. Like magic.

The pit in my belly suddenly had a name, a label, the sudden bright light switch of clarity shining on it.

I didn't want to do this alone. The entire time I'd been freaking out was because I didn't want to walk into this entire ordeal with no one to be my safety net. Not someone to fight my battles for me or speak in my place, but I wanted, desperately, to be able to have Matthew stand there with me so I would know that I wasn't alone.

"I understand that, trust me." I slumped down and let the back of my head rest on my chair. "But Logan ... you have to admit it's a little insane that you're here right now."

"Do you hate me?" Without looking, I could hear a slight grin in his voice.

"I don't hate you." Opening my eyes, I cut him a brief look. "But you coming complicates things for me. Especially if I can't smuggle you back out on this exact ferry without my family seeing you."

His smile was quick and fast. There and gone. But he wouldn't look at me.

We sat quietly for a while. Not once did he look at his phone, which struck me as odd. I wanted to pull mine out and scroll mindlessly, but for some reason, I felt like I was taking my cue from him.

"So this guy you're dating..."

My heart seized in my chest. I should just tell him—tell him that the guy was Matthew and tell him about Matthew's history with my family—but the words crawled to a stop when I heard a familiar laugh behind us.

If I thought my heart seized in my chest before? It just fell the fuck out of my body.

"Ava? Is that you?"

"Oh dear sweet baby Jesus be a fence," I whispered under my breath. Then I turned. "Hi, Mom," I said weakly.

Logan's face snapped to me, his eyes widening in horror.

Because I had no choice, I stood and gave her a listless hug.

I was screwed.

And not in a good way.

Right on her heels was my dad, wearing a dark suit and perfectly starched white shirt. His hair was a touch grayer than it had been the last time I saw him, just as the lines fanning out from his green eyes were a touch deeper.

"I-I thought you guys were getting to the island yesterday."

My dad patted my back absentmindedly. "Had to bump our flight, kiddo. I was called in on an emergency quadruple bypass when the on-call doc was already in surgery."

Logan stood slowly, wiping his hands down his thighs. The look on his face was stoic, but I could sense the unease in his rigid frame.

Did I feel bad for him?

I sure as hell did not. *This is what you get, Ward, when you show up on ferries that you shouldn't be on*, I thought bitterly.

That was when I saw the transformation in my mom's perfectly unlined, perfectly made-up face. Her pink lips, the same Elizabeth Arden Blushing Pink that she'd worn as long as I could walk, curved up slowly, slowly, slowly. Her eyes narrowed like they only did when she was actually, really happy about something.

And then, she pushed her caramel-colored hair in her signature sleek bob behind her ear and tilted her chin to show off her good side. "Well now, you must be Ava's beau."

Kill.

Me.

Now.

Logan gave me a brief look that I roughly translated to, *what the hell am I supposed to do?* I blinked a few times because I didn't know.

Maybe I could say he was a stranger I'd been chatting with.

Maybe I could say ... I didn't know! I didn't know what I could say because the universe had just wedged my numb body between Mount Rainier and another big mountain, making it impossible for me to move. To speak. To think, apparently.

He stretched his hand out to her. "It's a pleasure to meet you. I'm Logan."

My mom took his hand but then turned hers so her knuckles were facing up. Oh my sweet Lord, did she want him to kiss her hand?

"Mom," I said, shaking my head.

She shrugged like, *can't blame me for trying.* "Logan, what a wonderfully strong name. Please, call me Abigail."

My dad stepped forward and took Logan's hand in a firm shake. "Alan Baker." He rocked back and gave Logan a considering look, head to toe, as though he was a horse about to go up on the auction block. "Ward? That's your last name?"

"Yes, sir."

Oh goodie, my fake date was polite.

"Any family I might know in the Northern California area?"

Logan glanced at me, clearing his throat before he answered. "Not that I know of."

"And you play? On Ava's team?"

I rolled lips between my teeth and considered the possibility of survival if I were to pitch myself overboard and swim back to Seattle.

At that question, Logan actually graced my parents with a tiny smile. "You could argue it's my team more than Ava's since I've been there about five years longer. Though she does keep us all in line with an iron fist."

My father laughed heartily, and my mom tittered as though he'd just told her she was the most beautiful woman alive. I mock glared at him even though he was completely right.

"Right, right," my dad said, slapping him on the back. "That sounds like our Ava."

"Does it now?" I muttered.

"Can we sit with you?" my mom asked, rolling her suitcase to the chairs opposite of ours and taking a seat before anyone uttered so much as a syllable. As much as anyone could, my mother looked regal sitting in that blue plastic chair, her tan pantsuit perfectly tailored and her slim legs crossed so that we could see the nude patent heels with the bright red bottoms.

Logan and I took our seats, and he leaned in to whisper in my ear while my parents looked at something on my dad's phone. "Alan, Abigail, Ashley, and Ava?"

I exhaled quietly, then answered under my breath. "And my brother-in-law is Adam. Yes, our family matches. Keep your judgment away from me, if you please. It's not like I had any choice in the matter."

He smiled again, then settled into his chair before folding his arms over his chest. "They don't seem so bad."

"Bite your *tongue*, Ward. You've known them for thirty-two seconds."

He actually chuckled under his breath, and I considered what might happen if I punched him in the nuts. Maybe it wasn't fair, but Logan made a very convenient anger scapegoat in this whole bullshit situation. While my parents continued their private conversation, and Logan fell quiet again, I fought the urge to panic while I considered my options.

1- I excuse myself and call Matthew. Tell him what happened

and hope it didn't stress him out that I was parading one of his teammates around as my date. Unintentionally, but still.

2- I come clean to my parents right now while we were stuck on this boat for forty minutes or so.

And then there was the last option. I took a deep breath and felt that roiling pit in my stomach again. Only this time, it was accompanied by a hundred-pound weight on my chest.

3- I let the weekend play out. Make Logan go home tomorrow morning, fake an illness or something. My parents think they met my boyfriend, but he doesn't attend the ceremony in Matthew's place. When I get home on Sunday, I come clean to Matthew so he's not stressed the entire weekend.

Surreptitiously, I watched my parents. My mom must have felt my eyes on them because she glanced up. Then she winked, giving me a wide-eyed stare as she tilted her head in Logan's direction. *Nice work*, she mouthed. And just like that, her attention left me, zeroing back on my dad's phone and whatever was so fascinating to them.

For a moment, I hated her. I hated myself. Because that one small nod of approval felt like she'd handed me my weight in gold. I'd never heard them be proud of my job or what I'd accomplished professionally. I'd never heard them compliment anything about me. The closest thing I'd ever gotten was what my dad had said to Logan.

At the back of my throat, I felt the burn of embarrassed tears. Because I knew I'd choose option three. Even if it was for twelve hours, I couldn't deny the fact that I wanted my family to look at me and be impressed. To hold their interest, just for a few snippets of time.

Was this what it felt like to be Ashley? I wondered. An instant, guaranteed interest in every facet of my life?

Approval.

Pride in who I was and in what I'd accomplished.

It was so foreign that it felt like someone had dumped me into another country where they didn't speak the same language, and I was left without a translator.

But it wasn't about me. Not really.

It was really based on this person sitting next to me. Their interest stemmed and blossomed from the knowledge that I had, in their minds, a successful partner, and not that I was successful in my own right. I wasn't even sure how I felt about that except that for even a moment, I wanted to step into this feeling. No matter how brief it was or how shallow it might seem.

"Your brain is about to start letting off smoke," Logan mumbled.

I glanced sharply at him. "How did you ..."

He gave me a long look, which was no small feat considering he didn't turn his face to me. "I've worked with you for what? Six years? People forget that the quiet guy in the corner is usually quiet so he can figure everyone out."

I couldn't help my smile. "That sounds so creepy."

His brows bent in over his eyes. "Yeah. I suppose it does."

Click.

Logan and I looked over at my mom, who'd just snapped a picture of us on her phone. She smiled sheepishly. Fake sheepishly, but at least she was attempting to look apologetic.

"Sorry, you kids just look so lovely together. All that dark hair." She hummed, staring down at her screen, presumably at her picture of us.

Suddenly, I was in elementary school again, clutching my sparkly purple backpack in my hands on the first day of school and watching my mom take picture after picture of Ashley in front of the tree in our front yard. The bus pulled up, and I smiled, stepping forward so she could get one of me too.

"Come on, Ava," Ashley snapped. "You'll make everyone late."

My mom patted my shoulder absently. "She's right, dear. Go on."

I remember climbing onto the bus, telling myself that she'd get one later when I got home because moms always took the first day of school pictures, right? She didn't. At least, not that year. Not of me.

Just this once, I promised myself even though I heard the dark thread of my thoughts. It was selfish. It was dishonest. And it was shallow.

Still, despite all that, I found myself reaching my hand out and wanting to see how she saw me. Just once.

"Can I see it?" I asked my mom.

With a smile, she handed over her phone. On the large, crystal clear screen, Logan and I had our heads bent toward each other. I was smiling, and he was giving me a look that could only be described as soft and sweet. His hair was darker than mine, almost black in the light of the boat.

The tears that had pressed on the back of my throat earlier spilled up and over, just one sliding past my eyelashes and down my cheek. My hand wiped it away before she saw, but I felt Logan staring at me.

I didn't want this to be the picture on my mom's phone.

I wanted it to be Matthew and me. But the second they knew, the second they found out, I'd be pushed to the side again. Worse, actually. They'd erect a fence between them and me. A protective barrier to keep the unpleasantness away from their picture-perfect lives.

"It's a good picture," I told her thickly and handed her phone back with a shaky hand.

"Your skin looks wonderful, honey," my mom said. She tucked her phone back into her Louis Vuitton purse. "You're glowing."

My dad nodded, finally tearing his eyes away from the screen and giving me a moment of his attention. "Indeed, indeed. Prettier than you've ever been, kiddo."

Their words were like pouring a honey-sweetened vinegar over a dried-out sponge that had been left in the sun too long. My soul was parched for words like that from them, a husk I'd ignored for years out of necessity, but even if the initial moment they hit was sweet, the aftertaste was bitter.

Because I felt like a sell-out.

I felt like a whore.

Yet I replayed what they said, over and over, until I couldn't possibly forget these little snapshots of time.

For the remainder of the boat ride, I stayed quiet, because if I'd opened my mouth, I might have screamed. So loud and so long that it would've busted out the windows of the boat.

If I'd known what was waiting for us on the island when the boat docked, I probably would have, just to be able to prevent it.

CHAPTER 23
AVA

WASHINGTON WOLVES

"**N**ice hotel," Logan said as we walked through the lobby.

My mom fairly preened. "It's the best on the island, of course. Their outdoor event space has the best view of the sound, which is why Ashley is having her ceremony take place there."

"Unless it rains," my dad chimed in. There was an awkward beat of silence after his quite obvious statement. I glanced at my mom, who sighed.

"Yes, Alan, unless it rains." Her voice was even, but I almost laughed at how patronizing she sounded.

The plush carpet under our feet made our progress soundless. That alone made me feel like this whole thing might be a dream. Nightmare. Whatever. If a group of people walked through a hotel lobby and didn't make any sound, were they even there?

Just in case, I pinched the inside of my arm. Nope. Not asleep.

Our rooms were on different floors, thank goodness, because there was less of a risk that they'd see Logan leave in the morning, and see that he was quite healthy, despite whatever story I'd concoct.

For a brief window of time, while my parents went below deck to drive their rental car off the ferry, Logan and I were able to settle on a game plan. By that, I mean that I told him exactly what was going to happen.

He'd meet Ashley once she was done having dinner with Adam and his parents. She could ooh and aah and be green with jealousy, and then he and I would retire, claiming exhaustion from a long day at work. In the morning, he'd slip out of the hotel early and wait for the morning ferry. I would tell my family that he got sick overnight and had to go back, out of concern for me catching whatever he had.

Because my parents weren't stupid, he was going to wait in my room until it was late, then sneak into the room he'd booked for himself when he came up with this misguided excuse for chivalry.

With a quick sideways glance at his stoic profile, I had to admit that if I hadn't been so tied up in knots over how this weekend would play out, how the future would play out—so long as Matthew was in it—I might have been touched by what he was willing to do for me.

But unfortunately for Logan, the gesture was wasted. I just wanted him gone. I wanted him gone and on a boat and back in Seattle so I could breathe deeply again. Even walking next to him felt like some sort of betrayal even though I hadn't invited him.

That was the crux, wasn't it?

He hadn't touched me, not even in a casual way. He hadn't done anything inappropriate. He didn't need to. His being here and me allowing it was wrong. The closer we got to my room, the truer it became, until it was a dark, hulking entity creeping in the back of my head, haunting every other thought that tried to over-take it.

Wrong.

Wrong.

Wrong.

"Ava," my mom said, and I realized she must have called my name more than once.

"Sorry, what?"

"Your sister said she'd be done in about twenty minutes. Do you two want to freshen up and meet us down in the bar?"

Liar.

Cheat.

Fake.

I must have nodded or something because she smiled. "Excellent." To my abject horror, she leaned in to kiss my cheek, whispering in my ear as she did. "Don't take too long, if you know what I mean."

"We won't," I promised her from the very depths of my soul. Easiest thing I'd ever told my mom.

They turned down the hallway of the ground floor, their matching suitcases rolling behind them silently. Logan exhaled, and I leaned forward to push the button on the elevator.

"Have I said sorry yet?" he asked, gesturing for me to get in before him.

"I don't believe you have," I answered as politely as I could manage. Under the circumstances, I was proud of myself. Yes, in my job, I had to be capable of facing an erupting volcano of bad press and keep my cool, keep my message straight, and deliver it with authority. But those things were never personal.

This was as personal as it could get.

The car chugged up with a lurch, and we faced each other from opposite ends of the enclosed space. He rubbed a hand over the back of his neck, and for the first time, I noticed how tired he looked.

"I apologize, Ava." Logan shook his head. "I'm not sure what I was thinking."

After a beat of consideration, I lifted my hand and held it out to him. "Forgiven."

He took my hand with a smile, letting it drop after a firm shake. "I'm guessing you'll make me pay for this with interviews, right?"

"You don't even *know* how bad it's going to be for you."

We were both laughing when the elevator doors opened on the

fourth floor, and he took my suitcase for me while I fished the room key out of the paper envelope.

"This night cannot go fast enough," I said as I slid the card into the little black slot. The red light turned green, and I turned the handle, pushing the door open with an awkward lurch.

"I'll try not to be offended," Logan answered dryly.

When I walked into the room, I saw lights on around the corner, then squeaked in alarm when I saw the tips of someone's shoes. Someone's white tennis shoes. Just like in the ferry, I followed the line up, up, up. Dark jeans on long, thick legs, a solid color T-shirt over a broad chest, and a face that looked like it was carved from granite.

"Matthew," I breathed, a smile lighting my face before I saw the icy hardness in his normally warm eyes.

"Hawkins?" Logan asked. "What are you—" Then he stopped as if someone had pulled the plug on his vocal cords. "Oh," he drawled.

I took a step toward Matthew with my hands out. "Oh my gosh, I'm so glad you're here. This is insane. Logan was trying to help me and ..."

"And you forgot to tell me?" he asked, voice implacable. Then his eyes sliced to Logan. I swallowed nervously, seeing this seething, hissing rage hum under the surface of his skin. Where was my smiling Matthew? The Matthew who would wrap me in his arms and tell me everything would be okay?

"Matthew, hang on," Logan started. "I swear to you, this is not what it looks like."

"You expect me to believe that? Because trust me, I've heard a variation of that before in my life," he said quietly. Then he laughed a low, unamused sound. "This is her. Right?"

I looked back and forth between the two hulking men currently sucking up all the free oxygen in the room. It was the only explanation for why I couldn't breathe. "What are you talking about?"

Logan's face hardened. "I told you that in confidence, and I had no idea you were the guy. How could I have known?"

"Told him *what* in confidence?"

They ignored me.

Matthew took a step, and I felt the air around me pulse like a rogue wave, cold and icy and uncomfortable. "Leave, Ward. Now."

Logan hesitated, giving me a questioning look. But I didn't react. Couldn't react. My eyes went back to Matthew, and I wanted to burst into tears. This looked bad. It looked about as bad as anything could look to him. My hands pressed against my stomach. If I thought I had a pit before, it was bupkis compared to what was going on inside me. The whole time I'd felt it, the portent, the omen, the icky feeling, it was only a warm-up to this moment.

"I'm sorry," he said, then opened his mouth to say more but wisely snapped his jaw shut when Matthew narrowed his eyes dangerously.

He left the room, the door closing with a sharp snap, and I felt an icy flush of panic slide through my body when I realized I had no idea what to do with this Matthew. We'd never even come to close to irritation with each other, let alone real, justified anger.

"How-how did you get in here?" I asked quietly.

"Is that seriously the first thing you want to ask right now?" he asked right back. "Let's start with how long you've been lying to me? I like that question better."

My throat closed with hot embarrassment, my nose tingled when I searched for words.

"A little quicker, Ava," he bit out, color high in his face, "because it'll make me think you don't have a good story thought out."

I held his eyes and willed myself not to cry. "I've been caught off guard more than once tonight, and I'm really over the whole presumptuous male beating his chest and making decisions for me. You have a right to be upset right now, but don't be an asshole."

Matthew folded his arms over his chest and watched me impassively. If it weren't for the tightness in his hard-edged jawline and the slight flare in his nostrils, I would've thought he didn't care.

"Fine," he said tightly. "But please help me understand why my girlfriend just walked into a hotel room with another man because I'm not feeling all that charitable right now."

My stomach curled in on itself at how horrible it all looked, but I kept my chin up and held his eyes. "I *didn't know* Logan would be on the ferry. I swear to you, I didn't. And I would've made him turn right back around and go back if my parents hadn't been on the same one. They-they wanted to meet my boyfriend," I said helplessly.

He exhaled hard through his nose, a sharp nod lifting his chin. "And *why* would they think that was Logan?"

————

Matthew

She looked miserable. Tortured. On the razor edge of tears. But I steeled myself, locking every emotion tight and bolting it shut behind a thick wall of iron because the feeling of seeing her walk in the door with Logan right behind her and hearing a smile in her voice when the last thing I'd seen of her was not even close to smiling made me feel as if someone had reached down my throat and ripped my heart out in the blink of an eye.

Messy and brutal, but true.

It felt like betrayal. Had the smell, the feel, the metallic taste of it, the sticky residue all around me of deceit.

"B-because he came into my office the day Ashley showed up. The day you sent me flowers."

The day in her office, she'd been a wreck, but that was weeks earlier. *Weeks.* "And?"

Ava knit her hands together, but I could still see them vibrating even as her knuckles turned white from how tightly she was holding them together. "And I panicked because Ashley knew I was dating a player. Logan," she stumbled slightly over his name, and I had to fight the urge to rip something apart just to release some of the fiery, tumbling emotion inside me, "Logan walked in, and I panicked. I introduced him as my boyfriend so she'd drop it. The last thing I wanted was for her to take a sudden interest in the roster. I wasn't ready. *We* weren't ready."

I couldn't look at her.

I couldn't look at her without wanting to yell and scream and demand she explain herself in a way that didn't sound like she'd chosen to lie to me for weeks. The best weeks of my life. The happiest. The most settled. With her at the center, anchoring all that happiness into place.

"Why didn't you just tell me then?" I jabbed a finger in the air, and she flinched. "That's the part I'm missing."

"Because I thought that was it!" she burst out. "End of story, no big deal. I never had any intention of bringing Logan here because I couldn't stand the thought of being here with someone else if I couldn't be here with you. Even if my parents were suddenly falling over themselves to find out more about him."

I tipped my head back and battled the rising sensation, the clawing rage at her statement. Because I knew, I knew her parents were at the heart of this insanity. They had been from day one. When I looked back at her, those green eyes were glossy with tears, and it made me fight a different battle, resist a different urge. To hold her. Tell her it would be fine.

Because it wouldn't.

She was the first person that I thought would never lie to me. Not about something like this. No matter whether that was it. Or if she thought it was the end of the story.

It hadn't been.

She still didn't tell me.

"Then what?" I asked quietly, keeping my arms firmly over my chest.

"Logan offered to come with me, a-and I told him I was dating someone, and it was complicated, but I couldn't bring him with me." Ava took a step closer, and her spine straightened, her eyes cleared. "I *wasn't* going to bring him, Matthew. He showed up on his own, thinking he was going to help me, I don't know, some misguided white knight thing because he's got family issues of his own. I don't *know*," she said, visibly frustrated. "I can't read Logan's mind, but I didn't know he was coming. Ask him the next time you see him. I had *no clue* my parents would be on the same ferry with us. M-my dad had some last-minute surgery, and they had to bump their flights. Ask him! Once he was here, I figured that I would send him off to his own room later, and he was going to catch the ferry tomorrow morning. I'd tell my family he got sick, and you and I could deal with our own stuff down the road."

I nodded slowly, but inside, the rage inside me mushroomed into something else entirely. I knew why Logan showed up. He'd told me. She was the woman he had feelings for, the woman he knew was dating someone else, and he refused to let his shot pass.

What had he said to her?

How had he treated her?

Touched her?

Flirted with her?

Had she let him?

"Matthew, please, say something," she pleaded, taking a tentative step toward me. "Are you even hearing what I'm saying? Yes, it was stupid not to tell you, and I'm sorry, but it felt so little, so unimportant at the time."

My face was stone. My stomach was acid. My skin was on fire.

That was the thing no one told you about being lied to, about the little things, the things that added up, that snowballed, that grew and grew until that one white lie became a giant wall of ice. It should be cold. Feel cold.

But the slicing open of your pride was hot and fiery, a slow-burning trail of glowing orange magma that you couldn't stop, and it left a trail of ash behind that you could taste in your mouth for far longer than you wanted to.

I leaned toward Ava and felt a tiny, selfish twinge of satisfaction that she leaned back from whatever she saw on my face. "It wouldn't have been unimportant to me. That's what you're missing. This isn't just about you, and what you feel and want and are ready for or feel like I need to be aware of."

Ava tucked her lips between her teeth and watched me, her chest heaving on shallow breaths. Somehow, she kept the tears in her eyes, but they were there, threatening to spill over onto her cheeks. It was like she knew that if I saw her cry, I'd soften, I'd reach out to her, and right now, I was too pissed and feeling too betrayed to let that happen.

"Did you talk to Logan about this after that first time?"

When she didn't answer, when her jade green eyes cut away from me, I lost my breath. Because that was my answer.

"How many times?" I asked.

She swallowed roughly. "Twice. After that first time."

I nodded, looking down at my duffel bag. The one I'd packed thinking we could cocoon ourselves in the room when she wasn't needed with her family. It was stupid. Chartering a plane to beat her here was stupid. Bribing the front desk person with tickets so I could surprise my girlfriend in her room was stupid. Coming here to tell her that I was in love with her was the stupidest idea of all.

Because I thought I could predict everything she'd do, say, and how she'd react. She was supposed to fly into my arms, rain kisses over my face, and thank me for being here with her. Even if I couldn't come to the ceremony, she'd tell me she loved me back.

Instead, she walked into the room with another man.

"I'm going to go," I said quietly. "I can't do this right now. Not here."

"Matthew, please," she begged, finally closing the gap between us to lay her hands on my arms. "I get why you're mad, I do. But come on, you could have talked to me about wanting to come here."

"Talk to you?" I said incredulously. "Talk to you."

She blinked at the harsh tone of my voice.

"That would assume you'd actually be willing to talk about your family with me. Do you have any idea how frustrated I've been, Ava? I've wanted to talk about this stuff with you for weeks, and you avoided it at every turn."

Ava didn't argue, but I could see the rising frustration in the shift of her shoulders and the set of her jaw.

"Can you blame me for not wanting to have this conversation?" she asked, gesturing between us.

"No," I said honestly, and she drew back in obvious surprise. "I get it. I get that there are things in life that suck and are hard to talk about, hard to work through. I understand why you didn't want to talk about it. But I thought we had something between us that made it bearable to go through that stuff. That we had the kind of relationship where you'd let me shoulder some of that burden for you, Ava."

"We do have that," she said on a rush, coming toward me again. "Matthew, we do, I just ..."

I held up my hand, and she stopped. Maybe it wasn't fair. Maybe it was cruel. But at that moment, I couldn't handle any more convenient truths or reasonable explanations for why I felt so blindsided by her.

"I can't do this right now, Ava," I said quietly, then leaned down to grab my bag and strode away from her.

I yanked the door open and stopped short.

With her hand raised in the air was Ava's mom and not far behind her, her dad staring at his phone with a bored expression on his face.

We both froze, her eyes widened in her face as she realized who I was.

"M-Matthew Hawkins?" she hissed. "Ava, what on *earth* is going on?

My heart froze solid in my chest. Before anyone could react, Ava's mom shoved me back into the room and gave her husband a whispered command to get in the room and shut the door.

"Hey," I said indignantly, half shocked she was able to move me back in the first place.

"Mom, Dad," Ava stuttered. "What are you doing up here?"

Dr. Baker glanced back and forth between his daughter and me, color high in his face. His wife was gawking at me, mouth hanging open like a fish.

"You didn't show up for drinks, so we came to get you and ..." His voice trailed off when he caught the thunderous expression on my face. He cleared his throat.

"What is he doing here?" Ava's mom said.

"I have a name," I reminded her coolly.

Her eyes flicked to me, then back to her daughter. I'd all but been dismissed. I slicked my tongue over my teeth and gripped the handle of my duffel bag more tightly.

"Mom," Ava started, "there's been a huge misunderstanding."

"Is this some sick joke?" she interrupted.

Ava shook her head slowly. "What do you mean?"

"Is this about ruining your sister's day?" she accused, hand clutching at her chest. "Ava Marie, if you brought him here to cause problems ..."

"What?" Ava gasped.

"Are you kidding me?" I bellowed, unable to watch it play out anymore. "Do you actually believe she's capable of something like that? You know *nothing* about her."

Ava's face softened instantly, but I could still hardly look at her. Just because I was pissed as hell didn't mean I'd let them trash her in front of me.

Dr. Baker held up his hands. "Now, let's just all calm down. Matthew, this is a family issue."

"Don't you tell me what I believe, or what I know," his wife interjected. "She's *my* daughter, and where the hell do you get off thinking you belong in this conversation in the first place?"

I rubbed at my forehead wearily. "You are unbelievable. Not everything is about Ashley, you know."

Dr. Baker muttered something under his breath, and his wife gave him a quelling glare.

She turned her cold eyes back to me. "You need to leave this room, Matthew, right now."

I crossed my arms and gave her the look I only reserved for game day. I wasn't the kid she knew ten years ago, and I'd like to see her try to shove me out in the hallway now.

"Abigail," Dr. Baker said quietly.

"Do you think I won't call security?" she snapped at me.

"Mom," Ava said. "Please, just stop yelling at him. He's ... he's—"

"He's what?" she whispered dangerously.

Ava inhaled slowly, exhaled a heavy breath. "Mom, it's just ... it's not what you think."

Air rushed out of my lungs, hard and heavy. It took Ava a second to realize how that sounded. That during the one moment Ava could've grabbed my hand and claimed our relationship, she used the same line that was uttered when I found her with Logan.

A mistake. A misunderstanding. That it was nothing. She gasped and moved toward me.

"Matthew," she whispered frantically.

Anything hot turned icy cold. I felt the gates slam down as frost climbed up them in spidery webs.

I turned my head over my shoulder and gave her a last look. "She's right, Mrs. Baker. It's not what you think." I shouldered past them without another word, ignoring whatever commotion happened in my wake. "Not what I thought either, apparently."

CHAPTER 24
AVA

WASHINGTON
WOLVES

I ran after him, ignoring my mom's attempt to grab my arm and my dad's protest at ... I didn't even know.

"Matthew, wait. *Please*, just wait for a second," I called out just before he turned the corner. His frame was rigid, but he stopped.

I approached him cautiously with my hands lifted.

"That sounded so awful," I whispered, desperately wanting to lay my hands on his broad back. "I am so sorry that it sounded so awful. You know I didn't mean it that way."

Finally, he turned. It was slow and steady with no rush to meet my eyes or see whatever look was frozen on my face.

"Do I know that?" he said.

My breath was shaking. My body was shaking. He was standing right in front of me, but I could see him slipping away. "Tell me what to do to make this better."

His eyes searched my face as I lost the battle with my tears. His jaw clenched as each one slid silently down my cheeks.

Matthew spoke quietly and deliberately. "Right now, you can't. Not while we're standing in the hallway with them back there waiting for you. Right now, I need time. Because even though I can understand how all these dominoes fell into place—including the ones you have no control over—it doesn't change the fact that I chartered a plane here so I could look you in the eyes when I told you I'd fallen in love with you. And instead, I found you in a room with another man, and then was treated like a dirty secret in front of your parents, who are the sole reason you're so guarded, I couldn't get you to talk to me in the first place."

A sob escaped my lips, and I pressed a hand to my mouth so I could keep all the others down, the ones choking my throat and crowding my heart.

"Matthew," I said in a wretched, tear-filled voice. I wanted to tell him that I'd fallen in love with him too, that I couldn't imagine my future without him, but I'd fucked up so badly, all I could do was stand in front of him and cry.

He lifted his hand and used the pad of one thumb to swipe at the tears on my face. My fingers pressed harder against my lips so that I didn't clutch his hand to me and refuse to let go.

I couldn't let him leave without saying something, somehow letting him know the incredible space he'd taken up inside my heart.

He dropped his hand and reached for his duffel.

"Matthew, please, I'm falling in—"

"Stop," he said instantly, harshly, his forehead lined and bent with discomfort. "Not like this, Ava, please."

I sniffed noisily, and my head wobbled on a shaky nod. As he turned and walked away, I stood frozen in place until I heard the ding of the elevator.

My parents were talking over each other when I walked back into my room, but I couldn't hear a word. My brain was muffled with cotton, all their syllables and irritation and confusion bleeding together in one long, discordant sound.

All the words as they came out painted a picture so shallow, I could see through it. It certainly didn't give me anything to stand on.

It was flimsy.

Insubstantial.

When I closed my eyes and imagined his face, my heart squeezed so painfully, I worried for a moment that I would pass out.

"Ava Marie, are you even listening?" my mom hissed, grabbing my arm and pulling me back into my room. I ripped it out of the grasp of her bony fingers, and she laid a hand on her chest in shock. "You better start talking, young lady."

"This is insanity," my dad grumbled.

"Just stop talking," I whispered. "Just for one second while I try to breathe."

Their chattering had dried up my tears, but my whole body was shaking. I sat on the edge of the king-size bed, braced my elbows on my knees, and speared my fingers through my hair. It took me a second of deep, even breathing to realize they'd listened to me.

When I raised my head, my parents were staring at me with a strange mix of annoyance, anger, and disbelief written on their faces.

"Well," my dad said, waving a hand toward the door. "Care to explain why your sister's college boyfriend was in your hotel room? And where the hell *your* boyfriend is?"

I stared at him, trying to form words that would make this make sense. And I couldn't do it. Where did I start? They wouldn't even care what the truth was.

My mom's narrow-eyed gaze watched me carefully, sifting through what she'd seen and what she'd heard. After only a few seconds, I watched her make sense of all the pieces without me needing to say a thing. Her face smoothed out, and she exhaled slowly.

"Let me handle this, Alan."

Surprisingly, he did. He pursed his lips and shook his head.

"Honestly, Ava, the particulars don't matter." She swept her hands down the front of her pantsuit, effectively ridding herself of what had happened. "I don't know what that man was doing in here, but it's obvious, in retrospect, that—"

"That man?" I repeated quietly, gaping up at her. "*That* man? You guys loved Matthew. She cheated on him when they were supposed to get married, and now you're referring to him as *that man*?"

My mom laughed under her breath, holding up a hand when my dad started to speak.

"Ava"—she shook her head slowly—"if you have kids someday, you'll understand what it feels like, okay? Reality is a little different for us when we look at that situation than it is for you. *Clearly.*" Her snide tone set the hair up on my arms, and my fingers curled into fists. "Your poor relationship with Ashley has never been a secret, but I swear to you right now, if you ruin this weekend for her because of whatever you're doing with him, whatever reason he was here, I'll never forgive you."

Oh yeah, my tears were long gone. In their place was a strange numbness. I couldn't even find the strength to drudge up anger, any shred of righteous indignation, or a defense for myself. Apathy felt like a heavy blanket at that moment. The kind you burrowed under when you couldn't sleep and hoped that it lulled you with a false sense of security.

"You'll never forgive me," I repeated in a hollow voice.

"Not one word to her about this, Ava," she continued. "Do you understand me?"

My dad was looking down at the floor, his arms crossed over his chest. My mom's face was flushed, just a little, and I tilted my head to study her. I didn't look anything like her. Not her hair, or eyes, or the way her nose had a cute upturn at the end.

Any illusions I had about this weekend were snipped away. Like balloons freed into the big empty sky with precise snicks of a sharp pair of scissors.

Snip.

Snip.

Snip.

"I understand you perfectly," I said evenly. The double meaning of my words was lost on her.

She straightened with a huff. "Good. Now, we're late for drinks. That's why we came to your room in the first place." She gave me a cursory glance. "Now wipe your face and straighten your shirt. And pinch your cheeks for a little color. You'll do."

I laughed, and the sound brought my dad's head up for the first time in minutes. "I'm not going down for drinks."

"Oh yes, you are."

"Abigail," my dad said quietly but firmly.

I stood from the bed and took a deep breath. "No, Mother, I won't. I'll be at the ceremony. I'll keep a smile on my face because I'm not like Ashley. I will suck it up and not make a scene as she would have done if the roles were reversed. The kind that you would condone because it's her. The kind you'd justify because it's *her*."

My mom's mouth flopped open like she was a fish caught on a hook, and my dad grimaced.

"But tonight," I continued, "I'm ordering at least one bottle of obscenely priced wine from room service, probably some chocolate cake that I can cry into because I fucked up so badly tonight with someone *very* important to me, I'll be charging all of it to this room you're paying for, and you won't fight me on a single bit of it."

There was a saying that a smart soldier knew when to retreat. And my parents were not stupid. One prolonged look at my face, which probably resembled a cracked-out raccoon from the streaked mascara, and they started filing out of my room.

My dad turned before leaving and opened his mouth to say something, but I held up a hand. "Not tonight, Dad. Just ... not tonight."

My father, I looked like him. I had the same blade straight nose. The same eyes. The same smile when he chose to use it. Looking at him in the doorway, I wasn't sure I could pinpoint what I saw in his face, but I refused to name it as anything close to pity because I'd lose the tenuous hold on my weird, seesawing emotions.

Shame.

Embarrassment.

Despair.

Pain.

Love.

Disappointment.

Anger.

And nothing. Just nothing.

I could barely process all the things I'd felt in the past hour, the past week, or month, let alone try to name them and be mentally healthy about it.

Hence the wine and chocolate cake.

I slipped into my pajamas to await my delivery. I signed the bill with a blank smile. I crawled into my big empty bed, drank straight from the bottle, and ate the cake with my fingers like only the brokenhearted can.

After one bottle, I stared at my text thread with Matthew and tried to not sob ugly, fat tears. In my drunk state, I fancied that my tears were beautiful glistening trails going down my face. I told myself calling him was a horrible idea. I didn't even know if he'd made it off the island. He could've walked five minutes and found a different hotel to stay at. He could've chartered a plane or a helicopter to take him back to Seattle (Oh, the joys of being obscenely wealthy).

I rolled on my back, phone above me, and I settled for a text. Just one. Just one little text for him to wake up to.

That was when I almost lost it. Because if he had made it back to Seattle, I knew he was in his bed. I knew how he was lying—on his back with his hands crossed over his stomach because that was the best for his back—and I knew what time he laid his head down on those amazing, expensive pillows of his. And my entire body throbbed with missing him. With the reality of what had happened in just one short evening of my life.

Me: I miss you. I'm sorry. I'm horrible, and I hate all this, and yes, maybe I'm drunk, but it still makes all of the above true.

Me: I hate being in this place without you. Anywhere without you, really.

Me: Shit. I told myself I'd only send one text and now I'm on number 3, and I sound like a selfish bitch. Ironic, huh? I get if you need to be mad at me for a while. But we're not done, Matthew. Nobody feels the way we feel about each and can just be DONE. Not like this.

Me: Did I mention I'm horrible and sorry? And drunk? And that I miss you?

"Well," I mumbled, tossing my phone onto the empty side of the bed. "That escalated quickly."

For a moment, I stared at the second bottle of wine, the one that cost my parents somewhere in the sixty-dollar range, and decided to take pity on future me, so I got up and chugged some water, then fell face first back in bed.

The sheets were cold. So was my pillow. But with a heavy sigh, I was able to curl in on myself and fall asleep.

————

The next morning, I did an excellent impression of an Ava-bot. I hugged my sister as she flitted from one place to the next, successfully slipping away before she could engage me in conversation. I helped the event coordinator tie ivory ribbons around the bright white chairs on the emerald-green grass overlooking the sapphire water of the bay, backed by the gray and brown and white of the mountains.

The view was perfection.

I was a wreck.

My phone remained silent.

A smile stayed plastered on my face.

Inside, my heart and stomach were pretzeled around each other.

My head was off in the clouds, thinking of Matthew.

When the venue was ready, I stayed in the lobby until my mom gave me one warning glance, and then I walked serenely off to my room to make myself look presentable.

When I pulled the navy, one-shoulder Grecian chiffon dress off the hanger, I sighed. As I struggled to zip up the side, tightened the black belt around my waist, and slipped my nude wedges on, I realized that this weekend was one giant fake.

As I expertly sprayed my messy waves into place, I knew that any stress I had about this tiny chunk of hours meant nothing. The foreboding I'd felt was a Trojan horse.

The real issue—tucked inside and waiting to attack, to raze my city to the ground—was outside the ceremony, outside my parents, outside Ashley.

And all centered on my issues.

I'd closed off big, important pieces of myself to a man who loved me because I'd never learned how to be loved in the right way. The healthy, forgiving, accepting way. In front of me, I'd had someone who was all of those things, and I swallowed down truth after truth rather than risk the uncomfortable conversations with him where I might not know the answer.

I walked out of my room, black clutch in hand and head straight, and made my way outside. The weather was as if my sister had ordered it—slight breeze, bright sun, and temps in the low seventies. It was a small gathering, no more than twenty-five, and I only recognized my mom's terrible sister, Ellen, who hadn't spoken to Ashley or me since I was in diapers.

Maybe she was under the same orders as I was. Show up, put a smile on your face, and don't upset Ashley. I sat in my chair while my parents took their seats next to me in the front row. I watched Adam take his place up front under a simple wood frame arch covered with ivory and white roses.

Ashley wore a white fitted dress and came gliding down the aisle like it was made from gold and glitter and lined with the world's approval.

But she looked happy.

I had to bite down on my molars not to cry as I saw it.

As she approached Adam, who had the same shining gold hair that she did, she was beaming.

It was almost too much. My dad settled a hand on my back as if he knew I was contemplating bolting and gave me a soft shake of his head.

"Not now, Ava," he whispered. "Just a little bit longer."

I bit down on my lip and made it through their flowery vows, made it through their surprisingly passionate kiss, and their triumphant retreat down the aisle, where the four-course dinner waited for us inside the hotel.

Before we were ushered out behind them, my dad curled his arm around the back of my chair and leaned his head toward mine.

"Kiddo, I don't know what happened yesterday, and you don't need to tell me if you don't want to. But I'm- I'm proud of you for putting your foot down yesterday."

I jerked my eyes up to his. The attendant motioned for us to leave our seats, and I did, mind racing. We made it to the end of the aisle where Ashley and Adam were posing for some shots for the photographer. My mom never looked at me once.

I turned to my dad and gave him a questioning look. He rubbed the back of his neck, clearly uncomfortable.

"I liked Matthew," he said quietly. "But he wasn't right for your sister."

I snorted. Then I sighed wearily. "Why are you telling me this now, Dad?"

"Your sister ... your sister was always exactly like me. Liked the same things. Never surprised us." He gave me a brief look, then his eyes darted away again. "You were the opposite from the moment we knew you were coming. And, and I didn't always know"—he paused and cleared his throat—"how to handle that well. Doctors often don't. We like to be right, to be sure."

I blew out a slow breath and stared at the mountains. I'd made it all day without crying, and I didn't want to start now. "Where does that leave me? What am I supposed to say to that?"

He lifted his chin in greeting when someone called his name.

"Nothing if you don't want to. I just wanted to say it. Because the way you've handled yourself today, you didn't get that from your mother or me. That's ... that's all you. And that's a good thing. It means we didn't ruin those surprising parts of you."

I opened my mouth to respond when Ashley came over and gripped me in a tight hug.

"You look pretty," she said, then turned when I didn't answer. "Well? I think I do too."

I couldn't help but smile at her shameless compliment hunt. "You look beautiful. And happy," I added after a slight pause.

Ashley tilted her head. "Of course I'm happy."

"I'm glad."

My mom edged toward us, watching me carefully.

"Hey, where's Logan?" Ashley asked, looking around.

I opened my mouth, but there were no words there.

"I told Adam that he could finally find someone to take golfing when you guys come home for Christmas," she chattered, completely oblivious to my lack of response. Her eyes drifted over the group of people. "Seriously, though, where did he *go*? You guys already missed drinks last night."

My mom stepped up next to us, her eyes narrowed in my direction. *Don't you dare.* I heard it as clearly as if she'd said it out loud.

In the cage of my chest, my heart drummed rapidly. No more lies. I refused to lie anymore. It wasn't out of some misplaced sense of honor or desire to reconstruct a relationship with Ashley that made me decide on honesty. It was because of Matthew. He deserved my honesty. He deserved so much better than how I'd handled this situation.

"Ashley," I started.

My mom rushed forward, gripping my arm with bruising strength. "Ashley, we need family pictures while the light is good." Out of the side of her mouth, she hissed at me, "Not now, Ava."

Ashley looked back and forth between us curiously, then rolled her eyes. "Whatever. Is Logan going to be in the pictures with us? I mean, he sure looked serious about you. I'm fine with including him as long as we get a couple of shots without him, you know, just in case."

I laughed, then laughed even harder, which made my mom look like she was one step away from hysterics. Ashley gave me a weird look.

Using my fingers to rub at my temples, I took a deep breath. "No, Ashley, Logan will not be in the family pictures. And right now, neither can I."

"What?" they snapped in unison.

I exhaled, feeling a huge weight lift off my shoulders. "I need to go."

"Right now?" Ashley scoffed. "That's rude."

"You might be right." I pecked her on the cheek and gave my mom a tight smile. "Mom can explain where Logan is. Right, Mom?"

Her mouth hung open, and some strange noises came out. I gave her an air kiss too, patted my dad on the shoulder, and marched back to my room.

I had a ferry to catch.

CHAPTER 25
MATTHEW

There were plus sides to having your heart ripped out by the last person you expected. I was the first one in the weight room. The last one to leave. For the past two days, the guys seemed to sense that something inside me was just dying to be unchained because they gave me a wide berth.

Maybe it was because I had headphones in constantly while I trained except for when we ran plays, but it also could've been the look on my face that was straight-up murderous.

Drunk texts from Ava didn't help.

They made it worse, which I'm sure was the opposite of her intention. Seeing her words in black and white, reminding me of how many opportunities she had to tell me the truth and how many times she ignored them. Remembering the way everything unfolded in her hotel room, I had to fight not to throw my phone up against the wall.

Same thing when she tried to call me on Sunday. Twice. Both times, I sent her to voicemail because I just ... I wasn't ready.

On the Monday following our fight, the first official workday when I might run into her, I made sure to leave my apartment at dawn so that I could be sweating out my frustrations by the time she showed up. The hallway to the weight room wasn't dark, but it was hushed and quiet, like walking through a church.

Just as I was cueing up my music on my phone, ready to slide my headphones from my neck up over my ears, I heard the sound of heels tapping nervously on the floor. The next song, the one my thumb hovered over, was angry and loud, and the perfect music for lifting heavy weights, for whaling on a heavy bag to get my heart rate up. Not so much for conversation.

I glanced up, and she was leaning against the wall across from the weight room, carrying a to-go cup of coffee in her hands. Since I was walking quietly, not willing to be the one to disturb the silence, she hadn't seen me yet. Her foot, crossed over the top of the other, knocked rhythmically against the shiny floors.

The fact she looked normal, looked beautiful and polished and put together pissed me off. Where were the dark circles under her eyes? Like the ones under mine, the ones that darkened each night I tossed and turned and stared at the ceiling, even though I'd worked my body to the brink of exhaustion three days in a row.

I exhaled heavily, and her head snapped up.

"Matthew," she said nervously, licking her lips.

"Not here, Ava," I told her. I set my jaw and started toward the weight room. Just being this close to her while I was still so pissed had my heart pounding in my chest.

"Please, will you just give me five minutes?" She moved so that I had no choice but to stop. I could either cut around her or move her out of my way, and she knew I wouldn't do either.

My eyes closed as I struggled to keep my anger in check. Keep my hurt in check.

Her texts told me it was okay if I was mad at her as if I needed her permission to be pissed over the fact that my girlfriend lied to me about another man. As if I needed her permission to be really pissed over the fact that my girlfriend acted like she'd been caught by her parents when I was the one who'd always supported her.

When I opened my eyes, I gave her a warning look. "Not now. I need to get to work."

"It's six in the morning, Matthew, and we're the only ones here." Her eyes were big and pleading, and now that I was closer, I could see beyond her expertly made-up face. There were bags under her eyes that I wasn't used to seeing. Because she'd cried, I'm sure.

Because she was caught? Because she was truly sorry?

If I was willing to unearth all the bullshit I was feeling in the quiet hallway, I might have given her ten minutes. I might have walked back to her office and shut the door. Digging under that, I knew that the level-headed version of me would've hated that she cried. Hated that she was hurting.

But I was still really fucking mad over what she did. And I wasn't ready to set that aside yet or be the guy who only ever took things at her pace or discuss the things she wanted, when she wanted. I'd done that already and look where it got us.

"I don't care if we're the only ones here," I told her. She flinched back at the ice in my tone. "I won't say it again, Ava. Not now. I'm not ready to have this out, okay?"

When she didn't move, her feet firmly planted in the hallway and her chin lifted out of stubbornness, I moved to the side and went around her.

Her hand grabbed my arm, and I whipped around.

"Damn it, Ava," I yelled. The feel of her skin on mine lit the waiting fuse, like gasoline, igniting it instantly. "I get a say in this too. You don't get to force your timeline on me. *Not now.*"

She dropped her hand and stepped back, her face white. My whole body was shaking from that one burst of emotion, and if I didn't get the hell away from her, I would lose it completely and say something I regretted before I was ready to say it.

Angry hands shoved my headphones up over my head, and I stormed into the empty weight room. I flipped the lights on, cranked my music up, and got to work. Teammates came in, activity increased, and I stayed zeroed in on what I was doing.

Lift, down, breathe.

Lift, down, breathe.

Stop and wipe the sweat from my face. Stretch my arms. Roll my neck. Change the song.

Lift, down, breathe.

It was the only way I could keep that bubbling sense of an explosion from boiling over. My skin was tight. Christiansen came in and gave me a questioning look since he'd become my unofficial lifting partner. I shook my head and kept moving. Kept everything locked down tight, and brought the chains tighter around the hot pulse of anger as my blood pumped faster and faster with each rep. As the sweat built on my back and arms, dripping down the sides of my face, I knew it wasn't enough to keep the fire on low.

Ava lit the fuse, and I hadn't yet effectively stomped it out. Instead of being shut down as I had been earlier, before I heard her clear her throat and beg me to be ready to forgive her, I was simply waiting on simmer. The heat was there, low and unobtrusive, until someone cranked it back up to high and threw the flames back up my sides.

That someone turned out to be Logan.

He walked into the weight room, and immediately, his eyes sought me out. I was shaking my head before he started in my direction. He ignored me, standing in front of me while I finished my tenth squat lift. I kept my breathing steady and my muscles tense until I could safely drop the bar on the ground, where it bounced at my feet.

I looked him dead in the eye and went to move around him. The music was roaring in my ears, loud enough that I was sure anyone standing next to me could hear it.

His hand reached out and grabbed my arm. It was the second time—two times too many—that someone felt like giving me space wasn't important. Felt like unburdening themselves was a higher priority than my right to process things in my own time.

It was the only reason I could give for why I immediately turned and shoved his hand back at him without removing my headphones. His face went from annoyed to angry.

Slowly, and only because he was one of the team captains, did I pull my headphones free, but I left the music running.

"I need a minute," he ground out.

"No thanks." I turned away. "And don't ever grab me again, Ward."

Eyes turned in our direction, some wary, some curious, and some concerned. Christiansen stood from the bench and watched us carefully.

"Hey," he said firmly. "I said I need a minute. You can spare me that."

I closed my eyes and counted to five because ten was impossible. If he kept his trap shut for those five seconds, I could walk away. I could keep this from turning into a scene.

Except for those five seconds, I saw his face as he walked into the hotel room behind my girlfriend, the woman I'd been touching, kissing, sleeping with for weeks, with the intent of ingratiating himself into her life. Suddenly, he was the reason all this bullshit happened. He was the reason I was so fucking angry. Why I was coming here at dawn to avoid Ava because I wasn't ready to hear her excuses again.

"Hawkins," he barked out. My hands curled into fists. "Don't be stubborn. Let's go outside in the hall."

My eyes popped open, and my hands reached out to shove him back. He stumbled, not prepared for it.

"Whoa," someone said behind us. "Cool it, guys."

Logan stood tall and walked the remaining steps between us. I was taller than him by an inch or two, and I weighed more than him, but when he practically went nose to nose with me, I had to try not to blink from surprise. When he spoke, his voice was low. "I'll give you that one shot. Just one." His mouth thinned. "I didn't know it was you, okay? You think I would've gone if I'd known?"

"I don't want to talk about this here," I ground out.

His arms spread wide. "Where do you want to talk about it? Out on the practice field? In the showers? Give me one minute, Hawkins."

I poked him in the chest, and someone whistled. "I don't owe you shit because the way I look at it, none of this would've happened if you'd kept yourself out of my business. If you'd stayed away from her, *none* of this would have happened."

He laughed under his breath. "You don't think I regret going? I wish I'd never stepped foot on that damn ferry. But you're delusional if you think this is all on me."

I started to walk away. I tried.

"You forgive her yet?"

I whirled around, fire crawling up my throat at the sound of his voice asking about Ava. "It's none of your business, Ward."

Something about my voice, the pitch that was bound at the edges with a touch of violence made the entire room go quiet. The rest of the team was watchful and alert but not ready to interfere. Not yet.

He spread his legs and faced me without any fear, lifted his chin, and said, "What if I decide to make it my business? You know how I feel about her."

With a roar, I grabbed his shirt with both hands and slammed him up against the wall. He drove his elbow down onto the tender side of my forearm and drove his fist into my side when I was forced to drop my hand.

"You stay away from her," I yelled in his face.

Hands fell on my arms and shoulders, pulling me back as more bodies stood in front of Ward and held him back by the chest.

"And you think you deserve her right now?" he yelled right back. "Look at yourself, Hawkins. Stomping around here, glaring at anything that moves. You're like a kid who didn't get his way."

I struggled against the hands holding me back, but they held fast. "You don't know jack shit about me, Ward. You like to be lied to? You like the feeling of seeing what I saw on Friday? You don't know anything about me. Or her."

He was breathing hard, but he nodded at the guys holding his chest. They both backed off. Logan only took one step in my direction.

"Don't act like the only person who's been shit on, okay? Your story is no worse than anyone else's in this locker room. Hell, in this entire building." He narrowed his eyes and shook his head as though I'd disgusted him. "Because guess what? You don't know me either."

The tension seeped from my muscles, one scolding word after another until the hands on my shoulders, arms, and chest loosened their grip.

"You're right." I lifted my hands and let them drop. "We agree on that. I don't know you, and you don't know me. So why are you trying to tell me what to do?"

He huffed out a disbelieving laugh. "You don't get extra points for how long you hold on to the feeling of being wronged. If you're not man enough to set aside your anger and just listen—to her, or to me—then you really don't deserve her."

"Geez, who's the chick?" someone whispered, and I closed my eyes against a snappish response that wouldn't help anything.

I swallowed roughly, glancing around at the faces of my teammates. Fights happened in the locker room. On the field. It was impossible to have a group of guys this size, with this much energy and drive and ask them to play with barely leashed violence, and not have that seep into the non-game spaces. But it was the first time for me that I'd ever laid hands on someone I shared a jersey with.

Just like that, all the fight left me, and I was tired. Exhausted down to the bones holding up my body.

You don't get extra points for how long you hold on to the feeling of being wronged.

I couldn't answer Logan. Not right then, with the whole team staring at us. I exhaled slowly.

"Sorry for the commotion, everyone," I said.

Everyone but Christiansen dispersed, slowly making their way back to the machines, and a low hum of conversation filled the room again. He lowered his eyebrows in question, and I nodded.

I gave Logan a long look. "This won't happen again, I swear. I'm not the guy who starts fights."

He nodded slowly. "I know you're not."

"But," I told him, "even if you're right, don't tell me how to deal with my relationship, okay? Not after seeing you with her like that. Because you might be saying every single thing I need to hear to make this okay between her and me, but I won't hear a word of it. Not knowing what your intention was when you showed up on the ferry."

"Fair enough," he conceded.

I left the room feeling like I weighed twice as much as I had when I walked into it. This time, I was weighed down by his words, by hers, and by the heavy emotional expectation of needing to slug through everything that had happened.

It felt like someone was asking me to dig up a body, six feet under the wet earth, with my bare hands. But before I could make a single dent, I had to get my head right and know what I was willing to let go of and what I wasn't.

I just didn't know what those things were yet.

CHAPTER 26
AVA

Trying to stay focused at the office proved fruitless, so I gave up after a couple of hours. Anytime I turned a corner, I wondered if Matthew's face would greet me. If I'd see that remote, angry, unfamiliar expression on his face again.

Packing up my files, trudging home in the ridiculously appropriate rain, and working from my bed, wearing one of the sweatshirts he'd left at my place seemed like the best course of action.

Not for my sanity, of course, because between emails and phone calls, I'd stop to pull the fabric up to my nose and take a deep, masochistic breath.

Then I'd be reminded all over again of the train wreck of a weekend.

The one person I never wanted to hurt, I'd hurt beyond anything I could have imagined.

Control the narrative, I thought grimly. Yeah, that had worked out reeeeeally well for me. The only outcome I'd successfully influenced was if I'd been aiming in the direction of *How to Make Ava look like a Thoughtless Bitch*. In that, I'd been a smashing success.

Ashley had tried to call me twice. Twice she'd been sent to voicemail. My mom, predictably, maintained radio silence. If their travel plans had stayed the same, they were all still out on Orcas, enjoying a few rare days off together.

And there I was, burrowed under the covers while the sun set in the west, wearing a dark gray Stanford sweatshirt that fell to my knees, trying to wrack my brains over how I was supposed to prove to Matthew that I did love him while giving him the space he clearly needed.

I got out of bed to heat some soup in my USC mug, then crawled back in bed to eat it. As I was lifting a steaming spoonful to my mouth, my phone rang on the nightstand.

When I saw Matthew's name, I almost dropped the soup into my lap.

"Hi," I said on an exhale as soon as I picked up the call. With shaky hands, I set the soup on my nightstand.

"Hey," he answered, then cleared his throat.

The sound of his voice had me sinking down into bed and curling to my side. If I closed my eyes, I could pretend he was there with me.

"I stopped by your office when I was done with camp."

That had me sitting back up. "You did?"

Well, shit.

"Yeah." He paused for a second, and I physically bit down on my tongue to allow him that second to think. "I just needed to say a couple of things before work tomorrow, just in case we run into each other."

And there I went back down into bed. I didn't like that phrasing. It was my job to read into how things were phrased, and that was not the kind of subtext I was looking for.

"Okay," I said quietly.

"I know you're sorry for what happened. I don't need you to apologize again because I'm not blameless in this. I shouldn't have shown up in your hotel room like that," he started. "In my head, it was romantic, and I don't know, proved something big, something important about how I was feeling. So I'm sorry for that."

I shook my head even though he couldn't see me. I wanted to

argue, I wanted to say that if Logan hadn't been with me, I probably would've thought it was romantic too. Ill-advised, maybe, considering I could've walked into my room with Ashley in tow, but I would've thought it was romantic.

"There's nothing to apologize for, Matthew," I told him. "But I'll accept it because it means a lot that you're even willing to talk to me right now."

"That's the thing, Ava. I've *wanted* to talk about this stuff with you. About your past, about mine, about the shit we're going to face because we're together. I need that from you. I need to know that you're not going to shy away from the hard stuff that comes with this relationship."

"I *won't*, Matthew." I leaned forward and pinched my eyes shut. "I wish I could see you right now."

He sighed. "I think ... I think maybe it's good that we're having this conversation over the phone. I hate seeing you upset, you know that. It killed me not to hold you in that hotel, but I can't sacrifice what I need out of a relationship all the time because my instinct is to always make things easier on you. And that's what I've done."

They said hindsight was twenty/twenty. It was a frustratingly accurate statement as I laid in my bed and listened to the things he was telling me. I could see it clear as a freaking bell.

"Tell me what you need, Matthew," I pleaded quietly. "I know I can sit here until I'm blue in the face and say that you can trust me, that I'll never, ever do something like that again, but I know that's not enough. And you deserve more than lip service."

He was quiet on the other end of the phone. I tried to imagine where he was, what his face looked like, and how he might be sitting. A million miles could've stretched between us for as how far away I felt from him.

"I'm not asking you to destroy your family for me, Ava, you know that. I need to know that you'll trust me not to be like them and trust that you don't need to protect yourself from me the way you had to protect yourself from them. I need to know that you'll stand up for me the way I'll always stand up for you. I'll do every Christmas, every strained, uncomfortable holiday as long as I know you're right there with me, not lessening what we have to make it easier for everyone else. Yeah, my female fans might freak out for a minute, but I don't care. Let them. They're not part of this; you and I are the only ones who are. And I need you to trust in that as much as I do."

My nostrils burned as I listened quietly. "You need me to be okay with the ugly realities and not try to make them pretty falsehoods."

"Yeah," he said slowly. "Yeah, that's what I need."

"Okay," I answered quietly. "I hear you."

"I know, in my head and in my heart, that you'd never do to me what your sister did. What Lexi and I did to each other. I *know that*, Ava. But until this morning at work, I don't think I realized how much I still carry from those relationships."

I thought of what I'd carried around, what I'd unknowingly brought from my relationship with my family into my relationship with Matthew. Unintentional distance caused by invisible wounds. We all carried that around, to a certain extent, no matter where the damage came from. "Sometimes, I think knowing that is half the battle in overcoming it."

"I hope so." He sighed into the silence. "I miss you, Slim."

I curled on my side and brought the neck of the sweatshirt to my nose so I could inhale deeply. "I miss you too."

We wished each other a good night, and he disconnected the call as I kept my phone pressed to my ear. Before he hung up, he didn't tell me he loved me, and I didn't say it to him either. This wasn't the time for it. When I finally had a chance to say it, I'd be looking him straight in the eye.

As I finished my cold soup, fed Frankie, then washed my face and brushed my teeth, my brain spun what he'd said over and over. When I crawled back between the covers of my bed, I carefully picked up my phone and took a deep breath before I made a single phone call. It rang a few times, then the voicemail clicked on, which I was grateful for.

"It's me," I said. "I ... I need you do something tomorrow if you have time, and you're willing to hear me out. It's important. Otherwise, I wouldn't ask."

After I finished my message, I took a deep breath and set my phone down. Maybe it would be enough. Maybe it wouldn't. Either way, I had to try.

CHAPTER 27
AVA

WASHINGTON WOLVES

"You said the conference room across from your office?" the defensive coordinator barked into my desk phone. In the background, I could hear the shouts of the players and the hum of activity that I loved so much. So badly, I wanted to be out there watching, especially since it was the last day of camp before our first preseason game.

But more important things were afoot.

"Yeah, that's the one."

"Everyone is signing autographs now. We're done running plays." He cleared his throat. "But I don't have to actually *run* a meeting, right?"

I rolled my eyes a little. "No, Gary, I will be taking care of that. Just keep that between us, okay?"

"You got it, Baker. I'll send 'im your way. Mums the word."

After I hung up, I clicked my nails on my desk and watched the long arm of the clock tick closer to the S.D.G.T.

Scheduled Dramatic Gesture Time.

The two biggest moving parts included my invited guests, if they decided to take me up on my offer, and our defensive coordinator telling Matthew he was needed for a brief meeting in the conference room across the hall from my office.

Sorry, I wasn't putting him, my sister, my mom, my dad, and myself into my office, which only had one escape route. We needed space. Everyone would need sufficient oxygen to breathe for this.

My phone rang again, and I picked it up quickly, saying a little prayer that it was the front desk.

"This is Ava," I said into the receiver.

"Ava, you have three guests here to see you. Shall I send them back?"

I closed my eyes, and my shoulders slumped in relief. "Yeah, you can. Thanks for calling, Miriam."

Miriam and I had had a wee little chat about sending guests back without notice. There was massive relief in knowing Ashley wouldn't be popping her head around the corner at any given moment.

I stood from my desk and smoothed my hands down the front of my wide-leg black pants. There would be no notecards or PowerPoint for this little meeting I'd scheduled, but I'd be damned if it wasn't held on my turf.

My dad entered my office first, giving it a quick glance, then giving me a small smile. I hugged him briefly, staring over his shoulder as my mom's pinched face came into view. Ashley's facial expression didn't give anything away, and I had zero clue how much my mom had told her when I'd bolted from Orcas.

"What's this about, Ava?" my mom started, gripping her purse strap like it might need to be used as a weapon.

My dad pointed at the two seats opposite my desk. Mom took one and Ashley hesitated visibly before taking the second one. I sat down in my chair and folded my hands in my lap.

"I want to start by apologizing to you, Ashley. I'm sure you're not happy with me for leaving your party the way I did."

She raised an eyebrow slowly. "It forced Mom and me to lie to the rest of our guests when they inquired about you, so no, I'm not terribly thrilled. But I will accept your apology because you didn't make me demand it," she said magnanimously.

I turned my attention to my mother. "How much did you explain to her?"

"I told her that your ... boyfriend had to return to Seattle early, and you went to check on him."

Not a lie, but not exactly the truth either. Maybe I got my PR skills from my maternal side.

"That's true," I said, glancing at the clock.

"What I would like to know is why I had to make my husband wait at the hotel for this," Ashley said before I could get another word out.

A fair question, and thankfully one that I'd expected. "Is it enough—just for right now—to tell you that my reason will make sense once this is all done?"

She rolled her eyes a little but nodded. My mom looked one second away from apoplectic shock.

"Actually, do you guys mind if we go across the hall? That way you can sit if you'd like, Dad."

"It's fine," he said. "I can stand."

"Please?" I stated, then swept my arm to the doorway. No one moved.

With a sigh, I stood and started across the hallway, hoping they'd follow me. One of the front office staff passed, smiling at me as she did. After she moved past me, I stared down the hallway toward the locker room. No players were milling about, which meant Matthew was probably still showering.

Single file, with my dad once again in front, they entered the large room. The Wolves logo was painted on the wall, and red and black upholstered chairs faced a massive projection screen. It was one of the bigger meeting rooms we had, large enough to accommodate the entire team and coaching staff.

"What is this about, Ava?" my mom said once again, taking a seat in the front row and serving me with a dangerous look.

"You know what it's about," I told her quietly.

Immediately, she stood and started for the door. "Let's go, Alan, Ashley," she said over her shoulder. "This is ridiculous."

I blocked her path to the door and propped my hands on my hips. "Sit. Down."

"Bossy much?" Ashley muttered but watched me with unconcealed interest.

My mom stared me down, kept her chin lifted, and whispered under her breath. "You're going to destroy her by telling her this."

"Highly unlikely," I said right back. "She's happy. There's no reason for her to be destroyed by anything I have to say."

Mom's jaw tightened, and I was shocked I didn't hear the snap of her teeth clenching together, but after a second, she turned and sat down again.

Behind me, I heard the footsteps coming down the hall, and I pulled in a slow breath through my nose, letting it out through my lips. My brows bent in when a low hum of voices grew in volume.

Way too many voices.

I stuck my head out into the hallway and saw close to two dozen defensive players striding down the hallway. Matthew's head bobbed somewhere in the middle of the pack, talking to someone next to him. Gary was in the front and gave me two thumbs up when he saw me gawking.

I held up a finger to my family. "One second."

Gary stopped and smiled when I darted out into the hallway and pulled the door shut behind me. "Delivered as promised."

My eyes took in almost the entire defense—the *entire defense*—then rested briefly on Matthew, who had just noticed me. His eyes held mine, and I had to lick my suddenly dry lips. I could read nothing in those eyes, but he was still watching me intently.

I blinked, looking away.

"Gary," I said under my breath, leaning in so only he could hear me. "I don't need *all* of them. I said to send down Hawkins."

"Ohhhhhh," he drawled sheepishly. He scratched the side of his face. "Uhh, it was loud out there, so I couldn't hear everything you said."

"And you're deaf, old man," Carter, one of the defensive ends, said, and everyone else cracked up. Except for Matthew. His face had taken on a speculative gleam when Carter piped up again. "What's up, Baker? We in trouble?"

I pasted a smile on my face. "No trouble, just a little misunderstanding. I didn't need everyone, that's all."

No one moved. Except for Gary. He saw the look on my face and brushed past me. "Enjoy your meeting!"

Note to self- don't ask Gary for a favor ever again.

"You guys can go," I told them but held Matthew's eyes. "I just need to talk to Hawkins. Gary got the message mixed up."

And again, no one moved. I narrowed my eyes when two of the defensive backs traded a completely loaded look.

"Hawkins, huh?" Carter asked with a sly smile.

"Carter," Matthew said in a warning tone, moving toward me through the crowd of players.

"Does Ward have anything to do with this?"

My face paled, and I tried to keep my voice even when I answered. "N-no, why?"

Thank goodness Logan wasn't in the group of players.

There was a chorus of oooooohs at my response. I almost stomped my foot. "Go away, all of you."

Matthew approached me slowly. A few guys walked away, but a solid six or seven hung back, watching us with glee.

"What is going on?" I whispered to him.

He grimaced. "Well, Logan and I might have almost gotten in a fight in the weight room yesterday, and they heard us talking about a woman, so..." His voice trailed off. "I think they're putting some puzzle pieces together."

I slicked my tongue over my teeth and nodded. "Hmmm. Awesome, okay, well, I was trying to do this privately, but what the hell ever."

"Do what privately?" Matthew asked. He leaned in closer, and I had to shut my eyes against the smell of him. He was clean from his shower, clad in dark jeans and a charcoal Wolves shirt that molded to his body in a way that was positively sinful.

I hooked a thumb over my shoulder. "I'm going to apologize

preemptively for the things in that room that I cannot control, okay? But please, just give me five minutes after the inevitable freaking out is over."

Matthew searched my face but didn't answer right away.

"Please," I repeated. "Please trust me right now."

Finally, he nodded. "Okay."

Before I turned back to the conference room, I glared at Carter and the other players who started following us. "Don't even think about coming in that room, or you'll be on garbage pickup for every community event from now until kingdom come."

Carter grinned and saluted me.

"You look nervous," Matthew said just before we reached the closed door of the conference room.

"That's because I am nervous," I admitted. My fingers gripped the handle, and I took a deep breath before pushing it open and walking in.

My mom scoffed at my reappearance, Ashley narrowed her eyes, and my dad sighed in relief.

All reactions I expected when they saw me.

Then ... then they saw Matthew.

My mom pinched her eyes shut. My dad rubbed the bridge of his nose.

And Ashley, Ashley went white as a sheet. "What the hell is this?" she whispered.

"Ohhhhhkay then," Matthew said from behind me.

"What the hell is going on, Ava?" Ashley said, standing slowly from her chair and pointing a finger at me. "You better start talking *right* now."

I held up my hand and took a position at the front of the room so I could see all four of them. Matthew had his hands shoved into the pockets of his jeans, color high on his cheekbones, but he was keeping his attention solely on me.

"I'm going to try to keep this as short and sweet as possible," I said to my family. "What I have to say isn't up for debate or discussion. This is a courtesy conversation so that you know what to expect moving forward."

My dad crossed his arms over his chest and stared at the ground. Ashley's foot was bobbing furiously now that she was sitting again, and my mom looked like she was about to pass the hell out.

"It's him," I said, pointing at Matthew. Quickly, I glanced at him, heart squeezing at the intensity in his eyes.

"What is?" Ashley ground out, face pinched and eyes narrowed on me.

"All of it. The flowers you found, the message I was leaving, the man who's made me so happy, it's him. Anything else you thought was the truth was simply a misunderstanding driven by a ridiculous desire to be relevant to the three of you."

"Damn, that's some harsh shit," I heard someone mutter excitedly in the hallway. Matthew closed his eyes and shut the door with one hand.

"This is a circus," my mom hissed and went to stand.

"You can stand if you want, Mom, but I am not finished," I told her.

"Abigail, she's earned the right to be heard," my dad said implacably when my mom looked like she was going to storm out no matter what I said.

I gave him a small smile and kept going. "I regret lying about Matthew. I regret that I let my fear of your reaction influence my actions more than any one of you could ever know because I am in love with him." I looked at Matthew as my voice wobbled at the end. His jaw was tight, his arms now crossed over his chest, his brow furrowed at my words. "I am in love with you, Matthew Hawkins, and I'll risk any recourse, any complication, and any fallout for you to trust in that more than you've ever trusted in anything." I pressed my hands to my chest and met his stare. "I want this, between us, to be the truest and most constant thing you've ever known because that's what it is for me. And I know you were mad at me. You had every right to be furious over what happened, but I'll earn your forgiveness out of sheer force of will if I have to."

He huffed out a breath that could have been a laugh, or it could have been disbelief. But in his eyes, I saw my first glimmer of hope that this just might be working. There was a warmth there that I hadn't seen since he knelt next to my car in the parking lot just before I left to catch the ferry.

"This is insane," Ashley said under her breath, eyes wide and frantic when I glanced over at her. "I was *engaged* to him, Ava. Don't you think that's a little ..." Her arms flailed out when she couldn't find the words. "I don't know, incestuous or something?"

I laughed. "No, Ashley, I don't think that. I think there's a reason he ended up here and why our pasts unfolded the way they did because he's it for me." I looked back at him. "You're it for me." I shrugged.

"Ava Marie," my mom said in a low voice, "if you think that—"

"Quit talking, Abigail," my dad interrupted.

My mouth fell open. My mom blinked, and Ashley stared at my dad like he'd lost his mind.

"Excuse me?" she whispered.

He sighed. "I said quit talking. It's not about you. Or me. If Matthew was able to move on from what Ashley and Adam did to him, then why the hell can't we?" He straightened the front of his suit jacket and gave Matthew an assessing look, then brought his eyes back to me. "Anything else you need to say, Ava?"

"Uhh"—my eyes ping-ponged between my mom and dad —"nope. That was pretty much it."

He nodded, then held out a hand to my still seething mother. "Let's go. Ashley, if you need to stay, we'll wait for you out in the parking lot."

My mom acted like she wasn't going to leave, but Ashley gave her a look. "Mom, I'm thirty-three. I hardly need you to fight my battles. Please go."

Before my parents left the conference room, my dad paused in front of Matthew and held out his hand. Cautiously, Matthew took it for a hard shake. My dad nodded at me, and then they were gone.

And then, there were three, I thought with a tiny bubble of panic slipping up my spine. As soon as my parents were gone, he and Ashley regarded each other warily.

What must he be thinking? What if this entire thing was a giant mistake? I tapped my fingers along my thigh.

"What are we supposed to do now, Ava?" Ashley asked. There was nothing snide or hidden in her voice, but her hands were knit tightly together, and the diamond in her ring glinted from the lights in the ceiling. Her knuckles were white; that was how tightly she was keeping herself in check.

"I'm just letting you know that he's in my life if he'll still have me." I kept my eyes off Matthew's face. "I don't expect anything beyond you accepting that, even if you're not comfortable with it."

Her blue eyes glanced from me back to the man standing by the door. What was *she* thinking?

"Okay," she said, standing slowly.

"I know this is weird, Ashley," I told her.

Her eyes fell shut. "Am I free to go now?"

I took a deep breath, unsure of how her stoic reaction made me feel. But I remembered what Matthew had said to me just a couple of days earlier. It wasn't always about me, or when I wanted to talk about things, or how I wanted to process them. If I wanted Ashley to respect this, then I shouldn't push her. I nodded. "Yeah. Thank you for hearing me out."

Ashley nodded back, clenched her jaw together behind closed lips.

She gave Matthew a quick look. "I'm glad you two are happy," she ground out. A shaky hand swept across her forehead. "But right now, I just want ... I need to go talk to my husband about all of this. Ava, I'll talk to you ... later."

Then she calmly walked out of the room.

The door shut with a quiet click, and I let out a heavy breath.

Matthew still said nothing.

Then he took a step toward me, unfolding his arms from his chest. His eyes bored into mine.

"Say it again," he said.

My breathing picked up, quick and erratic as I backed into the wall behind me. "S-say what?"

He stopped within reaching distance of my body. "Say it again, Ava. Now that there's no audience, no prying eyes, and no one to stop me from kissing you once the words are out."

My face flushed hot with relief, and I smiled a little. "I'm in love with you, Matthew Hawkins."

Matthew braced his hands on the wall, effectively caging me in. His forehead rested against mine, and he exhaled. "Again."

I smoothed my hands up his chest and gripped his neck tightly. "I'm in love with you."

He kissed my temple, then my cheek, the tip of my nose, on either side of my mouth, just shy of my lips, which sought out his. He chuckled.

"Again," he whispered over my lips.

"I'm *so* in love with—"

His mouth cut off my words, his tongue swept into my mouth with authority and precision, drawing a moan from my lungs. I wrapped myself around him, my arms twined around his neck as his mouth ate at mine. His hands gripped my back, my bottom, and slowly, he turned the kiss into something slow and sensual, moving his frame against mine in a way that had me wishing we weren't in a bright conference room across from my office.

As soon as the thought zipped through my brain, a sound broke through the fog of imagined sexy times.

It was applause. Obnoxious whooping and hollering.

Matthew broke away when he realized I'd stopped kissing him back. We both turned our heads toward the sound, and through the tiny window in the door, we saw about four faces pressed up against the glass. Carter had his phone up, capturing the whole thing with a wide smile on his face.

"Awwww, yeah baby, get it done, Hawk," he hooted.

Matthew's frame shook with laughter as their faces backed away from the glass to give us privacy, and I buried my face into his broad chest. He kissed the top of my head and wrapped me tightly in his arms.

Nothing, nothing had ever felt better. And nothing ever would, I knew with certainty.

"Have you heard it enough now?" I said, tilting my chin up so I could look into his face.

He chuckled, dipping down for another searching kiss on my waiting lips. When he pulled away, we were both breathing hard.

"I'll never be able to hear it enough," he whispered. "I love you too, Ava."

My mouth stretched in a happy smile.

"Can we get out of here now?" I asked.

His grin was devious, and I narrowed my eyes.

"What is that face?"

"Nothing," he said lightly.

But then he dropped his arm, sweeping it under my knees as I shrieked with laughter. "Matthew, don't you dare! They'll never let me live this down."

He smacked a kiss on my lips. "I'm planning on that, beautiful girl."

Carter was so kind as to open the door for us, and when we left the conference room, there were easily a dozen players waiting. They roared their approval as he swept into my office so I could grab my purse, then followed us down the hall like our own personal parade out the front doors.

"Your place or mine, Slim?" he asked as we approached his truck.

I sighed, tightening my hold on his neck.

"Anywhere," I told him honestly. "I'll go anywhere as long as I get to be with you."

EPILOGUE

WASHINGTON WOLVES

Ava

Four months later

"I don't think I can watch," I said from behind my hands, which were covering my eyes. Allie yanked them away from my face ruthlessly.

"If I have to watch, then so do you." She waved her hands in front of her face. "I can't breathe."

Normally, we'd be up in the owner's box, but at the beginning of the fourth quarter, we made our way down to the sidelines because this was a moment when we both needed to be as close as possible.

Robert Sutton Stadium—newly renamed during the offseason after Allie poured millions of dollars into renovations and improvements—was packed to capacity at seventy-two thousand, four hundred and fifty-six fans. They were on their feet, stomping, screaming, and slamming hands against the seats in front of them because we were up by seven with one minute and thirty seconds left in the NFC championship.

If we held off Green Bay, we'd be in the Super Bowl.

My phone buzzed angrily from my back pocket, where I'd shoved it as security led us down to the field. Since I had time, I whipped out and grinned at the text from my dad.

Dad: Matthew's got this, kiddo. Don't look so nervous.

My dad had watched almost every game of the season—a show of support that meant the world to Matthew and me—and even if he missed a game or two because he was in surgery, he always texted me when he watched the highlights. Normally, he never caught sight of me on camera. Today made sense, though, since I was standing next to the owner, who was recently engaged to the quarterback.

The quarterback currently sitting on the bench was unable to help his team any more than he already had. Luke's head was bent down, his hands clasped between his knees, a deceptively casual pose for a man who I knew was probably vibrating from the need to be doing something. Anything.

While the commercial break wound down, and our defense lined up on the grass, the noise level got higher, and higher again when Matthew turned and jacked his arms up, calling for more and more from the people wearing black and red.

From where I stood, I could hear his roar of demand before the fans gave him what he wanted. The muscles of his arms were coated in sweat and dirt and grass when he crouched down into position. The offense lined up, quarterback pointing and yelling, trying to be heard over the deafening sounds of our fans.

They were hungry for this. Starving and ravenous for a win that would mean the world to a city that had supported these players for years. Normally, I would've taken a second to glance around the stands to soak it all up and see the tangible fruition of all our hard work in these moments before the outcome was known.

Every event, every tweet and picture and signing and practice and moment that endeared our players to those fans led up to this.

But my eyes stayed glued on Matthew.

I never knew that I could want something so badly for another person. In my mouth was a coppery tang of blood from where I'd accidentally bit my lip when he sacked the QB in the third quarter on fourth down, stopping a scoring drive in its tracks. My hands were raw from wringing them together, and my throat was coated with thick, grainy sand from all the yelling I'd done in the past three hours.

The ball snapped crisply into the QB's waiting hands, and the defense shoved forward, pulled like a rip cord into action. The receivers ran downfield in hopes to catch whatever bomb he was planning to unleash on us.

Matthew dropped back suddenly, instead of rolling around to try to grab the quarterback, and I narrowed my eyes. The ball zipped forward, and he lunged sideways, arms outstretched, taped-up hands extending to an almost inhumane length.

From midair, he snagged the ball and hugged it into his barrel chest, then he slid to the grass while his teammates piled on top of him in celebration of his game-ending interception.

Everything around us erupted.

The players on the bench.

The fans in the stands.

Allie and I screamed, clutching each other tightly. She was wiping happy tears, and I struggled to breathe through the violent eruption of adrenaline coursing through my body.

Luke was standing on the bench, hands raised in the air, and a massive smile splitting his face. All he had left to do was take the field and kneel the ball, and we were going to the mother effing Super Bowl.

Matthew finally stood up from the ground, and the crowd somehow got even louder. The entire stadium shook from the sheer force of energy pulsing from every square inch. He tossed the ball to the official and jogged off the field so that the offense could finish what he'd just set into place.

Briefly, he caught my eye, and I caught a flash of white teeth behind his helmet, underneath the grit and grime coating his face.

Then his coach snagged him for a hug, and he was swamped by all the players on the bench for hugs and back slaps and ridiculous victory dances that would end up in a gif somewhere.

Allie sighed and slung her arm around my shoulders. "Holy shit."

I burst out laughing. "Yeah."

"They're going to be so exhausted tonight, aren't they?"

I watched Matthew toss back some Gatorade, admiring the way his thick throat worked on a swallow. "Yeah."

He threw the crumpled cup aside, and his eyes zeroed in on me as the clock wound down. Luke had kneeled once. He'd only need to do it once more, and the game would be done. The players would storm the field, shake hands, say their congratulations, and Matthew would start in on the post-game ritual that would keep him occupied for the next couple of hours.

As he started toward me, fire banked bright in his eyes, and I wished we were alone at our apartment. It used to be his, but Frankie and I decided we wanted a shorter commute to work, so we'd moved in during the bye week.

Matthew shouldered his way through the players, and as soon as he was close, I leaped into his arms, wrapping myself as tightly around him as I could.

"You did it," I said into his ear, placing a kiss under the sweaty line of his hard jaw. "I'm so proud of you."

He pulled his face back and grinned happily. "Think you can put up with two more post-game massages, Slim?"

It was our ritual once he got home even though he'd already been worked on by the team masseuse. Of course, our massage took place in the massive sunken tub in the bathroom and was done stark-ass naked while I worked on the kinks in his shoulders and back.

I kissed him hard, and the fans in the stands directly behind us whooped and hollered.

"I'll do a million post-game massages," I told him fiercely when I pulled away. "You've earned them tonight, big guy."

He dropped his forehead and rolled it against mine. "Love you, Slim."

I smiled when he kissed me again. "Love you too."

He set me down just as the game finished and cupped the back of my neck with his hand. "You know one of these days, I'm going to ask you to marry me, right?"

My smile widened because we'd been playing this game for about four weeks.

"Is it today?"

His answering smirk was delicious. "I don't know. Today isn't over yet, now is it?"

I watched him with narrowed, suspicious eyes because that was a new answer. Then he ran off to celebrate, and I tipped my head back to breathe in everything I was feeling. Confetti rained down on my face, and I caught a shiny red piece in my hand.

As I was rubbing it between my fingers, smiling at all the celebrations surrounding me, I saw Matthew making his way back over. He'd wiped off his face, which was covered with a devious, heart-flutter inducing smile.

With both hands, he gripped the sides of my face before he kissed me, before he wound his tongue around mine as I sagged against him.

His voice was low when he spoke against my lips. "Yeah, it's going to be today. I was going to try to be patient so we could be alone, but then I see you standing there, looking so beautiful and perfect and *mine*, and I can't wait." He held my eyes as I started to cry. "I can't wait another minute, another second, because I can't imagine anything feeling better than this moment right now."

"Matthew," I whispered brokenly.

He dropped down onto one knee, and everyone around us

started chattering excitedly. My hand was shaking as he gripped it in his own.

"Slim, I want you to be my wife. I want to wake up every single day knowing that you're there, that I get to be there for you, and that I can love you through anything we might face because I know you'll do the same for me." His eyes glistened brightly under the harsh lights of the stadium, and I could see it even through the sheen of my own tears. "Will you marry me?"

I fell to my knees and wrapped my arms around his neck.

"Yes, yes, yes," I whispered through kisses. He buried his head into my neck and sighed heavily with relief. I started laughing. "Were you really going to do this later?"

He smiled as he lifted his head. "Yeah."

"My crazy man," I said, cupping the side of his face. "This was perfect."

"There's a ring at home for you, I swear."

I kissed him softly, and his arms tightened around my back as he held me to him. "I don't even care about the ring," I told him.

His eyes searched mine, face full of such tenderness that my heart flipped over backward. "So I can return it then?"

I smacked his chest, and his answering laughter was all I needed.

The End

THE MARRIAGE EFFECT

———

Paige McKinney

I turned back to the bar, risking a glance at the guy next to me. His profile might have been carved from rock for as much as it gave away. He lifted his water and took another long drink. I didn't know what it said about my brain, but I felt a tingle of absurd happiness that he was ignoring me completely.

Hello Challenge, my name is Paige.

As I stood there, I heard the sound of Colt shuffling away.

"I think you broke his heart," the bartender said, flicking her eyes to where Colt had just been standing.

"Highly doubtful," I answered. "He's a twentysomething professional football player. I think his *heart* will mend just fine before the night is over."

"Another lemon rosemary bourbon sour?" she asked, wiping the surface of the bar with deft movements.

The large frame of the man sitting next to me shifted slightly, and I tilted my head in his direction, wishing I could see his face more clearly.

"What's he drinking?" I asked.

"*He* has a name," his grumbly, rumbly voice answered. "And after that little speech, don't you think it's a bit hypocritical that you didn't ask what it is?"

The second I heard him speak, his name clicked into place in my head.

Of course.

That voice was one not heard often because he stayed under the radar, hated doing any press, and was, without a doubt, one of the best safeties in professional football. The casual football fan wouldn't have any clue who he was. He could probably walk through most cities in America and not be recognized.

But I recognized his voice all the same. The first time I heard it, I thought that someone yanked it from the pits of hell, but in a really super-duper sexy way.

Before I turned, I pulled a stool out and perched on it. Then I pivoted to the side so I could see him fully.

"Logan Ward," I said, appreciating the slight start of surprise he gave when that was the next thing out of my mouth. His eyes flicked in my direction, and oh goodness, they were green. That was not something I knew about him, and it pleased me to the depths of my very bored soul to discover it. "See? No hypocrites to be found at this bar."

He didn't say anything, only took another drink of his water.

Everything in me screamed to wait, to allow him to be the next to talk, but honestly, I was never the best at listening to the voices in my head that tried to curb my more irrational impulses.

"Do you think I broke Colt's heart?"

"Nope."

"Do you think he'll remember my lesson when he approaches the next woman he wants to talk to?"

"Nope."

I laughed. "That's a shame."

Finally, Logan turned his chin far enough that he was almost, sort of facing me. Now that was a face that a camera would love. Strong jaw, straight nose, eyes so bright and thickly lashed that I was only a little jealous. It was also a face I hadn't seen very often, save behind his football helmet. He rarely made appearances at the social functions.

"Do you critique every man who approaches you?" he asked.

"No," I said easily. I shrugged one shoulder. "But the thing is, most women feel like they can't be honest when a man comes up to us in a social setting and says something stupid or annoying or cheesy. And my thing is, how will they ever learn? We're taught to smile and be nice and be charming because that's what a good girl does. But if a guy comes up to me and smacks me on the ass and hands me a drink that he so graciously bought, shouldn't I be allowed to tell him that I don't particularly appreciate the gesture?"

Logan answered that with a lifted brow. "Yes, you should."

"Thank you. If I had daughters, I'd want to teach them to be kind but also be honest about how they should be treated. If I had sons, I'd want to teach them how to be respectful of the people they want to speak to. Do you have sons or daughters, Logan?"

As I spoke, he started shaking his head, the tiniest beginnings of a smile on those firmly sculpted lips. "I have sisters. Lots of them."

"And you're not drinking?" I teased.

"I don't drink." His mouth settled into a firm line.

He stood, pulling some cash out of his wallet and tucking it into the tip jar.

"Leaving already?" I asked, feeling an irrational tug of disappointment.

"Yup."

"Aren't you going to ask my name?" I said.

His eyes stayed steadily on mine as he put his wallet into the back pocket of his dark cut jeans. "Who says I don't already know it?"

My mouth popped open as he turned and walked away.

Need more Logan and Paige?
Grab your copy of The Marriage Effect, a marriage of convenience romance.

ACKNOWLEDGMENTS

Fun fact about me: If I woke up tomorrow and 1- was a man and 2- had the talent to play professional football, I'd play defense. There is something INCREDIBLY appealing to me about being the one who needs to knock the quarterback on his ass, the one who snags the ball out of the air for an interception, the one who can force a fumble and turn the game on its head. Writing a character like Matthew—whose career is inspired by the incomparable JJ Watts—was a lot of fun for me because of that. Other than Peyton Manning, some of my all-time favorite players have been on defense. So to players like Von Miller, Bob Sanders, Charles Woodson, and Dwight Freeney, I thank you.

I always struggle when I sit down to write acknowledgements, because I often wait until the last minute, and I want to write giant, effusive paragraphs to properly thank each person who helped me mold this book the best possible version of the story. Occasionally, I manage enough time to make that happen, but this is not one of those times.

To my family, for unwavering support.

To Fiona Cole (the other integral half of the #dreamteam) and Staci Hart for putting those first crucial and critical eyes on this, and not letting me rock in the corner when I *desperately* wanted to.

To Kathryn Andrews, Kandi Steiner, Caitlin Terpstra, and Michelle Clay for giving for giving me honesty and support and suggestions that put the final polish on Ava and Matthew's story.

To Najla Qamber for another beautiful cover.

To Jenny Sims at Editing4Indies and Amanda Yeakel for proof-reading.

To Enticing Journey for all their exceptionally organized promo help.

To my reader group, bloggers and bookstagrammers for loving and believing in my books.

To my God, my Lord and Savior.

OTHER BOOKS BY KARLA SORENSEN

(AVAILABLE TO READ WITH YOUR KU SUBSCRIPTION)

Three Little Words

By Your Side

Light Me Up

Tell Them Lies

Love at First Sight

Baking Me Crazy

Batter of Wits

Steal my Magnolia

Worth the Wait

ABOUT KARLA SORENSEN

Karla Sorensen has been an avid reader her entire life, preferring stories with a happily-ever-after over just about any other kind. And considering she has an entire line item in her budget for books, she realized it might just be cheaper to write her own stories. She still keeps her toes in the world of health care marketing, where she made her living pre-babies. Now she stays home, writing and mommy-ing full time (this translates to almost every day being a 'pajama day' at the Sorensen household...don't judge). She lives in West Michigan with her husband, two exceptionally adorable sons, and big, shaggy rescue dog.

Photo credit: Perrywinkle Photography
Find Karla online:
karlasorensen.com
karla@karlasorensen.com
Facebook
Facebook Reader Group

Made in the USA
Las Vegas, NV
19 May 2024

90133610R00156